COLD
SNAP

COLD SNAP

A VIKING CAT MYSTERY

Codi Schneider

SPARKPRESS

Published by SparkPress, a BookSparks imprint,
A division of SparkPoint Studio, LLC
Phoenix, Arizona, USA, 85007
www.gosparkpress.com

Published 2021
Printed in the United States of America
Print ISBN: 978-1-68463-101-8
E-ISBN: 978-1-68463-102-5
Library of Congress Control Number: 2021904800

Interior design by Tabitha Lahr

To my darling (and dashing) husband, Thomas.
You're almost as snuggly as the animals.

Contents

The Crime of Awfulness

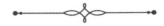

Crime doesn't often visit the town of Gray Birch, Colorado, because it can't squeeze itself over or between the mountains. They're too high, you see. And too close together. Even the clouds here have to tuck in the abdomen just to pass by. I'd certainly never seen Crime in my seven years as a resident. Not until last summer. Well, *spring*, really. It all happened last spring under the cloak of a white sky that didn't so much murmur *mystery* as *conundrum*. And this crime, this conundrum, blew in with the snow—just as cold, just as shocking.

But first, before I recount this tale, an introduction. You may call me Bijou. Though Brynhild or Freydis would be more fitting because, despite my French name, I'm 100 percent Norwegian Forest cat. Possibly 99 percent. I know this because I have the beautiful long fur. And the strength of ten bears. Also, I've earned exactly 103 tabby stripes for bravery.

My ancestors, dear reader, were Viking cats. Rapturous specimens and decorated longship mousers possessed with the Ancient Bloat of Respect. That bloat now resides on me. Some might say I'm overweight, but I know better. This bloat has been passed down through posterity and hangs proudly between my knees. And like all forms of respect, it must be fed frequently.

Now, as a modern-day Viking cat, you'd think I'd bat the jowls of Crime with rapid-fire paws. But when I trotted along the riverpath that shockingly snowy night of June 1 and stumbled upon the beaten and bloodied corpse, I wasn't in my most Vikingest state. I was too full of maple cupcakes and bubble ale. For instead of anticipating Crime that night, I'd anticipated, and greatly indulged in, the grand opening of Witching Flour, Gray Birch's new bakery. And I wasn't alone; nearly the whole town had come out for it.

The corpse was, as corpses tend to be, very dead. It laid supine on the riverpath, propped up by an unenthusiastic shrubbery. The side of its head was matted with blood and rogue spindrifts of river spray, and one hand lay palm-up on the ground, its fingers extended as though reaching for something important. Something unseen.

Donning my imaginary Viking helmet and hefting my imaginary Viking shield, I crept closer. Overhead more clouds gathered, crowning the mountains and murmuring the many merits of more snow. The flakes coming from these springtime drifters were heavy and thick, cloaking the surrounding flowers in buttercream. This storm, I knew, had angered the townspeople. They were desperate for summer, their knobby knees revealed beneath paisley skirts just that night. Possibly, I thought, closing in on the shrubbery, this much blood would anger them as well.

My paws sinking into winter's spite, I circled the shrubbery to investigate the matter of identity. Reaching the riverside, I stopped to face the corpse head-on. Now we

Viking cats have many expectations, but I had not expected recognition. I stared at this face I knew, but there was a failing to see eye to eye. Its eyes were empty and mine full.

For a long moment, time stood still, all noise and all thought drowned in the shock of falling snow.

And then, with a buzz of oddly composed clarity, I knew it was imperative I search for that same something important and that same something unseen those stiff, white fingers reached for. I knew now what it was. *Who* it was. He could be hiding. He hated violence. He hated cold and darkness. I called for him, but, of course, he couldn't answer. Lifting my paw, I pushed off, searching every bush and bramble, checking every hollow and tree well, arching around rocks and stuffing myself in spaces never meant for a Viking's vastness. I gave extra care to check the river, my eyes piercing the moonless waves and coils—the water slick and soft as it slid over its rocky bed.

But there was nothing. No tracks in the snow, no scent upon the wind, no sound but the whisper of my own paws. Returning to the shrubbery, I forced myself to face those poor, sightless eyes head-on. Then, without warning, a war cry ascended from my lips, ballast to the weight and thump of my dropping heart.

Swallowing, I found my throat arid. Unfamiliar with the ways of Crime, I racked my brain while my stomach roiled. All the while, that poor, dead face stared at me with a horrid, tactless derision.

Then I saw it. The tiny circle of red webbing. His collar, silver tag faceup, the name, *Fennec*, engraved across the slick surface. It lay half-buried in the snow, inches from the corpse's outstretched fingers.

Any air I still possessed flung itself from behind my incisors and legged it for Lapland. A rush of sound filled my ears as though the whole of the river had drained into their canals. Dizzy, I tipped to the side and made a snow cat on what was recently a burgeoning mushroom.

A Viking, I mused, staring up at the tumbling flakes, really should possess more fortitude. Possibly though, Crimes of Awfulness took getting used to. There had never been any murders or dognappings in this town before. There were a few hundred stone cottages nestled in the forested valley between the mountains, yes. There were mild-to-medium cases of altitude sickness and honeyed lattes peppered with cayenne, yes. Murders and dognappings, no.

Swiveling my neck, I looked again at that once kindly face I knew and loosed a lament that could chip wood. I was just a splat in the snow. A gray-and-black-striped mop, wrung out and left to dry under the watchful eye of a blizzard. Bijous weren't meant for shock. They were meant for swording, fjording, and consuming great quantities of salted cod.

The minutes floated by as I mused darkly on offenses against the law, letting the snow mound on my midriff and waiting, *waiting* for Trauma to vacate the system.

Bobi Pinn: I certainly don't think Witching Flour's grand opening got—what did you say?—*out of hand*. Sure, there was some champagne flowing and people were partaking, but what's wrong with that? Gum, Lieutenant? It's cinnamon.

Tahereh: This can't be happening. A dognapping and a *murder*? I mean, stuff like that just doesn't happen here. Gray Birch isn't a murdery place. It's droll, not violent.

Dr. Flora: This is *outrageous*. The way people treat animals in this world is disgusting. That poor puppy. I just gave him his shots, you know. Poor baby was terrified. I might go and give myself a few shots now too. I can't help thinking, Lieutenant, that I could've stopped it somehow. Seen something or . . . I don't know.

Dirk Square Jaw: It's gotta be a woman who did it. Women just can't let things go, can they? Probably felt jealous over a romance. Or a scarf. Got hysterical. You know how it is, Lieutenant. I don't gotta explain life to you.

Spencer: Yes, I attended Eddy's grand opening for Witching Flour and . . . I'm sorry, may I have a tissue? This is all such a shock. I mean, my Bijou found the poor soul. Oh dear, I think I've started to cry.

Police Lieutenant Lou Tennant: Hold on now. Why is there a cat in here? This is an official police interrogation. Margaret? Hello? Can someone please remove this damn cat?

2

The Potbellied and the Pit Bull

Two months earlier . . .

"Bijou!" Spencer called. Her wool socks slid across Fox Burrow's warped oak floors. "Bijou Bonanno! We have new guests!"

Starting from my position atop the giant bag of new dog food, I spat out a mouthful of mixed plastics. Five more minutes and I'd have a hole chewed clean through it. But as co-owner and manager of the prestigious Fox Burrow Pet Inn, I couldn't leave guests unattended.

Descending the dune of kibble (feeling each bump and crunch under the paws), I trotted from the brightly lit kitchen through the warm hallways of the three-story Victorian Spencer and I had turned into our inn. Despite creaky eaves and a few graying boards, she sat strong at the end of Sourdough Drive, her blue siding and white shutters snuggled within a grove of willows, pines, and cottonwoods.

On my way to reception, I paused to nip off the tip of a wandering ivy plant. The pruning of plants was just one of my many duties as manager. Others included (but were not limited to) welcoming all guests, fluffing their beds, testing their meals for poison, and regaling them with bedtime stories of ancient Viking battles won and won.

In fact, as manager, I held so many duties I'd felt it prudent to hire an assistant. But even Duty was displeased with the lack of applicants, and so Spencer's mentally negligible Pomeranian, Skunk, fell headfirst into the role. Her latest dating profile said: *Hi, I'm Skunk! Single, female, pun-loving Pom residing in the mountains but dreaming of the tropics. Petite with big hair and a passion for peanut butter and patchouli.*

Passing the living room, I felt the heat of a crackling fire in the hearth and arched my lumbar. Outside, the wind had picked up with the descent of the sun, and, like all Norsecats, I appreciated a grand flame.

Trotting into the front room used for reception, my first view was of Spencer's feet, clad in her favorite blue-and-white polar bear socks, tucked out of sight under the desk. On the other side of the desk, toes nearly touching hers but for the thin partition, were a pair of Vans shoes.

"Of course we have a room for all of you," Spencer was saying, tucking her long blond hair behind one ear. "We designed the Hachiko Suite specifically for people who want to stay with their pets."

"Oh, that's a relief. You're a lifesaver." Jacking up my head, I saw a handsome, dark-haired man with glasses sitting across from Spencer. "I apologize for walking in so late and making such a last-minute request. The apartment I'm renovating is in much worse condition than I initially believed, and the town's main inn—the Doe?—already turned me away." The man had dimples that flashed periodically when he spoke. But Spencer didn't notice. Her blue eyes, so like the sea, were studying the booking calendar on her laptop.

"It's no problem at all," she murmured. "The Doe doesn't allow animals, and the Hachiko Suite isn't booked as often as our other rooms. You said you didn't yet know how long you'll be with us?"

"Could be a couple of weeks. If you can put up with us that long."

Spencer smiled at her screen, the freckles across her cheekbones forming a chain like pieces from Barrel of Monkeys. "I'm sure we'll manage." She typed a few lines of information, the keyboard clicking amicably.

Us? Who else was here? All I could see was this last-minute man-guest, and a good manager always knows *exactly* who arrives at her establishment. Rocking the bloat back and forth, I built momentum and then sprang onto the desk for a better vantage point. "Oh, Bijou, there you are," Spencer said, unfazed by my sudden appearance. "This is Eddy. Eddy Line. Eddy, this is Bijou."

"Hey, Bijou." Smiling, Eddy leaned forward and held out his hand (tanned with clean half-moon nails), which I greeted with a polite sniff and rub. His scent was a soothing mixture of sun, salt water, and fresh baked bread. His brown eyes focused on me from behind their round glasses. "Bijou . . . is that French? You seem like more of a northern kitty to me."

I blinked and then pranced vehemently. Very few bipeds pegged my Vikingness so soon, if at all. "You may call me Freydis," I informed him.

"Whether she's French or not, I like the name Bijou," said Spencer, closing her computer. "It means 'jewel.'"

"Ah, well, she *is* like a polished gem," said Eddy. "Shiny and round."

I tried to figure out if that was a compliment or not while Spencer laughed, her gaze at last settling on him. And she gave a start. It wasn't a big start. In fact, only someone who knew her as well as I did would have noticed. But it was enough to tell me this was the first time she'd truly *looked* at him. What's more, he was a guest himself, not just his pets (if they existed), and I watched that fact sink in and circle behind her eyes. Then, as expected, Apprehension settled on her and she began to straighten the pens on her desk.

Eddy, meanwhile, gestured to the floor beside him, and both Spencer and I peered over the edge of the desk. "These are my boys, Fennec and Hamlet. They're both sleeping. It was a long drive from California for Hamlet and I. Fennec here only had to make the trip from Denver though. We just adopted him."

Sitting next to Eddy's leg was a carrier with black mesh on the top and sides. Inside, two small shapes curled around each other, one covered in sandy fur, the other pink, bald, and wearing a sweater.

"Oh my," Spencer said. "They're both just babies. Is Hamlet a potbellied pig?"

"Yep. And Fennec is a pit bull. I think they love each other already."

"I can see that." Spencer's eyes were bright, the animals instantly relieving some of her apprehension. "What's that red pattern on Hamlet's sweater? Balloons?"

"Pomegranate seeds." Eddy grinned. "My grandmother likes to sew him sweaters she thinks the youth of today will enjoy."

"Ah, you're lucky you still have a grandmother."

"I know. She called me yesterday to say that she read in *Husbandry Over Husbands* magazine how prone potbellied pigs are to obesity. She warned me that he can't have fruit. 'One grape, Eddy,' she said, 'and he'll bloat like the fat disciple, Jude. Or was it Judas? Jesus spoiled that one, you know. Too much unleavened bread.'"

Spencer's laugh rollicked around the room while I sat with my toes lined up at the edge of the desk and stared down at my tiny new guests. Something, a feeling perhaps, had taken hold of the claws and worked its way up. A swine had never before come to Fox Burrow. A miniature horse, yes. Several gerbils and a hamster, yes. A mini lop named Dolly Parton, of course. A hundred dogs and cats, to be sure. But never a swine.

With a sigh that could swaddle Oslo, I jumped to the floor for a better view of the thing and found myself perturbed. No, it was worse than that; I was in a moral gymnasium, and I hated swordless exercise. Swines were pink, and not only did I disapprove of the color pink, I was fairly certain I disapproved of swines. They belonged in the barn with the rest of the cloven-hooved. Surely now that she'd seen him, Spencer would rescind her offer of the Hachiko Suite. It was our nicest room, and this boar would leave it in squalor.

"So the Hachiko Suite is number four on the second floor," said Spencer, handing Eddy a large brass key. "You'll be up there with the cats. That's their floor, each with their own suite of course, while the dogs are on the first floor, and Bijou, Skunk, and I are on the third."

"Skunk?" said Eddy, pocketing the key.

"My Pomeranian. I'm actually surprised she's not here. She loves greeting new guests."

I was having trouble feeling anything below the whiskers. Spencer had officially agreed to lodge this pork chop in luxury, and she'd done so without discussing it with me. This was not how clans stayed united. But, summoning patience—a Viking's least best quality—I told myself it could still be fixed.

In his sleep, the swinelet let out a grunt that bullied his dormant neck skin. Also, his nose looked more like the back end of a baboon than a breathing device. Furthermore, his eyes were peeling open to stare at me with something akin to intelligence. Looking into them, I realized someone was home. "You are a swine," I informed him.

He wagged his tail happily. "And you're a cat, and he—" he pointed at the still-sleeping puppy, "—is a dog."

"This isn't a game," I said, annoyed. After a moment I followed his gaze to where it'd landed on the bookshelf. "What are you looking at?"

"There's a book on airplanes."

"No, there isn't."

"Yes, there is." He jutted his nose at a thick tome with a Bell P-63 Kingcobra on the cover.

"That's a bee," I said.

"No, it's not—" His argument was cut off by Skunk bounding into the room, late, as usual, and completely unaware of the situation. She'd been napping in her favorite upstairs cabinet, the one containing Spencer's prized collection of essential oils, and so she smelled like a fairy burp.

"What'd I miss?" she asked, her tiny white muzzle protruding from a lion's mane of black hair.

"That." I pointed at the pig.

"Is it a shih tzu?" she asked, still looking at me.

"I'm a Hamlet," said Hamlet.

Skunk turned and her greeting froze on her tongue. I could see it dangling from the edge with one arm. A quiver started in her tail and worked its way hand-over-hand to her nose. Confusion had taken hold, and with confusion came fear. She flicked panicked eyes at me. "What is it, Bijou?"

I folded my tail around my paws. "I can explain it to you, but I can't understand it for you."

"It's pink."

"Yes."

Her eyes clouded over, a sure sign of Thought. I could see Dilemma forming between her ears. Pink was on her list of favorite things. Foreign objects were on her list of least favorite things. Before her stood both. I sighed. An assistant manager, I thought, really should be more decisive. I waited to see if she'd stand her ground or leg it for wide-open spaces.

It was Spencer who made the decision. Rising from her chair, she scooped up the Pom and, tucking her comfortably beneath an arm, announced we would all be great friends.

Well, my brain waved the red flag of warning, but I watched as Dilemma cleared from Skunk's eyes and her tiny tongue lolled to the side in a smile. "I've always wanted a pink friend, haven't I, Bijou? In fact, I said so just the other day."

Eddy's phone buzzed and he pulled it from his pocket. "Sorry, I should take this. It's my contractor."

Spencer waved her free hand. "Of course, answer it."

"Hi, Mike." A frown marred Eddy's face as he listened to the voice on the other end. After a moment, he sat back in his chair and ran a hand over his face. "Seriously? Okay. Yes, I'll be right over." Slipping the phone back into his pocket, he looked at Spencer. "Gas leak. One of Mike's guys must've hit a pipe earlier today, and the neighbors just called it in."

"Oh dear, that's not good," Spencer said. "You go on, and we'll get Fennec and Hamlet settled and comfortable here."

"Are you sure? They might be a bit nervous without me. Fennec especially. He has some fear issues, and, you should know, he's a deaf-mute."

Spencer's eyes widened. "Really? Poor boy. We'll take extra good care of them both, I promise. They'll be happier eating dinner and getting cozy here than waiting in your car, don't you think?"

Clearly anxious about leaving them alone, Eddy's jaw twitched. But then he nodded, softening. "You're right, they'll be much happier here. Thanks, Spencer." Rising, he gave me a pet before jotting down his phone number on a tattered envelope sitting on the desk. "Call me if you need anything. Though I really shouldn't be gone long. I'm not going far."

"Where is this apartment of yours?" Spencer asked, glancing at the envelope before slipping it into the top desk drawer.

"Well, it's not just an apartment, really," said Eddy, zipping up his coat. "I actually bought the old firehouse on Main Street and am turning just the upstairs into an apartment. The bottom floor will be a bakery."

"Wait, *you're* the person who bought the old firehouse?" Spencer said, her eyebrows climbing. "Everyone wanted that old place, but I'm glad you got it. This town needs a good bakery."

"Hopefully I can provide it. That is, if the place doesn't blow up or crumble down first. I'm calling it 'Witching Flour.'"

"Witching Flour." Spencer smiled. "How clever." She waved toward the door. "Better get to it then."

Skunk, who'd been completely riveted by Hamlet, only realized there was also a puppy after Eddy had gone. With unbridled excitement, she raced around the house, her toenails screeching as she slid around corners and into walls. We could hear her breathless pants ballooning and popping as we walked upstairs to the Hachiko Suite. In front of me, Spencer moved carefully with the carrier so as not to jolt Fennec and Hamlet. I lugged myself after her, each paw dipped in a weighty pillar of concrete.

The second floor contained six cat suites (three bedrooms each divided in half) plus the much larger Hachiko

Suite at the end of the hall. Walking this hallway, we could hear our guests eating their dinner and sipping their catbernet behind closed doors, their purrs tumbling through the walls and into our ears. A blue-and-silver carpet runner ran the length of the hall, and everywhere plants dangled and lanterns flickered.

Entering the Hachiko Suite, Spencer immediately set down the carrier and lit the gas fireplace—flames unfurling across the wall like blue-and-orange blossoms. Then she moved to draw the thick, creamy curtains over the windows before drifting about, lighting numerous candles on bookshelves well out of Fennec's and Hamlet's reach. Hints of black cherry and vanilla floated through the room. For over a year now, Spencer had been very into hygge, and she swore it changed her life. The long Colorado winters had always been hard for her, and hygge helped. Though the concept was more Danish than Norwegian, I very much approved. The two countries had once been a single kingdom after all, and the art of being consciously cozy was extremely feline.

Kneeling on the thick, cream-colored rug, Spencer reached toward me, and my fur tingled with the anticipation of pets. But, horribly, her hands flew right over me like dirigible double-crossers and landed on the carrier. Unzipping it, she called to Hamlet, who happily trotted out. "Aren't you cute!" she said, scratching him between the ears.

"I think the word you mean is *hideous*," I said, donning the frosty cloak of the maltreated. "Not *cute*. Though your confusion is understandable. I myself struggle at times with words that start with C and H. It was a dismal day three summers past when I called myself a hat."

Spencer didn't reply. Instead she peeked in at Fennec and stroked him gently between the eyes with a finger. "Oh, there's nothing like a good puppy sleep," she whispered.

"Soak it all in, buddy. And when you wake up, you'll see you're in a safe place. No one will hurt you here."

At her touch he stretched clumsy, too-large paws and sighed, his downy puppy coat like a sandbar in the sea of black mesh. Leaving the carrier open so he could come out when he wanted, Spencer rose and began to set up a playpen in the corner of the room with a patch of potty grass inside and a bunch of blankets and rubber chew toys. Then she retrieved a litter box and litter from the hallway supply closet and set up a bathroom for the swine, who used it right away. I watched him do it with a raised brow, pondering the ethics of feline appropriation.

"Okay," said Spencer, looking around. "I'm going to fix you guys some dinner. You want to come help, Bij? Skunk will look after them."

I looked over as the Pom galloped into the room, waving the flag of joy. Yes. Yes, I was coming. But not to help make dinner. There was much to ponder, and pondering, I thought, made up the difference between the very intelligent and the very dumb. Also, I couldn't watch the inevitable squalor. Turning tail, I followed Spencer unhappily down the stairs.

We Norsecats look splendid in armor. Particularly helmets. And this was why, alone in the firelight of the living room, I stuck my head into an empty succulent pot. Instantly I felt connected to the ancestors and to that fjord of blood that ran all cool and slushy in my veins.

I would've stayed in the pot all night, listening to the dulcet tones of seafaring pillagers and to the *kabump kabump* of a dozen wooden bows breaking through cresting waves. But alas, Hunger descended, and we Viking cats have appetites rivaling the American pygmy shrew. Like them, we

need great quantities of food to keep our phenomenal metab-
olisms going. Daily we eat three times our own body weight,
and even one hour without food can usher in certain death.

Having not pondered nearly enough, yet too hungry to
ponder, I left the ancestors behind and made my way to the
kitchen, arthritic floorboards creaking beneath my paws.
Outside, the evening alpenglow faded through the windows,
softening Fox Burrow's dormant hoopskirt of a lawn. This
lawn, so lush in the summertime, backed up to the Arkansas
River (the golden vein of Gray Birch's tourist-driven econ-
omy) and beyond that sat the low mountain of Napping
Cowboy. West, across the valley from the Cowboy, stood a
massive range of mountains, each crowned with snow. One
of these, the largest of all, was a lone prince with three faces,
and he overlooked the town with gray, Loki-like eyes.

Upon entering the kitchen and maneuvering around a
stove that looked as though it'd rather be anything else, I found
Spencer measuring out food for Fennec. Beside his bowl was a
dinner of mashed bran and lettuce for the swine. "You know,"
she told me, "cats and pigs have a lot in common."

I propped up an eyebrow. Other than being quadrupeds,
I couldn't think of a single commonality. Besides, just the
other day I'd walked to the extra-far spigot on my hind legs.

"Hamlet and Skunk will make marvelous friends,"
Spencer continued. She took care not to look at me. To be
casual. "You could be too. Now, I can tell you're unsure
about him, and that's okay. But, well . . . I love you, Bij,
more than anything, but sometimes you can be just a wee
bit barbaric."

Taking that as a compliment, I snuck seven and a half
morsels of dog food when she wasn't looking.

"I mean, he's just a baby. Completely harmless and
smart too." She reached over and smoothed the furrows

between my ears. "Anyway, just think about it. For now, can you go give Miss Tut her turndown? She's such an early bird, and remember, she bought the Purrfection package, which includes a second glass of pinot meow or catbernet along with her aromatherapy." She finished filling Fennec's bowl and rubbed her temples. "God, I need to call Tahereh tonight. It's been so long since we've had a human guest, I don't remember how to do it anymore. We need food. Our website says a gourmet breakfast is included in the price of the room, doesn't it? As it stands, Eddy is in for a crusty bread heel topped with some very old jam. Hardly appetizing." She paused for a moment. Then, "Maybe Pete would like to join us? I'll call him too."

A tiny bray escaped between my incisors. Pete Moss was our groomer and general doer-of-all-jobs-needing-doing. He was a lovable, if reticent, man who would in no way contribute to the breakfast conversation. And while he had soft hands and the soul of a goddess, he looked like a reanimated bog body. In fact, I was fairly certain he *was* a bog body. If Spencer was looking for someone to break the ice at the breakfast table with her and Eddy (which she was), she'd picked the wrong man.

Sneaking seven and a half additional morsels of dog food, I lifted my paw and pushed off to see Miss Tut, who was one of my favorite guests. She came every spring for three months while her humans flew to the hot sands of Hawaii. While old, she was the most elegant of Siameses with eyes like pilot lights and a soul like John Quincy Adams. Her suite was one of my favorites, too, with a giant window overlooking the unbroken forest to the south.

After ten minutes in Miss Tut's company, I'd quite forgotten the case of the undercooked bacon and been given a history of the Whig Party and reminded that every time a bald eagle calls, a patriot is born. Miss Tut knew all about US history and even tried to enlist in the military twice before her hip froze up.

Now, as a Viking cat, I care more for Norse doctrine than American politics. But Miss Tut enjoyed sharing her pinot meow, and though not my favorite drink (which was ale), a good manager always did what she could to indulge her guests' delights.

Drunken Warbler

Cats named Bijou are normally debonair, and I'm no exception. It's the French side of me that Spencer implanted with her appellation. I can't help it, though it does at times clash with the sheer force of my Vikingness. And clash it did that first night Hamlet stayed at Fox Burrow.

Eddy still hadn't returned and it was bedtime. That most holy time when cat and human (and Skunk) curled up together in trust and friendship. Since kittenhood (after Spencer rescued me from that cold box in that cold alleyway) I'd laid on a pillow next to Spencer, her long blond hair draped over me like a blanket. That pillow was my throne. My sanctuary and my shrine. It was when I felt closest to the Norsegods, Freyja in particular. My beloved Freyja (goddess of love, war, death, and more) who rode in a chariot pulled by cats. In fact, Freyja and her cats were stitched on the pillow along with my favorite bedtime poem.

Fluffy kitty
Norse kitty
Tiny ball of floof
Viking kitty
Slayer kitty
Fjord meow poof

And now, after kneading that throne to the brink of luxury, Spencer announced the puppy and the *pig* were lonely and scared in the Hachiko Suite and so would join us up here. In our room. On the bed. Well, my tail nearly detached at this announcement. Never had guests been allowed into our upstairs quarters.

"Poor things," Spencer said, heading toward the stairs to retrieve them as the pig's yellow-bellied grunts vibrated the floorboards. She passed by our room's giant circular window, the moon turning her robe lily-white. "I'm surprised it's taking Eddy this long. It's after ten for God's sake . . . but no, I shouldn't call him. We've got a handle on everything, don't we?" She turned to me, her lips firm. "Now you be nice and curl up with them, Bijou."

Curl up with them? *Curl up with them?* As in welcome a swine to my pillow? What kind of spell had this pig cast on Spencer? No, this lodged a protest deep in my throat. A protest that I loosed upon her as soon as she returned holding both the carrier and the pink barbarian. "Fennec still won't come out," she lamented, lugging the carrier to the bed. "He gobbled up his dinner, but only after I put it in the carrier with him. And now he's cowering in the back, terrified." She placed the carrier down by Skunk, who licked it. "Good girl. See if you can comfort him, Skunk." Then Spencer turned and placed the little rubicund terrorist on my pillow. "Scoot over, Bij."

I protested louder. Vikings didn't spoon barn animals. Well, maybe some did. But not the ones destined for Valhalla.

The swine brushed his dewy nose against my shoulder, his bare buttocks descending on Freyja. Well, this was simply too much for Bijou.

Lighting the dynamite beneath my paws, I waited for them to blow. The fuses were short. In .2 seconds I'd shot straight to the ceiling, my legs locked and splayed, my tail inflated. I swam the paws through the air and was out the door and down the stairs before Descent was finalized.

Skunk's surprised yelp ushered me out the cat door and onto the frozen, yellow grass. There, I blinked and imagined the screech of a perfectly plump pillow deflating. How had this happened? I'd been in for a perfectly cozy night, and now my sacred sleeping arrangement was besmirched. Never had a guest so mistreated their manager.

Nostrils flared, I swiveled my neck in search of a new berth. The dark bulk of our old horse barn caught my eye. But if the pig wasn't sleeping there, *I* certainly wasn't. I was a proud Viking and as such, didn't require any old barn. I welcomed the elements and would cushion my head with rock and cover the fur with hailstones.

Yet as the wind increased, I decided I didn't want to sleep *entirely* out in the open. Even the ancestors sought a smidgen of shelter in the night. To my left stood the new agility course Spencer and Pete Moss had built last fall. It was situated within a low, white painted fence and pushed up against the edge of the property. Just past it, beyond a hedge, stood the neighbor's squat brick house that belonged to Police Lieutenant Lou Tennant. His security light was on, bathing much of the course in soft, yellow warmth, and I fluttered toward it like a moth.

The obstacle that afforded the most protection was the dog chute. It lay torpid on the ground, blue and frosty and baffling to all manner of canine. Stepping gingerly toward it, I tapped it three times with a paw faster than lightning. Assured it wasn't, in fact, a snake or giant cucumber simply *posing* as a chute, I slithered my way inside. It smelled like a tent and Skunk's essential oils. Skunk loved the agility course. She bounced around it daily, her hair flying, her tongue flapping in a sickening attempt for treats and praise. Clenching my jaw, I forced myself into the prone position. Dethroned by a sow, I was desperate for Sleep, the great healer.

Slowly, I nodded off. A dream taking shape and cloaking my eyelids with silk. This wasn't so bad. Not really. My northern blood ran true, and I welcomed nature like an innocent clergyman a longship.

I was undulating with the North Sea when a many-legged horror penetrated my sleep, porcupining the fur. The thing was hard shelled and halfway up my nose by the time I pierced it with my imaginary sword, Dewclaw. Fleeing from the chute, my ears chilled like champagne glasses in the night air. I'd been under the impression that beetles hibernated in winter. But now that one had proved both wakeful and guilty of unlawful entry, I dared not return to sleep.

After a moment, I decided there was only one place to go. The Drunken Warbler would still be open and it wasn't far. It sat in the heart of town, past the end of Sourdough Drive, left on Pecan Street, and then right on Main. Foggy would be happy to see me. He appreciated quadrupeds like myself—the ones with many layers and great depth. Like puff pastry. And a little appreciation, I thought, would be much appreciated right now.

Foggy Lawson, the fifty-year-old proprietor and bartender of the Drunken Warbler, greeted me at the back door after I scratched it. We were old friends, Foggy and I, and though I didn't often come to the pub alone, he served me my favorite ale right away.

"Skol," I cheered, taking a long drink until my chin hairs were as white as his. Burping discreetly behind a paw, I looked around the pub from my stool at the counter. The Warbler wasn't crowded. Not at this time on a Thursday night. But a few souls dotted the rich oak booths, and I exchanged nods with Bobi Pinn, Gray Birch's most chop-happy hairdresser. She had pink tresses that night and sat in a corner booth, chatting with pretty, young Dr. Flora, the vet at Flora's Fauna. Both were nursing hot toddies. I crouched down a bit on my stool, not wanting Dr. Flora to see me. She'd poked and prodded Bijou enough in life already.

I spared a sideways glance at Foggy, but he seemed unconcerned with Dr. Flora, even though not long ago they'd ended a five-year engagement. They'd seemed happy together for most of those years, despite the significant age difference and despite rumors that Foggy often attended anger management. And they seemed happy enough now, separated. Bipeds in small towns often found odd ways of getting along—some of which included frequenting each other's establishments and complimenting one another's "briskness of servitude" and "generous tipping practices."

The door opened and the grande dame of the town, Demelza Corn, swept inside, followed clumsily by Brooke Binder, owner of the Snoozy Poet bookstore. They joined Bobi and Flora at their table, signaling Foggy to bring more drinks.

"Ah, the Toddy Club meets again," said Foggy, giving me a wink. "It's up to three nights a week now." He reached over and rubbed my ears with calloused fingers. "Are they still trying to recruit Spencer?"

I assured him they were and that she remained unpersuaded.

"Speaking of Spencer, where is she tonight, Bij? On a date?"

I scoffed into my ale. Spencer never dated. Not for years. Not after she had her heart shattered and the pieces dipped in vinegar. Last year, on her thirtieth birthday, she'd told me that dating was like looking for a grape in a peanut field. Being single, she said, was about fermenting your own grape into a strong, fruity wine. This was why we were both partial to malbec.

"Yeah, didn't think so." Foggy chuckled. "I've known Spencer since she was a kid, and she's always been the independent type. Although, it's certainly nice to have someone to cozy up with on cold nights. I hope she knows that."

But she *did* have someone to cozy up with. She had me. Well, usually.

While Foggy mixed and delivered more toddies, I watched the nightly news play silently on the television behind the bar. A young, heavyset man with a carpet of pale hair laughed on the screen. But there was something distasteful about the way his smile stretched . . . like a string of cheese melted between two stale cheeks of bread. The chyron below said, DENVER MAN SINKS THREE YACHTS IN GULF OF MEXICO.

Ever the interested sailor who never sailed, Foggy turned on the sound when he returned and we learned from a serious woman with a serious voice how the man, Chauncey Kane, was the son of a billionaire. While partying on his multi-million-dollar yacht, he'd crashed it straight into two other multimillion-dollar yachts moored passively off Cancún.

"No, I take no responsibility at all," the man said. His

voice was awfully thin for being so arrogant. "I'd certainly *like* to apologize, but it wasn't my fault. They shouldn't have dropped anchor where they did."

"But they were in a marina," said the reporter, baffled.

The man shrugged and Foggy muted the television again. "What a fool," he said to me, rolling his eyes.

While the night matured like vinegar in a cask, I lapped my ale and watched the flow of townspeople drift in and out. Conversations floated through the air, and I listened to snippets of one and then another while Foggy poured, mixed, and shook.

"See here now, ladies absolutely *love* me," Dirk Square Jaw crooned, leaning up against the wall and speaking down to the lady seated below him.

"Uh-huh, yes, I'm sure they do," the lady said, trying to inch away.

"See? I got you interested already." Dirk grinned, showing snippy little rows of teeth.

As the woman made her getaway, my ears picked up another conversation. This one from the toddy table. "Have you spoken with William recently, Demelza?" Bobi's husky voice carried across the room, as did her loud slurping. The ladies were in three deep now, and Brooke Binder leaned forward to hear Demelza's reply, her giant spectacles slipping from her nose.

"I write to him every week." Demelza sighed, smoothing her steel-gray hair. "But he rarely writes back and *never* calls. You know how prisons are. I wonder if they're keeping my letters from him. I can't imagine why, they're perfectly innocent, just an old mother writing to her grown son, but there you have it."

"And you have no idea when he might be released?" asked Brooke, breathless.

"Didn't you say he was up for parole soon?" said Dr. Flora.

"He is," replied Demelza. "But one can't get one's hopes up."

"Well, I for *one* hope William Corn remains in jail a good long while," Foggy grunted to me as he came back behind the counter. "He may be in there for tax fraud, but he was a bully through and through. Once he even tried to take this from me when we were boys, but I broke his nose." Discreetly, he fished for something hanging inside his shirt. "You'll appreciate this, Bij." He pulled a shiny object out and bent slightly so I could see it. It was a gold ring hanging from a cord around his neck. Very valuable from the looks of it except for a deep gash raking its midriff.

"This was my grandfather's. It was scratched by an ornery barn cat when he was a boy, and that convinced him it was lucky. He wore it around his neck during the Second World War and lived to tell the tale." Winking, he stuffed it back inside his shirt. "Now it's my lucky little secret. I never take it off."

As Foggy delivered another round of drinks, I caught a blur of movement from the doorway of the ladies' restroom. Sniffing, I detected a hint of perfume and something else . . . something sour with greed. Or was it just hunger? Maybe a patron was craving truffle fries. I knew I certainly was, and I rapped the counter seventeen times to let Foggy know.

Later, so late it was early and Foggy and I were the only ones left in the pub, a rumble filled my throat as he scratched me behind the ears. Within it, I told him about the many difficulties of my night. He nodded along to my account, his eyes half-closed, and topped off my ale with an extra measure of sympathy. "Here now. You can't trot on three paws, Bij."

I completely agreed, and soon both my chin hairs and his resembled a certain Northman's named St. Nick, and I discovered that a bar top could be quite as comfortable as any old pillow.

Cardboard Note

"I see I've driven you to drink."

I opened one crust-infused eye and saw a bleary blonde staring down at me. Swallowing, I found the throat bone-dry. It needed rain.

"Bijou," the blonde spoke again, her hands on her hips.

I tried to lift my head and found it cemented to the bar top.

Spencer sighed and placed a warm hand on my fur. "I've been searching for you for hours. Skunk woke before dawn and you were still gone. Now, instead of getting breakfast ready, I've been traipsing all over town, worrying more and more, and here you are, fast asleep." Her long mane shook. "I should've known."

I opened a second crust-infused eye and mumbled, "You can't trot on three paws."

She scooped me up, holding me against her puffy winter vest, and I breathed in her warm Spencer scent. And that rumble, so mysterious, so affecting, overcame me again.

There was nothing, *nothing* like being hammocked in your best friend's arms.

Foggy, who was asleep in a booth with his hat over his face, lifted a hand in farewell as we exited, and Spencer carried me across the town square, turning right up Pecan and then left on Sourdough Drive. All the way, she took care to shield my face from the morning sun, which blazed so bright and self-important it nearly broke its arm patting itself on the back.

Skunk waited for us by the mailbox, all four feet prancing about as though she wore stilettos. Instantly I shared my complaint about the sun.

"It thinks it's hot stuff," she agreed, looking straight at it and promptly falling into a ditch.

"Hot stuff." I cracked a grin, but it caught on my snaggletooth.

Oh yes, my snaggletooth . . .

Full disclosure, it's the most hideous thing about me and I detest it. It makes Bijou look like a two-cent mackerel caught on the line. I quickly snuffed it out with my lips.

Buried within my Spencer cocoon, I listened to her boots crunch up the frosty gravel drive. All the while I harbored no memory of the reason I'd abdicated my pillow last night until Reason himself appeared on the porch wearing a thick lavender sweater.

Hamlet looked as refreshed as Sleeping Beauty in Eddy's arms. My memory suddenly flooded with last night's horrors, and I inquired (without hope) as to the condition of my Freyja pillow.

Except I didn't actually *say* anything. See, an abundance of ale has the unfortunate side effects of gelding one's speech and battening down the eyelids. I glared at my reflection as we passed Eddy's 4Runner and Tahereh's little Mazda3.

"Thank goodness, you found her," Eddy said, trotting down the steps and looking exceptionally handsome in a black sweater and jeans. He seemed scruffier than he had yesterday. And taller. In fact, Spencer's head only came up to his chest as he stopped in front of us.

"I'm Hamlet," said Hamlet, looking down at me.

I blinked. Yes, I was aware.

Then Recognition settled in his eyes. "Oh, Bijou! It's you. You look different this morning. Bit older. Bit more lumpy around the eyes."

Summoning my best scowl, I dared him to say more.

"Bit haggard."

Skunk, having emerged from the ditch, deflected my ensuing scowl by tripping Spencer so that it hit not the swine but an innocent town deer munching grass nearby. "What did I do?" the deer cried, his deciduous horns nearly stripped of their velvet.

"*Skunk.*" Spencer stumbled a few steps before regaining her balance on Eddy's arm. "Thanks," she said, handing it back to him like a lightly used handkerchief.

Amused, Eddy turned to me. "Good morning, Bijou." The tip of his nose was red with cold. I nodded a greeting as we started for the house, Skunk now racing ahead, her floof streaming.

Entering Fox Burrow was like walking into a warm, fleecy hug. The old inn smelled of dark coffee, vanilla, and caramelized sugar, and Tahereh could be heard tinkering around in the kitchen. From the supply room down the hall came the sound of kibble raining into bowls, and I knew Pete Moss had taken over Spencer's breakfast shift.

"Morning, morning." Tahereh Safi-Beckett's long black hair swung as she popped her head out of the kitchen. "If you can, try and move around quietly as the baby's finally relaxed enough to nap."

Turning, we saw Eddy's deaf-mute pit bull puppy curled on the sofa in front of the blazing hearth, snuggled with a stuffed yellow duck. His tiny red collar was bright with new-ness, unmarred by even a speck of dust, the name *Fennec* engraved on the silver tag.

"Finally," Eddy said. "He didn't sleep at all last night, even after I got home. He just hid and shivered, poor boy."

Corralling Skunk before she could pounce on him, Spencer ushered everyone back into the kitchen, closing the French doors. Though deaf, the little pit bull could still be woken by our scents and vibrations.

Tahereh walked over and gave Spencer and I a one-armed hug, her cheeks smudged with flour. "Glad to see you're home in one piece, Bijou."

Spencer rolled her eyes. "It never ends with her. She was at the pub with Foggy. Anyway, thanks for coming over. Poor Eddy would've had nothing to eat otherwise."

"No problem. And as your best friend, I'll only charge you double." Tahereh's dark eyes were twin pools of humor. "Maybe triple since it's still the slow season for us caterers."

"You really didn't need to come just for me," said Eddy, swiping a wayward chocolate chip from the counter and munch-ing it happily. "I could've gone downtown for something."

"But breakfast is included on the website," said Tahereh. "And Spencer never lies on the website."

"No, never." Spencer grinned.

"Well in that case, may I get a splash of that coffee?" Eddy pointed to the French press roosting importantly on the counter.

"Nope, not until I put it on the table with the rest of breakfast," said Tahereh, bending to check on whatever was in the oven.

"Are those your famous banana scones?" asked Spencer, peering over her shoulder.

"With chocolate chips." Tahereh donned oven mitts, ready to pull the scones from the center rack. "Plus my homemade coconut milk cream and a cardamom citrus fruit salad. Sound good?"

My stomach growled.

"Bijou thinks so," said Spencer, kissing me between the ears. "Shall I go fetch Pete?"

Setting me on the floor, Spencer disappeared through the doors while I swayed slightly and urged my knees to unknock. By the time they did, Spencer was back. "He's coming. Okay, Bijou, I know you want your breakfast too. No, not you, Skunk. You already ate."

By the time I finished a delicious, if small-portioned meal, I felt much better and joined the others around the sun-drenched breakfast table. They were nursing second cups of coffee and I circled their legs, ignoring the swine, and hoping to vacuum up any crumbs that might fall.

"No, the shelter in Denver didn't know much about Fennec," Eddy was saying, spooning more cream onto his scone. "Only that a police officer rescued him from a guy who was knocking him around like a tetherball on the sidewalk. Apparently the guy went to jail. Not for kicking him, mind you, but because they found drugs in his backpack. Disgusting how animal cruelty is less of a crime. Anyway, Fennec had only been at the shelter for a day when I came along and found him. Obviously I'm still working to gain his trust."

A cloud had settled on Spencer's brow. "How can people be so cruel?" she said. "I simply don't understand it."

Eddy shook his head. "I don't know. And it's interesting because there aren't many deaf-mute dogs like Fennec. At the shelter they told me most deaf dogs bark loudly because they can't hear their own volume. But Fenn doesn't let out a peep. It's like he's scared of being heard. Scared of being noticed. Plus, get this, he has a weird tattoo to boot."

"A dog with a tattoo?" said Tahereh. "Who ever heard of such a thing?"

"I never noticed a tattoo," said Spencer.

"It's on his belly where there's not much hair," said Eddy. "A kind of geometric dog head. Big and very crudely done. You'd have to roll him over to see it."

Spencer set down her fork, a segment of grapefruit still speared on the end. "Okay, I don't like the sound of that at all. Thank God you rescued him, Eddy."

Circling the table, I closed in on my eleventh crumb. Before nabbing it, however, I ran into a dusty brown boot and nearly shot out of my fur. Pete Moss. I'd completely forgotten he was here. The man was invisible. He didn't talk; he listened. A special talent of the bog people, no doubt. As I gobbled up my crumb, he reached down and rubbed me with a gnarled finger.

"By the way, what time did you get in last night, Eddy?" Spencer asked. "I was half-asleep when I brought the boys to you. I assume you got the gas leak fixed at Witching Flour?"

"Witching Flour?" said Tahereh.

"Oh, right, I haven't told you yet. Eddy here is the one who bought the old firehouse on Main. He's turning it into a bakery."

"Oh, I'm glad to hear it! This town needs a good bakery, and the firehouse is so charming. I was sure batty old Demelza Corn would get her way and turn it into another Monstera shop."

Eddy's brows met as though for the first time. "Monstera shop?"

"Monsteras are houseplants," explained Spencer. "Also known as Swiss cheese plants. Very pretty, very large. Demelza's obsessed with them."

"She's had her eye on the firehouse for years hoping the owner would sell," said Tahereh. "But I don't think she ever knew who it was. It was all wrapped up in a trust or something."

"It was actually very difficult to buy," said Eddy. "The owner couldn't decide who to sell it to. In the end, all interested buyers had to write a letter explaining our hopes and dreams for the place. I guess mine won. Though I feel a little bad now, knowing I crushed the dreams of an elderly lady."

"Don't," said Spencer. "This would be Demelza's fifth Monstera shop. All of her previous ones failed because she yelled at her customers and charged ten times more than each plant was worth. Believe me, the people of Gray Birch will be happy to have a bakery instead."

"Absolutely. Don't sweat it," agreed Tahereh. "Demelza fancies herself the queen of the town and nearly always gets her way."

"In fact, she can behave rather badly when she *doesn't* get her way," said Spencer.

"Yes." Tahereh added more cream to her coffee. "She loves teaching her live-in grandson all about bad manners."

"Huh," said Eddy, tapping the table softly, a frown marring his face. "Well, that certainly *is* interesting."

"Why?" asked Spencer. "Don't tell me she did something to you already?"

"Well, the gas leak. Turns out it wasn't an accident. We found a note duct-taped to the pipe where it had obviously been cut."

"A note?"

Eddy nodded. "Written on cardboard with a marker. *You Are Not Welcome. Leave Town.* And from what you're telling me, Demelza definitely doesn't want me here in *her* firehouse."

Brooke Binder: Well, I heard there was a note of some kind when Eddy first moved here. But I don't know that it was *threatening* per se. I heard it was written in marker and was actually more of a light encouragement of sorts. Or maybe I just dreamed that. I dream a lot, you know. It's not as exciting as dusting the bookshelves, but it's a close second.

Spencer: That note was definitely threatening because it was attached to a severed gas pipe. I mean really, Lieutenant, it's not rocket science.

Dirk Square Jaw: Did he really have to open a *bakery* in that old firehouse? No wonder he got a threatening note. I mean, it's such a prime location, and now it'll only be used by stuffy old women in mothball coats who need a daily dose of sugar just to feel alive. He should've opened a welding shop. Now there's a well-rounded business idea.

Mike the Contractor: None of my people cut that pipe. They're an honest lot. Wouldn't hire anyone I didn't trust with my life. Construction is a dangerous business after all, lots of accidents, but that pipe ain't one of them. Someone had it in for Eddy the moment he crossed the town line. Never did like Demelza much, but she's better than that grandson of hers. I've caught him dropping dead squirrels into my wet cement a dozen times.

MARGARET: I'm sorry, Lieutenant. I don't know how this cat is avoiding my traps, but I fear it's pushing me to the very brink of propriety. The butterfly net *must* be extracted.

Scholastic Tail-Wagger

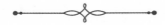

The next day, I followed Spencer down to the laundry room to oversee her washing of the dog beds. "Okay," she said, checking her watch. "We have an hour until Tahereh and Harry pick us up. That's just enough time to finish washing these and get ready."

Jumping onto the windowsill, I arched against the filigrees of early morning frost that clung to the windowpane. After Eddy had returned from installing ovens at the bakery last night, he and Spencer had been invited to go skiing the next day with Tahereh and her husband, Harry. As a Viking, I very much approved. After all, Scandinavians invented skis, and zooming across snow is quite natural for us Norsecats.

Taking a last sip of coffee, Spencer set down her mug, rolled up her sleeves, and picked up a soft green dog bed. Soaking it in a sink that looked as though it ate krill, she doused it with soap, and I wrinkled my nose as the stench of canine permeated the room. "You know," she said, scrubbing the bed vigorously, "Eddy really should be more concerned about that note. It was sabotage, clear and simple. But he says he doesn't need to involve the police. Which I suppose I understand. He's new to town after all and doesn't want to immediately step on toes . . . but someone already stepped on *his*."

Thinking of toes, I began to bathe my own. It'd been nothing but Eddy this and Eddy that all morning. Normally I wouldn't be interested, but I was starting to like the man . . . despite his affection for swine. Luckily that swine had slept in his own room last night, returning my pillow to me, and it had taken 105 cheek rubs to replace his scent with my own.

Gazing out the window, Spencer twisted the water from the dog bed and frowned. "Why is Skunk yapping at Widmer?"

Widmer was a handsome black Lab staying at Fox Burrow for the spring. His humans were avid hikers off tackling the Ozark Highlands Trail and he, an avid bear slayer. I glanced out the window where he napped on his patio. Skunk, meanwhile, pranced about on the other side of his fence, batting her eyelashes and wafting her freshly oiled fur in his direction. "She's not yapping, she's flirting," I said. "And skirting her many duties."

Spencer cracked open the window. "Squelch the bellows, Skunk." The Pom attempted to justify herself with more yaps. "Skunk!"

A cold breeze drifted by the window as Pete Moss glided into the open from nowhere. As he headed to calm Skunk I reflected on the idea that he must be dead anytime he wasn't in motion.

"Thanks, Pete!" Spencer yelled. Shutting the window, she let the wet dog bed drop to the floor like a kid thumping on AstroTurf.

I finished my bath while outside the mountains melted into the blue cream sky like white chocolate chips. It was a perfect day for skiing, and I pondered going along. Curiosity curiates the cat after all, and I was more than curious to see how Eddy handled the slopes.

"You are not welcome. Leave town," Spencer muttered, squeezing the soap bottle hard enough to make it gasp. Her blond braid swung where it hung between her shoulder blades. "That's a threat, clear as day."

Skunk decided to come along as well, and her elbow dug into my ribs as we hid beneath the pile of ski jackets in the back of Harry's old Volkswagen bus. See, there was no choice *but* to hide. Spencer didn't approve of us going skiing. It was too cold, she said. And too dangerous. Well, maybe for Skunk, but not for me. Cold and dangerous is a Viking's most natural state.

The van coughed several times before starting, and I praised Freyja the swine hadn't wanted to come, preferring to stay with Fennec. We'd seen the puppy's tattoo last night. He'd fallen asleep again by the fire, this time on his back, and we'd all gaped at the crude lines of ink. They were thick, especially the fangs of the dog head. The needle used must've been extraordinarily painful on his soft underbelly.

"Ah, good girl, Vanna!" roared Harry as the white bus finally coughed to life. Jovial and outdoorsy, he and Eddy hit it off right away. Pulling away from the inn, the two spoke affably about "German vehicles" and "wiring problems."

"I wish Delphiki were coming," whispered Skunk, referring to Tahereh's tiny terrier and her bosom friend. I, for one, was perfectly happy she wasn't. Together, Skunk and Delphiki were like the fingers of a tornado—my face, their prairie.

It was only thirty minutes from Gray Birch to Butterfly Ski Resort, and the road snaked up and up, the trees on either side thickening, the snow deepening. By the time we arrived, however, my muscles were cramped and the air around me was soured with Skunk breath. As the van bumped through the frozen parking lot, Skunk and I prepped for our escape. It would take a bit of luck to slither out unseen, but I was confident it could be done.

Sure enough, five minutes later Skunk and I bounded freely beneath rows of parked cars while Spencer and the others pulled out their ski jackets, blissfully unaware. The snaggletooth popped out, and Skunk and I grinned at each other. We both loved this resort for different reasons. Me, because the hum of the ski lifts sounded like a horde of Viking arrows shooting through the sky, and Skunk, because of dreamy ski patrol dogs. Both of us, however, loved that the ski lodge offered a wide array of food and drink.

Naturally, our paws led us to the lodge first. Trotting upstairs to the Treeline Café, we took care not to get our toes stepped on by any biped wearing ten pound death (ski) boots, and it was a relief when we entered the café unscathed. A comfortable drone of voices filled the room, as did a roaring fire, and in one corner, a thickly bearded crooner holding a harmonica.

Outside I saw dozens of ski runs, segmenting the forest like petrified avalanches. Bipeds on skis and snowboards flew (or flung) themselves downhill, some expressing an instinct for survival more than others.

As we slunk under tables, vacuuming up crumbs, I spotted James Halvah, Gray Birch's handsome young beekeeper sitting alone at a table. His face was drained of blood, and he spoke angrily into his phone. "You want to *tell* him? And how do you propose we do that?" One hand clenched the edge of the table, his knuckles white. "You know our history. You know what the consequences will be. No, no. *You* listen to *me*. We can't tell him. Not now—not ever." With a growl he ended the call, tossing the phone onto the table.

I turned to Skunk with boosted brows. I'd never known James Halvah to be an angry man. He'd always seemed very agreeable. But then, I hardly interacted with him. The most had been a few months ago when he tried to woo Spencer. Who could he be so furious with? The Pom, however, wasn't paying attention. Her snout was smashed against the window, her gaze glued to something outside.

"My God, Bijou," she panted. "What is *that*?"

"What is what?"

"It went in there." She pointed at a lumpy, multihued chalet of sorts. It sat, squat and homely, on the edge of the trees, sunlight shining off its dappled shoulders. The sign hanging over its door said *Ski Patrol.*

I sighed. "Leave the patrol dogs alone, Skunk."

"No, you have to see." She pulled me toward the exit, and I reluctantly followed her out of the lodge and across the snow to the patrol building. Up three steps we went to a door that screamed *paint me* as loudly as it could. Skunk cocked her ear against it while I scaled an adolescent pine to peek in the window. All was quiet. The front room was empty.

"No one's here," I told her. "Let's go back."

"Not until you see."

Groaning, I scrambled from the tree and then stood on Skunk's haunches in order to open the door. Thumbs, I thought, wrapping both paws around the knob, would be highly useful in such situations. In fact, a lack of thumbs was the sole reason Viking cats hadn't planted their flag on Mars or Tatooine or any other perfectly habitable planet.

With a practiced twist of the wrists, I succeeded in getting the knob to turn, and we tumbled inward. Four vacant treatment tables lined the front room along with shelves full of first aid supplies. Scanning them for snacks, all I spotted were a few tea bags and a lonely jar of honey.

"I can't eat honey," said Skunk, following my gaze. "It binds the teeth and constricts the throat, and no one wants to date a mute Pom."

"Just find your thing," I said. "Then we can get back to the lodge and real food." Following her through a narrow hallway, I pondered the many wonders of a mute Pom.

The next room we stumbled into was a dusty office, and 90 percent of it was taken up by a Saint Bernard with the name "Ullr" on his tag. He was sprawled on the floor, a sun patch covering his back like a saddle. A thick book lay open between his paws, and he looked up at our arrival.

After a moment's contemplation, he cleared his throat and began to recite aloud, "Being stuck in an avalanche is like being stuck in a giant washing machine filled with snow." His voice was deep and sagacious, and I felt a subtle fluttering of awe. "As an unintended passenger of such a frozen cascade," he continued, "one must swim, reach, and hope for help. The best way to survive an avalanche is not to be in one. The second best way is to obtain a Saint Bernard." He closed the book and rose. "I'm Professor Ullr."

Behind me, Skunk fainted.

I licked my lips, which were in need of a heavy dew. "I'm Bijou."

"Ah, yes." He appraised me, a veritable vortex of knowledge within his dark eyes. "I hope you'll remember what I've just read."

"I'm sure I will." I appraised him in return. On his collar, resting beneath his chin like a bow tie, was a small wooden keg. Intrigued, I stepped the paws closer.

"Well proportioned!" Skunk sprang back to life, her eyes bleary, her mouth unaware. "Virile!" She tottered in a circle twice before relocating Ullr, who she'd twice taken for a wall. "It's *him*," she whispered hoarsely to me. "See? Isn't he tremendous?" But the professor wasn't paying her any attention—his gaze was on me.

"Tell me, Bijou," he said, "what do you know of persistent weak layers and wind loading?"

"Both disrupt the digestion," I replied solemnly.

He nodded, his head massive in every way. I stepped slightly out from under it. "Also, these are two signs of unstable snow." He pushed imaginary glasses up his substantial nose. "Most importantly, Bijou, an avalanche's favorite sound is *whump*. If you hear *whump* while on a persistently weak, wind-loaded slope, call your local Saint Bernard forthwith."

"*Whump*." I tried out the avalanche's favorite sound, and a cold tingle slid down my spine.

"Professor," said Skunk, using me to support her weight. "I want you to know I'm very single. And very partial to long walks and peanut butter."

Ullr glanced at her and seemed surprised to see a dog in lieu of a mop.

A moment passed and while doing so gave us an awkward wave. Clearing her throat, Skunk continued. "Please, tell me about you. Your likes, dislikes, pet peeves, dreams." She sat and stared up at him, her chin resting between my ears. "I want to know everything."

"Very well," he said at last. "I'll tell you one thing: I dislike lions very much. Specifically when they invade my resort."

"Lions," I said. "Up here?"

"Regretfully." Ullr broke eye contact with Skunk with some difficulty, her orbs bulging with resistance. "Two in particular have been prowling this forest. Great big lions with colossal paws. Quite peculiar in their coloring too. Fur more blue-gray than tawny. Makes me wonder if they're not real lions but the ghosts of ones."

"Blue-gray." My heart slowed to a sickly staccato beat.

"I've expelled them from this mountain multiple times. Told them to follow the light and let go of their earthly regrets. Lions are too dangerous to be around all of these people. Even ghostly ones."

"You're saying you've spoken with them?"

Ullr puffed out his chest. "I do not *speak* with lions. I command lions."

"Yes, yes." I flapped my paw. "But what exactly did they *say*? Did they give you their names?"

The Saint Bernard narrowed his eyes and lowered his head so that I felt his hot breath on my whiskers. "You don't want their names, little cat. You don't want to find them. You don't want to be their dinner."

For a moment I considered telling him about the two great god-cats who pulled Freyja's chariot. Cats with blue-gray fur bigger than him. Asmund the male and Aslog the female. Both of whom I'd dreamed of meeting since kitten-hood. I *considered* it. In the end I simply confessed that my brain was rattled by hunger, while Skunk confessed that hers was rattled by love.

Ullr lifted his head to look out the window. "Just as well, I am tired of speaking of lions, and I have more important things to think about. Like the fact that there is no powder today. The skiers are disappointed there hasn't been a recent snow. Some are already thinking of summer."

"Summer is my favorite," said Skunk.

"In summer," said the professor, "it is vital one does not attempt to cross a rain-swollen stream. Wait it out. The stream will recede as soon as the rain stops." He looked at me. "Remember this, Bijou."

I nodded, though I'd barely heard a word the scholastic tail-wagger had said. I was too busy thinking of the mysterious lions with fur colored blue and gray.

Magnum Vikus

We were exiled from the ski patrol when a skier with a twisted knee was rushed in. Immediately Ullr was all business, offering the woman whiskey from his personal keg while Skunk and I slunk out the back.

Now I wandered aimlessly across the snow, swiping Dewclaw randomly at its groomed rows, the ridges as perfect as sweeping longship oars. Skunk danced alongside me, stardust in her eyes.

Instead of returning to the lodge, I found myself pulled into the forest where the deep snow lurked, and I paused my rumination long enough to warn Skunk away from the tree wells.

"I've fallen in love, Bijou," she replied dreamily. "I can fall into nothing else."

I nodded and continued to walk. Possibility, an ever and again draconian mistress, had smacked me twice upside the head. Two colossal lions with fur not tawny but blue-gray.

Could it be? The prospect of their nearness tantalized, dragging Skunk and I farther and farther into the forest until the trees pressed together cheek by jowl, blocking out sunlight.

In the distance, the cries of skiers sounded on sun-washed slopes, mostly hail-fellow-well-mets followed by laughter. But here in the wildwood, shadows weaved like lacework, and pine cones clicked a woodland symphony. As we rounded a stump, a squirrel scolded us from his branch just as a rabbit exploded from a nearby bush, its paddle-feet kicking up clouds of snow.

"Hare!" Skunk bugled, bounding forward.

Instantly, I lifted my paw like a stop sign, and her nose rammed into it. "Halt."

Obediently, her front paws skidded through the snow, brake pads smoking. However, this had the unfortunate side effect of launching her hind end high into the air so that she flipped over me, our snouts vis-à-vis, our eyes meeting like the orbs of heaven and hell.

She came to rest on a hillock of pine boughs. But instead of deflating like a balloon as I'd expected, she looked at me with spinny eyes while waving the flag of delight. Apparently Love's joy knew no bounds.

"I'll not have you running off by yourself and getting lost," I told her.

"I could only get lost in Ullr's eyes," she protested.

"Even so, the forest is fraught with tragedy," I warned.

And, sure enough, three gullies and five frenzied blue jays later, we encountered that tragedy. I'd collected a cluster of sap between the ears and there it stayed, gleefully barnacled and spewing taunts only freeloaders could comprehend. "Detach the invader," I ordered Skunk.

But suddenly, it seemed the Pom had lost her fragile hold on sanity. Ignoring me, she stared uphill, a quiver taking hold of her toenails and working its way up. She let out a sharp *yap*, *yap*, *YAP* that pierced my eardrums and floofed the fur so much we both looked like unsheared mutton.

I did my best to shush her and find the screw that'd rattled loose, but it was like trying to bag flies. I wished I'd never allowed her on this walkabout. Pomeranians possessed very little in the way of wilderness skills, and now she'd gone and sold her soul to the nearest thicket.

As suddenly as the yaps started, they stopped. In place of them gushed a series of growls so low I could practically see the octaves descend. Never in all my years had I heard such a sound emit from Skunk. I glanced over my shoulder to make sure a Doberman pinscher hadn't come into view, but all I saw was a clan of traumatized pine cones, each one fatter than the last.

Swiveling my neck back around, I cranked it uphill in time to see Skunk's bushy black bustle bounding toward a wooden shack. Two sets of skis and a snowboard leaned haphazardly against it, and clouds of smoke flowed from its countless cracks and crevices. As I rushed after her, a high-pitched scream came from within.

"It's on fire, Bijou!" Skunk howled as I caught up to her. "And there are people inside!"

Well, it is often said that Disaster brings out the best in Bijou, and this was no exception. Powering up my lungs, I bellowed like a whiskied jarl and found myself the architect of a fire alarm not even the deafest bipeds could ignore. Skunk joined in, and together we shook the very foundations of the shack. Bits of debris rained down on us, and the Pom's bays choked on a pebble roughly the width and length of a lentil.

As she hacked, a pimpled face appeared in the entrance, cloaked in smoke. Red eyes widened in terror as I launched toward it, my claws extended to pull it to safety. With a yelp it swatted me away. Landing on my feet, I launched at it again, bellowing, "LET ME SAVE YOU!"

"No!" it screamed, and ducked back inside.

Airborne, I flew through the smoke screen, coming to rest on my head in the middle of the shack floor. Silence greeted me. Hefting myself upright, I felt both the weight of my imaginary helmet (donned at exactly the right moment) and the wound in my pride (my dearest organ).

No flames crackled in the shack, and Disaster did nothing more than yawn and buff her nails in the corner. Three teenagers stared at me, a boy and a girl sitting cross-legged in grungy snow pants and the pimple-faced boy I'd tried to save, his eyes still wide with remnants of my valor. All were surrounded by a thick haze of their own cigarette smoke.

In the silence, a soprano, much like that of a dying hyena, assaulted the ears, and I winced.

"Squelch the bellows, Skunk!" I shouted. "I'm fine. There is no fire. I repeat. There is no fire!"

"Fight the fire, Bijou!" she howled.

"There is NO fire!"

But she continued to howl, and I caught "Sea of flames" and "Immolation" as she started launching snow through the entryway with her hind legs.

The silence in the shack was broken by a chuckle slow as molasses. *Drip ha*, *drip ha*. Then the pimple-faced boy screeched a laugh identical to the scream we'd heard earlier. That boy, I realized with a start, was Pim Corn—more specifically, William Corn the Third. He was Demelza Corn's disreputable grandson, and the cigarettes he and his friends had been smoking completely polluted the shack.

I'd heard enough stories about Pim and maimed critters to know I had to play it cool. Once I'd even seen him shoot an unsuspecting rabbit with his slingshot in the town square.

The rock he'd used had been specially chosen for its wholly jagged edges and death-to-bunnies ideology.

"Dude," said the other boy, looking at me. "Is that thing *wild?*" He had black hair and a handsome face and clearly knew how to carry a football from the way he suddenly lurched forward and stuffed me under his arm. Horribly, the many layers of my underside accordioned within his grip, and I reacted by speedbagging his face.

"Put it down, Kyle," said the girl, rolling her eyes. "It could be rabid."

"Yeah, I mean, did you see the way it attacked me in the doorway?" said Pim.

Working up bubbles of saliva, I exposed the snaggle-tooth. Immediately Kyle dropped me like a sack of salmonella, shouting, "Is that *froth?*"

I shot for the exit just as Pim, who was laughing hysterically, said, "You're such a sissy, Kyle. I've been bitten by hundreds of squirrels, and I'm fine."

"Oh, did that tingle go away then?" asked the girl.

"Kinda. I only feel it when I have to do chores and stuff for Gram. Like the other night she handed me a shovel and told me to dig at some construction site downtown. I felt it something nasty then."

Outside, I screeched to a halt by ramming into Skunk, who was soliloquizing a funeral prayer.

"Bijou." She stared at me, her voice hoarse. Then, with a great shake of her mane, she said, "No, it can't be. You died in the fire, and I don't want your ghost. Don't be like the lions. Follow the light, Bijou!"

"I'm bored," said Kyle. "Let's go ride."

"Only boring people get bored, Kyle."

"If I burn sage, will you go away?" Skunk whispered.

"Skunk, I'm not a ghost," I growled, turning to meet her eyes, which were plumb full of Pomeranian persistence.

"But you look wan."

"That's from hunger."

The return of my existence took a moment to sink in, but when it did she resumed her caterwauling, pausing only to slobber swaths of joy across my face. At the noise, however, a string of paranoid profanity emitted from the shack, including cries of "rabies" and "direwolves" and "butcher it."

"Time to go, Skunk," I said, hooking her collar with a claw just as Pim emerged, his ski goggles askew and slingshot in hand. "Skunk!"

Pew. A pebble whizzed overhead, and Skunk snapped at it as though it were a wayward bee.

"Skunk Anita Estelle Bonanno!" I leapt away from the shack, dragging her with me. "Run!"

Skunk zoomed over the forest floor like she'd never zoomed before. I, however, preferred to do my zooming in the treetops. Behind me, I could hear branches cracking and bark ripping as pebbles flew in pursuit. I upped the speed from Zoom to Scamper, which was more boundy, enabling me to reach farther destinations.

Even so, I felt a sharp *ping* on my tail and was expecting the jagged edges of Death any moment when the forest abruptly ended and I dropped, my legs splayed, into an unsuspecting ski run. Luckily, Skunk was there to break my fall, and she tumbled down the leeside of the mountain.

"Oiy! Watch it there!" a man yelled, flying past me on his skis.

"Hey, cat!" a snowboarder cried, flexing his board to jump over me.

"Jesus take the wheel!" A woman in a yellow snowsuit screamed as she tumbled past me, her skis flying off, her poles, goggles, and earmuffs littering the snow.

Fur porcupined, I looked uphill and saw a river of bipeds on sticks flying toward me. The green sign across the way said *Sleepy Hollow,* and I knew it was one of the busiest runs on the mountain. Increasing my bravery, I performed several rapid calculations in my head. *Distance + Application of Ski Wax - Motivation* x *Weight of Biped = Certain Death.*

Turning, I galloped downhill, away from the stampede and toward Skunk, who was emerging from a fledgling snowberry bush. When I reached her, we rapidly checked each other for injuries before pulling one another toward the trees and away from the flood of oncoming annihilation. At the edge of the run, Skunk stopped suddenly, her eyes lighting up. "Eddy? Bijou, look! Look, it's Eddy!"

Sure enough, sandwiched between the front and back of his ski jacket was Eddy, speeding toward us. He handled his skis quite well, and a dimpled grin of joy decorated his face. Right behind him flew Spencer, and then, farther back, came Tahereh and Harry.

"We're not supposed to be here," I reminded Skunk as she opened her maw to call out. "Hurry behind that tree so they don't see us."

"Bijou?" Eddy slid to a stop, peppering us with snow. He pushed up his goggles and rubbed his eyes. "Skunk?"

It was over. We were finished. Spencer had zoomed right by, but now she'd stopped and was hiking back toward us, her face morphing into a mask of fury. We could still run. I turned to Skunk, my fur tingling. "We could still run." But the Pom had already scampered to Eddy and rode the pogo stick around his legs.

"What are you doing here, girl?" he asked, scratching behind her ears as she wildly licked his glove. "How in the world *are* you here?"

"Bijou Bedelia Bonanno!" Spencer's nostrils flared as she came toward me, and cloudy exhalations puffed from her mouth.

"Uh-oh," Eddy murmured, giving me a sympathetic look.

Spencer stopped near Eddy and leaned on her poles, glaring at me. "Come over here right this instant."

I backed away until my hindquarters winterized the base of a blue spruce.

"*Bijou.*"

Turning, I hugged the tree between my forepaws, digging the claws in deep.

Spencer sighed. "Really? Again? It's like that, is it?"

"Um, this has happened before?" said Eddy.

"Three times. You'd think I'd learn to check the car."

"Everything okay?" Tahereh and Harry joined us, their cheeks rosy with cold. Then, appraising the situation, they added, "Oh. Oh, no. Sorry, Spence."

"They're going to get themselves killed. Or lost, which up here is pretty much the same thing."

That was simply untrue. A Viking never got lost unless she meant to make a discovery.

"Want me to get her?" Eddy asked, stepping out of his bindings.

"Yes, please," Spencer grunted, chasing Skunk, who was bounding from person to person, thrilled. "Bijou wants nothing to do with me when she knows she's in trouble."

Eddy's boots sank deep into the snow as he made his approach. Reaching the spruce, he dropped to his knees. "Come on, Bij. You know you're too hungry to stay here, and Spencer will be less angry if you come with me now."

That was true. I *was* too hungry. In fact, Hunger currently hollowed my stomach so much it felt like a ladle
waiting to be filled. Slowly I released my claws and allowed
Eddy to scoop me up and carry me back to his skis, while
below Skunk's jealousy made crop circles in the snow.

Shaking her head, Spencer snatched up the Pom and
plucked ice balls from her paws. "I will discuss this with both of
you at home," she told us. Then, turning to the others, she said,
"Sorry, everyone. Looks like our day up here will be cut short."

Assuring her it was fine, they all insisted they wanted
nothing more than to cozy up by the fireplace with large
mugs of mulled wine anyway.

As we began our descent, Eddy frowned and whispered to
me, "What in the world lodged itself between your ears, Bij?"

Back at the van, Harry opened the rear door so Skunk and I
could be placed inside. Halfway through lifting it, however,
he stopped. "Uh . . . do you guys see this?"

As one, we swivelled our necks downward to see two
colossal, four-toed paw prints etched in the snow.

"Those are way too big for a dog," said Harry doubtfully. "Unless Clifford was here."

"Definitely not a dog," said Tahereh, crouching to
examine them. "I studied wildlife conservation at my uni-
versity for a semester, and I'm pretty sure this belongs to a
mountain lion."

"I've never seen a mountain lion track that big," said
Spencer.

"And there are only two," said Eddy, looking around.
"Where are the other two? It couldn't just have two paws."

Everyone shrugged. "What a mystery," said Spencer,
taking me from Eddy and placing me in the van with Skunk.

"And another example of why the two of you *cannot* come up here and run around. Do you want to be eaten whole?"

I didn't reply. I was too busy staring at the paw prints, my head spinning.

"*Ouch*," yelped Skunk. "Something just bit me."

I turned to her. "What?"

"Something just bit me. Right there." She pointed toward where she'd been sitting on an old blanket.

Unsheathing Dewclaw, I flipped the blanket back, revealing the sharp corner of a large book.

"That wasn't there before," said Skunk. "I slept on that blanket the whole way up here, and it was like a cloud."

Pushing the blanket farther back, I revealed the book in its entirety. It was an aged, black thing, etched with flaking silver scrollwork. "*Magnum Vikus*," I read the title aloud, noting that the cover was festooned with etchings of drinking horns and Viking runes.

My heart performed multiple flips as I quickly pulled the blanket back over the book.

"Where did that come from?" Skunk whispered.

I signaled her to be quiet and looked once more at the giant paw prints stamped on the snow. And this time I saw them. I saw the two blue-gray hairs perched in the divots of the largest footpads.

As Harry shut the door I was spanked by certainty. It was *them*. Aslog and Asmund. Freyja's god-cats had paid me an earthly visit. They'd felt the presence of another Viking. *My* presence. They'd come and left me a message, and whatever it was was hidden in this book I now incubated.

Lost in Thought, I didn't notice the stench of Skunk's breath the whole way home.

DR. FLORA: *Who?* Mr. Halvah? Oh, he often comes into the office to ask me health questions about bees. Unfortunately that's not really my speciality, though once I suggested a sunnier location for the hive. Tell me, Lieutenant, do you have any dogs? And do they antagonize porcupines? That *is* my speciality.

DEMELZA CORN: Of course I know James Halvah. I've lived in this town my whole life, Lieutenant. I know everyone. Mr. Halvah's honey is exquisite, and I bought a gallon for my annual tea party just last month. The ladies said it was the best yet. Very refined. You see, that's the thing about me, Lieutenant. I appreciate the finer things in life such as tea parties and Monsteras. I'm not like so many here who enjoy sleeping in the dirt and playing in filthy river water. Keep your hands clean and your nose high, I say.

SPENCER: Yes, I went on a date with James Halvah once. He was very nice. But it just didn't work out.

TAHEREH: I'm the one who set Spencer and James up. But that was months ago. I thought they'd make such a good-looking couple. But Spencer's very particular and I love her for it. She knows what she wants, and she refuses to settle for anything less. I understand. I didn't settle for Harry either. He came in and swept me off my feet.

MARGARET: The butterfly net was thwarted, Lieutenant. Awaiting further instructions and am requesting a trough of wine in the meantime.

A Haircut Named Heinous

When we got back to the inn, I had no choice but to leave the book in Harry's van. It was too heavy to move unassisted, and Skunk had tumbled out of the door and disappeared as soon as the engine stopped. I would have to return for it before Harry left, and with a more helpful canine to carry it. Deserting the thing while still not knowing Asmund and Aslog's message, however, was the worst sort of torture.

Now I was stuck in Fox Burrow's grooming room while Spencer and Tahereh scrubbed layers of forest debris off Skunk and me. With a yelp, Spencer pointed to a tiny spider clinging to Skunk's whiskers. "An early bloomer," she groaned, trapping it in a glass and freeing it out into the cold dusk.

"Spencer, it's not coming out," said Tahereh, tugging vainly at the sap barnacled between my ears. This had the unfortunate effect of making me smile, frown, smile, frown, and soon all emotion everywhere pooled in my eyes.

"What's not?" Spencer turned and analyzed the situation. Then, with a deep breath, she pulled clippers from a drawer.

I stiffened. "No."

Spencer raised her hands in fake capitulation. "Now, Bij, this is the only way. I swear I'll make it look good."

"No."

Tahereh lovingly stroked my back. "You look beautiful with any haircut, Bijou. You've got one of those faces, you know? So symmetrical."

"Absolutely, unequivocally, no."

"Very symmetrical," Spencer agreed. "In fact, you could go completely bald and no one would notice. You're that pretty."

This was a lie. The snaggletooth I possessed would only cultivate luster when paired with a bald spot.

Spencer plugged in the clippers and advanced while Tahereh's grip tightened around my midsection.

"The sap can stay," I said, lurching for liberty and failing. "Really, there's no need to detach it."

The clippers hovered above, tittering like a wrathful, wingless bee. Frantic, I looked to Skunk for aid. But the Pom sat on the adjacent grooming table, her fur so floofed from her blowout she was unsighted by overenthusiastic bangs. She would offer no assistance at all.

The clippers' descent was a funeral march, and I prepared to make this an out-of-body experience. I'd done it once before. While meditating on whether to eat a semi-toxic yew plant, I'd hovered above myself and gained a new vantage point. One that allowed me to notice a nearby June bug, which proved much more toothsome.

"I'm sorry, Bij." I heard Spencer's voice as though from a great distance. "I'm only doing this because I love you."

Yes, well. Love comes in many forms, and this one looked remarkably sinister.

Detaching my mind from the body, I floated above and watched myself flinch as the clippers dropped to the gray-and-black silk between my ears. The mound of sap was annihilated in an instant. As was a high percentage of pride. In fact, so much pride left with the sap I seriously considered never rejoining the body.

There, below, was my very own bald spot. Shiny pale skin peeked upward and blinked against the sudden light. Surrounding this unsightly exposure was fur so cropped it reminded me of a scythed wheatfield. Surely the gods were laughing in Valhalla.

"Oh, Bijou, it's not that bad," Spencer said.

"It'll grow back before you know it," said Tahereh, releasing me.

Feeling the inaugural gusts of air on the naked patch of skin, I stumbled off the grooming table, reluctantly reuniting mind and body. A true Viking, I decided, should remain whole, no matter how hideous.

Spencer, who'd scolded me the whole way home from the ski resort, finally took pity. "My poor girl," she said, petting me. "It seems you two had quite an adventure in the forest. Would you like a glass of white kittendel with dinner?"

"Ale," I mumbled, pushing into the warmth of her hand.

Spencer leaned down and kissed my bald spot. "White kittendel it is."

The spicy scents of star anise, cinnamon, and cloves permeated the inn as we emerged from the grooming room and entered the kitchen. Eddy and Harry stood by the stove, Harry watching Eddy glug red wine and brandy into a pot. "This one knows what he's doing," he said, thumping Eddy on the shoulder.

Eddy grinned and added a handful of fresh orange peel. "This is my grandmother's mulled wine recipe."

"Oh, speaking of grandmothers," said Harry, turning to Tahereh and slinging an arm around her shoulder, "Google helped me translate an e-mail from yours. She's very excited to see us and wants to know what size socks you wear."

"What?" said Spencer. "You were finally approved to visit your grandmother in Iran?"

"Can you believe it?" said Tahereh. "After two years of being ignored, Grandma went to Tehran herself and stayed there for two weeks arguing with the Ministry of Foreign Affairs to get us authorization numbers. We just learned that she succeeded and we can buy our plane tickets. We're planning to go in August."

"That's amazing news! Way to go, Grandma." Spencer set me down in order to give Tahereh and Harry a double hug. "You finally get to meet her."

Tahereh's smile warmed the kitchen more than the wine, which was starting to bubble. "I simply can't wait."

"A few more minutes of simmering and we can celebrate with this," said Eddy, tapping a purple-stained spoon on the side of the pot before putting on the lid.

"Let's go sit by the fire," suggested Spencer.

Skunk and I both howled.

"Oh my God, I wouldn't forget you." Rolling her eyes, Spencer walked to our (childlocked) food cupboard while Skunk and I performed tippy-taps.

The melody of kibble raining into our bowls brought out three things: my snaggletooth, Fennec, and the pig. The third thing made the first thing disappear, and I chugged my white kittendel in search of solace.

Skunk, meanwhile, looked up from her bowl to spot Fennec peeking shyly over Hamlet's sweater (gray with golden snitches), and she immediately began to quiver with excitement.

Her cry of *PUPPY* was muffled by my tail, which also blocked her from bowling him over. For a moment, the terrified puppy looked as though he might leg it for quieter shores. But Skunk, realizing this, calmed herself and used her nose to push her food bowl toward him.

The puppy hesitated, his triangular ears flopping forward as he looked at the food. But instead of eating, he only ducked his head further.

"Try pluck first," I suggested, my mouth full. "Then work your way up to bravery." But of course the poor little deaf-mute couldn't hear me.

"Here." Skunk tipped the bowl over and swept the kibble toward him with her tail. "Now you can eat without moving."

"A lifelong dream of mine," I said.

Slowly Fennec's tail, previously limp and noodle-like, climbed upward, the very tip wobbling back and forth. Puppy's first wag.

"That's right," Skunk and I encouraged, "eat it all up now."

Suddenly, with a hop-and-pounce, Fennec gobbled up the food, the entirety of his body wriggling with delight. Skunk and I shared a toothy grin.

"Where's the pig?" Skunk asked, looking around. "We shouldn't leave him out."

I shrugged, focusing only on the puppy. "Who cares about the whereabouts of a swine?"

The crackle of the fire in the living room called to us as the wind rose outside. Spencer and the others were all gathered around it, laughing at something when we entered. They looked over at us, their eyes bright. "Hey, look at you, pal!"

Eddy said to Fennec. "Making friends." Shyly, the puppy wagged as Eddy stroked his velvety ears before checking his watch. "Oops, the wine should be more than mulled by now. I probably boiled the alcohol right out. Be right back."

Suddenly anxious with Eddy's exit, Fennec hid behind Skunk. But when Eddy returned moments later with four mugs and settled himself on the floor, the puppy rushed forward, his too-big paws scrambling clumsily over his knees and onto his lap. Eyes soft, Eddy cradled him, tucking him halfway inside his sweater. "He's never done this before," he whispered, looking at Spencer. "I think he's starting to feel safe here."

"I think he's starting to feel safe with *you*." Spencer smiled, tucking her feet beneath her on the sofa and sipping from her mug.

"I knew I wanted him the moment I saw his little face poking out between the bars," said Eddy. "The shelter workers were pleased. They said a few other people took one glance at his breed and tattoo and moved on. But I didn't even look at any other dogs."

Spencer gazed into her mug for a moment before refocusing on him. "Sometimes," she said softly, "you just know."

Eddy nodded, his big hand stroking Fennec's nose but his eyes fastened on her. "Sometimes you do."

From the corner of my eye I saw Harry plop a five-dollar bill into Tahereh's outstretched hand, a self-satisfied grin stretching her lips.

Outside the wind began to howl.

Hildisvini

Later that night, I got Widmer to carry *Magnum Vikus* up to Skunk's oil cabinet, the book resting heavily in his jaws. A storm had blown in with the wind, and during the short walk we'd been pelted by pea-sized balls of hail. I'd donned my imaginary helmet, but Widmer had nothing. He hadn't complained though. In fact, the only comment he'd made was to say that hail was nothing compared to being walloped by an overweight black bear.

Thanking the Lab for his service, I sent him back to his suite (with the promise of a dog biscuit later during turn-down). Then I settled inside Skunk's essential oil cabinet to read. It was dark and quiet inside, if robustly perfumed, and the laughter of everyone downstairs was muffled below the pink towel Skunk used as a daybed.

Curling on this towel now, I opened the book to page one, the arthritic paper crackling, the gnarled letters popping. To my dismay, four silver runes and a horn fell from the cover and landed on the towel, adorning it like tinsel.

Carefully, I began to read, handling the pages as delicately as the whiskers of a newborn kitten. At first the words were difficult to decipher, for they weren't really *words* but Viking runes, ancient and complex. Closing my eyes, I focused on the northern blood flowing through my veins, summoning my ancestors for aid. After a moment they came, stampeding into my mind's eye, bellowing, belching, pounding their shields and flexing their bloat. Miraculously, the runes transformed from wind-scattered bones to meaningful messages. Thanking the ancestors, I bent eagerly over the book.

On the title page it said, *Magnum Vikus.* Below this was the subtitle: *A Beginner's Guide.*

A beginner's guide to what? I read a little further.

On how to be a Viking, said the runes.

What? I jerked upward, smashing my head against the bottom shelf of oils. Was this Asmund and Aslog's message? That I needed lessons on being a Viking? No, I must read further. Peering at the pages with bulging orbs, I read rapidly.

A Viking earns her full name through actions and deeds. Yes, I knew that. Eventually I would be called Bijou Dragon's Bane.

Vikings have servants called thralls who can eventually earn their freedom. Yes, yes. That's what Skunk was.

Viking women have the same rights as men and can be warriors. Yes, obviously.

Human Vikings gift kittens to new brides as an essential part of a new household.

Human Vikings sailed with their cats. Thus these warrior cats spread across the world, hitched aboard wooden longships.

Viking ships are often called Fjord Elks.

The Norse god Odin rides a great eight-legged horse named Sleipnir.

Yes, yes, *yes.* All of this I knew. My fur poofed, I read on. Ah! Here was something close to my heart.

Freyja's chariot is pulled by two great cats, Asmund and Aslog. (My snaggletooth emerged.) *But most precious to Freyja is her beloved battle-boar, Hildisvini.* (My snaggletooth retreated.)

Her battle *what* now? Boar as in swine as in pig? Never had I heard of this god-swine. Not in all my years of Norse paganism. Flipping rather less carefully through the book than before, I found a section dedicated entirely to this "Hildisvini."

Just then, Skunk opened the cabinet and stuck her nose inside. "Harry and Tahereh are leaving, if you want to say goodbye."

"Skunk." I flicked out a claw and dragged her inside. "Have you heard of Hildisvini?"

The Pom performed a two-blink reboot. Then her eyes crossed in Thought. "Well . . . I know the Hildisvini from stanza seven of the Lay of Hyndla, if that's what you mean. Freyja rides Hildisvini to Valhalla in order to visit Odin while Hyndla rides her wolf. I understand they made very good time."

I stared at the Pom, who often suffered from bouts of unhinged spew. "Stanza seven. Stanza seven? Skunk, do you even know what a stanza is? And how do you know anything about the Norse gods?"

She shrugged, her tongue lolling. "I read."

No, no, *no.* I needed to consult the book. There must be more. I fell upon it like a large-portioned meal. Each inkblot, a snack.

"Have you really never heard of this god-swine, Bijou?" asked Skunk. "Not in all your years of Norse paganism?"

Ignoring her, I focused on the runes, reading all about Hildisvini until there was no more to read. Stunned, I sat back. Skunk, it turned out, was not wrong. Hildisvini *was* spoken of in the Lay of Hyndla, and he was famous as Freyja's loyal battle-boar. In fact, according to the book, it was a tremendous honor for a Viking to be presented with a pig as a companion. It showed exceptional favor with the gods.

I gazed at Skunk, speechless and cross-eyed. Could it be true? If so, it changed everything.

"Mistakes," I said slowly, "may have been made."

"Yes, for instance, maybe you shouldn't have called Hamlet 'thick as a blobfish' this morning," Skunk replied.

"Or spent twelve minutes in the succulent pot asking the ancestors about sacrificial protocols to the gods," I mused. How had I never known about Hildisvini? Had my education been so remiss?

"Your education has been remiss," said Skunk. "It took this Asmund and Assfrog to teach you."

"Aslog," I said.

"Assfrog?"

"Aslog."

"Assfrog?"

An inelegant silence ensued.

"Well . . . I'm off to bid farewell to Tahereh and Harry," said Skunk, ducking away. I could hear her toenails click speedily down the stairs.

Long after she left, I sat staring at a nailhead that had donned a black turtleneck of Pom hair. What else didn't I know? What other essentials could this *beginner's guide* teach me? I wished I were angry. Instead I felt like disgorging a hair ball. If there'd been a ruler in the cabinet, I'd crack it across my knuckles. I'd been a very bad student.

I stayed in the cabinet for hours, watching starvation crawl closer and closer. Finally, I could stay no longer. Despite everything, I needed food. Descending the stairs, I felt weak and I paused at the bottom to catch my breath.

"Are you okay?" asked a blushing voice.

I lifted my head to see the piglet peeking out from under the stairs. His sweater had collected numerous dust balls, as had the end of his nose.

"Ah, Pig," I said evenly. "I'm feeling momententarily unsteady and could use some assistance getting to my food bowl."

Stepping his hooves forward, Hamlet lent me his shoulder, and an accord was reached in my legs between Blood and Flow. Walking slowly toward the kitchen, I searched for something to say. In the end, I settled on what felt most appropriate. "Did you know your name means 'small village'?"

He nodded solemnly.

". . . And do you enjoy small villages?"

He shrugged. "I think so. They're very . . . I don't know. What's the word?"

"Clanlike?" I suggested.

"Clanlike . . ." He wagged his curly tail slightly. "Yeah. They seem that way."

My snaggletooth emerged. "And tell me, Pig, what do you think of the north?"

"I suppose it's better than the south."

Praise Freyja. It was true. Pigs had Viking blood, too, just like cats. Extending my paw, I patted the baby swine on his notable jowl. "It's an honor to know you, my friend. I apologize it took us so long to properly make an acquaintance."

He hopped with an abrupt delight, the dust balls falling away. Sizing him up, I saw he was full of pink potential. In fact, I estimated it wouldn't take long to conjure up some imaginary armor to replace those sweaters of his. Forgetting about my bald spot, forgetting *all* bad things, I asked if he wanted a glass of white kittendel in celebration.

He looked at me, his eyes bright. "Do you have any ale?"

Skunk insisted Hamlet was too young for ale, no matter what he said about Eddy's grandmother letting him sip her cooking sherry. It'd been Skunk and Fennec (who she'd insisted was on her side) against Hamlet and I, so we all went to Miss Tut for the tie-breaking vote.

"Oh yes, he's much too young," she purred, looking at us through blue canted eyes. And then she proceeded to remind us that West Point, New York, was the most important strategic position in America during the Revolution.

"If the British had won West Point, they'd have used the Hudson to split the colonies in two," she informed us, licking balayage fur. "Can you imagine, our farmer boys divided? We'd have lost the war."

"Loki stole Freyja's necklace once," I said, attempting to relate.

"Oh, Bijou," she called as we filed out the door, "a kippah could cover that bald spot. Or you could, of course, fashion a comb-over."

Down in the living room, the hearth cradled sizzling embers, and we found Spencer and Eddy asleep together on the sofa. Still wearing ski sweaters, their mugs half-full of tepid mulled wine, they clearly hadn't meant to fall asleep. But a flushed contentment cloaked the room, brushing their cheeks and deepening their breaths—her head on his shoulder.

Skunk, Hamlet, Fennec, and I glanced at one another, the same thought circulating in our eyes. Then, one by one, we climbed onto the sofa with them, each of us finding a nook or cranny to settle within. I curled in the crook of Spencer's arm, kneading the soft threads of her sweater and smelling her sweet scent mixing with Eddy's salt and flour one.

It took no time at all to drift off, cozy and warm, while outside the wind wailed. This, I thought drowsily, was truly clanlike. More than small villages, more than anything. Or, as Spencer put it in her half sleep before dawn, this was hygge. And the fiercer the storm grew in the night, the more hygge it became.

Die, Jerk

May should've ushered in spring, but it didn't. It procrastinated while our valley between the mountains remained cold, brown, and leafless. As a Viking, I loved snow, but when the snow melted I expected green.

"I expected green," I informed Skunk as we trotted past Widmer's patio. Woken from his nap, the handsome black Lab barked three times to inform us we were not bears. Twice meant we were. Once meant the javelin had been thrown, and we'd best move aside. We thanked him as we passed, promising to return later for a visit.

"Well, I expected Ullr to have found me and proposed by now." Skunk sighed. We slowed as we approached the agility course where Fennec scampered through the triple bow-wow barrel before clearing a set of hound hurdles.

"I really expected the apartment to be done by now," Eddy was saying to Spencer. He was perched on the white three-rail fence encircling the course.

"I didn't." Spencer laughed, leaning against his knee. "The contractors in Gray Birch are notoriously slow."

"I don't mind staying here longer if you don't." Eddy ran a hand through her long blond hair, and she let out a sigh like a baby dragon producing its first flame.

"How come nothing jiggles when Fennec runs?" complained Hamlet, leaving his position between Spencer's legs to sit beside Skunk and I.

"He may not jiggle, but he's still clumsy," I replied, my snaggletooth appearing as the puppy tackled the teeter-totter and teetered right off.

"Not even a yelp when he faceplants," said Eddy, watching the puppy rouse himself and shake off the dirt. "He still hasn't made one sound since I got him."

"Ah, but he expresses himself in so many other ways," said Spencer as Fennec galloped toward the tri-level jump.

"Good boy, Fenn!" Eddy called.

"Are you guys ready to go to Witching Flour?" Spencer asked, turning to the three of us. "We're off just as soon as Fennec's worn out."

We all nodded eagerly. We loved Witching Flour.

"And he should be worn out right about . . . now," said Eddy. And sure enough, Fennec went from full gallop to full nap in a blink, and Eddy hopped off the fence to retrieve him from between the weave poles.

The day wasn't so cold that we couldn't walk to the bakery, and we set out directly, Eddy carrying the snoozing puppy. Hamlet, splendid in his newly imagined armor, spent the whole walk sparring with Skunk. I, meanwhile, watched his developing swordplay with approval. I'd taught the piglet many things in the recent weeks, including how to properly lunge and parry. Twice weekly we sat together in the oil cabinet and studied *Magnum Vikus*. Hamlet, it turned out, was quite bookish, and he memorized the section on battle songs even more quickly than I did. I, however, took my book learning into the world and was much more skilled at finding medicinal plants like *Nepeta cataria* (commonly known as catnip, catswort, and catmint) than he was.

As we neared the old-firehouse-turned-bakery, we passed buildings short and tall, clapboard and brick, folded together arm in arm. Townspeople milled about, everyone enjoying a leisurely Saturday morning. Greetings were exchanged by all, and merry murmurs and clinking glasses sounded as we passed Cocoa Pod, Gray Birch's most popular café. As we walked by the café's window, Tahereh and Harry waved from their table inside.

To the west, the mountains loomed extra close, their shadows purple, their peaks fashioned with comb-overs of dilatory snow. Sighing happily, Spencer intertwined her fingers with Eddy's. She'd told me once that the company of a man had to be sweeter than her own solitude. It was clear now that Eddy was made of sugar, and she bit her lower lip softly after their first kiss and every one thereafter. Closing her eyes, she turned her face toward the sun. "I'm so ready for summer," she said. "So ready to surf the river."

"It's thawing," said Eddy. "Slowly but surely. Give it another couple of weeks and maybe we can go." Having lived in California his whole life until moving to Gray Birch, Eddy was no stranger to surfing—though *river* surfing was something else entirely, and I looked forward to seeing how he handled the never-ending wave.

Walking across the town square, we arrived at the firehouse. Gangly, it loomed over the Snoozy Poet bookstore, which squatted beside it, and was as red as Clifford the Big Red Dog. Two huge garage doors made up its front and they were closed, their glossy new windows papered over, giving the place an air of secrecy.

Leaning against those garage doors, staring at their papered windows, was Brooke Binder, proprietor of the Snoozy Poet and Toddy Club member.

She was sipping from a bottle of orange juice and looked over with huge, spectacled eyes when Spencer greeted her. "Oh, hello," she murmured dreamily, "I was just admiring the new windowpanes." She offered us each a sip of her juice, which, in turn, we each declined. "So much secrecy encircling this building now," she mused. "What with these papered-up windows. The whole town is buzzing about it. Could be something to tell the grandkids about."

"It's not *that* secretive," said Eddy, smiling. "You know it's a bakery."

"Yes," purred Brooke, "but what *kind* of bakery: extra butter or gluten-free?"

Eddy shrugged. "You'll just have to come and see for yourself when it opens."

"And you don't have any grandkids," said Spencer, laughing. "For that you'd first need kids."

"Oh, I don't think I want kids." Brooke wrinkled her nose. "If I wanted to hear the pitter-patter of little feet, I'd put shoes on my cat. But I *do* want to be old. Doesn't being old sound wonderful? There are so many possibilities. Singing to elevator music, taking multiple attempts to get over a speed bump, sleeping separate from your teeth."

"I suppose that's true," said Spencer, while Eddy grinned. "But tell me, how's the Poet doing? Did you get enough business over the winter?"

"Oh, yes," said Brooke, pushing up her enormous glasses. "I closed the shop every Monday, you see. Then I spent that day keeping records and fighting dust. It was all quite exhilarating." Her pea-green scarf flapped in the breeze as she took a swallow of juice and coughed. "Ugh. Pulp." Clearing her throat, she looked at Spencer. "How is your mother? We all miss her in the Toddy Club since she and your father moved to Florida."

"She's well," said Spencer. "I'm sure she misses you too."

Brooke's eerily magnified gaze suddenly dropped to me. "Why hello, kitty. You remind me of my old cat, Plumpy."

What? No, I'd met Plumpy, and I'd never seen a more pitiful or rotund beast. Lobbing up the stink eye, I knocked it out of the park.

"Well, maybe you're not *quite* so plump as Plumpy, but let me tell you, not a single diet ever worked, and I tried them all. After she was gone, poor broad, I realized she'd managed to chew a hole in her plastic food bin. For years she'd been sneaking extra portions. Silly old dame." Lost in memory, Brooke Binder took another swallow of juice before promptly spitting it out.

I felt Spencer's gaze on me and turned to see her looking thoughtful, as though given some great insight. This subject needed a rapid change in course.

Lifting my paw, I pointed out the blood-red graffiti on Witching Flour's smaller side door. The graffiti that said *Die, Jerk*. The graffiti no one had noticed but me.

"Oh my God," said Spencer, a hand fluttering to her mouth. "Really? Who would write that?"

Eddy studied it, his head tilted. "Well, if the phrase itself leaves much to be desired, the spraymanship actually shows talent. I'm impressed."

"Oh yes, *that*." Brooke flicked her gaze at it and then away. "So distasteful." Pouring the remainder of her orange juice into a particularly scurvy-prone shrubbery, she tottered away, her clogs three sizes too big, her scarf three sizes too ugly.

Approaching the graffiti, Spencer used her sleeve to try and rub it off. "Don't worry about it, Spence," said Eddy, coming up behind her. "I'm sure it was just kids. I'll paint over it."

She stepped back with a sigh. "First the gas pipe, then the note, and now this. Nothing rattles you, does it?"

"Spiders do. Spiders rattle me very much."

"Well, I speak fluent Arachnonese," said Skunk. "For instance, that spider just there on the doorframe by your head says welcome. And also that her many children are hungry."

Pulling out a key, Eddy unlocked the door and pushed it open.

"Is everything okay inside?" Spencer asked, peering over his shoulder.

"Aw, it's a mess," said Eddy, a teasing grin tugging the corners of his mouth. "A total hellhole. Completely ruined."

Skunk cleared her throat. "Mrs. Webster says she doesn't appreciate you referring to her home as a 'hellhole' seeing as she's just cleaned it this morning. She says that same comment killed her husband and now she's a single mother with many mouths to feed."

Oblivious to the countless souls scuttling above him, Eddy stood in the doorway for a moment before stepping over the threshold. The rest of us followed, my fur tingling with the possibility of a thousand spindly legs dropping onto my spine. Skunk, meanwhile, pranced gaily beneath all those legs, her eyes shiny, her mouth unhinged as she stared up at them, her tail waving the flag of the bilingual.

As Eddy flicked the lights on inside, I took in the beauty of the old building. The facelift Eddy had given it was immediately apparent. What had been dilapidated was now reinforced, fresh-faced, and clean. The old hardwood floors were once again svelte and ginger colored, the brick walls, cardinal.

Display counters lined the walls, and they were painted the color of a shallow sea, imitating Spencer's eyes. Industrial lights dangled from above, fashioning the bakery slightly steampunk, and I experienced the abrupt (and not unwelcome) desire to wear a monocle. Best of all, a silver fireman's pole still adorned the center of the room, reaching up through a man-sized hole to the second floor.

"The tables and chairs should arrive this week," said Eddy, walking through an archway into the cozy brick kitchen where several balls of dough were rising.

Besides remodeling, he'd spent the last weeks altering his recipes for Gray Birch's high altitude. Up here, cakes, brownies, and breads often found themselves falling into great depressions.

"Good," Eddy grunted, poking the fat spheres of dough. "These look much better already. I tweaked the recipe by using less sugar and baking powder and adding more liquid."

Washing his hands and rolling up his sleeves, he began to punch and knead the dough with efficient fists and well-mus-cled forearms. Scaling the empty cooling rack behind him, I watched keenly over his shoulder. Norsecats, I thought, would make wonderful bakers. We possessed the perfect paws for such work: circular and flat, with cushioned yet firm teardrop pads.

Through the archway, I saw Spencer grab a chalk marker and turn her attention to the huge chalkboard on the wall behind the counter. Stepping onto a stool, she pursed her lips for a moment before writing out *PASTRIES* in bold, scrolling letters. Beneath that she listed:

Cinnamon Roll $2.25
Danish (chocolate, cherry, almond) $2.50
Éclair (gluten-free) $2.00

Croissant $2.25
Scone $2.00

The more Eddy tested his recipes, the clearer the menu became, and Spencer enjoyed the job of menu artist. Moving across the board, she wrote *BAGELS* in bold script.

Bagel, plain $2.25
Bagel with schmear $2.50
Bagel with vegan schmear $2.50
Bagel with jam $2.50
Bagel, loaded $3.00

His cheeks smudged with flour, Eddy stepped through the archway and watched her for a moment before saying, "You know, I think in another month or so she'll be ready to open."

Spencer turned on her stool, the marker suspended in the air. "Really?"

"Yep. We're making really good progress."

"Eddy, we should throw a grand opening party for the whole town. Think how fun that would be."

He blew a dusting of flour from his arm and smiled. "That's exactly what I was thinking. Which means I should probably start looking to hire an employee or two."

Hopping from her stool, Spencer marked her jeans slightly with the liquid chalk. "If you set an official date for the opening, I can design a bunch of flyers to put up around town and place in the *Gray Birch Gazette*. We need to get this place on social media too. Start spreading the word. Everyone will want to come."

"Except for whoever cut my gas pipe and wrote *Die, Jerk* on my door," Eddy said, disappearing back into the kitchen before she could say anything about "having caution" or "mustering Lieutenant Tennant." Glancing at me where I sat on the cooling rack, she rolled her eyes.

Thirty minutes later, the dough had transformed into gooey cinnamon rolls and a heavy, three-part knock sounded on the kitchen door, which led to the alleyway. Skunk, who'd been soaking up the heat from the oven, hurdled toward the door like a tumbleweed. "I'll get it! I got it! MOVE OUT OF THE WAY."

"Oh, hi, James," said Eddy, opening the door and snatching Skunk, who torpedoed through his legs. "Come on in."

James Halvah, the handsome, normally *non*-angry beekeeper, entered the kitchen with a two-gallon jar of honey under each arm. "Your delivery, as promised," he said, setting them on the counter with a *thump*.

Eddy bent to study the golden liquid. "These look fantastic. Thanks for delivering them."

James Halvah didn't reply but instead stalked around the kitchen, weighing it with a critical eye. Suddenly he turned from where he'd been analyzing the cat on the cooling rack. "You don't remember me from before, do you?" His eyes had turned just as stormy as they'd been at the ski lodge.

Eddy straightened and looked at the other man quizzically. "Should I? Did we know each other before I moved here?"

"Oh, hey, Halvah." Spencer stepped through the archway, chalk dotting her cheeks along with her freckles.

The beekeeper looked at her, startled. "Spencer? I didn't know you were here."

"I'm just helping Eddy design his menu board." Noting the mood, she stuck the marker in her pocket with the lid still off. I watched a white splotch spread through the denim like a blossom of blood. "Is everything okay?"

Halvah deflated. "Ah, well, I didn't mean to involve you in this."

"Involve me in what?"

"Yeah, I'd like to know too," said Eddy, his brows suspended.

Halvah hesitated, and a silence, awkward in every conceivable way, stumbled through the room.

"Okay," said Eddy slowly, "tell me when we knew each other, James. I'm very curious."

Halvah crossed his arms. "Camp Fell."

"Camp Fell." Eddy's eyes widened. "Camp Fell! That's right, you were one of my counselors. I remember now. We called you Moose."

"Just one of the many joys of that job."

"Hold on," said Spencer. "Eddy, you went to Camp Fell? That's just thirty minutes from here."

"My parents sent me when I was twelve, and that's when I fell in love with the mountains. That's when I knew I wanted to move here someday."

"But you got kicked out," said Halvah, crossing his arms.

Eddy threw Spencer a sheepish look and shrugged. "I guess I did."

"You got kicked out of camp?" Spencer said, laughing. "What'd you do?" She turned to Halvah. "What did he do?"

"He ironed melt-a-beads into my hair while I slept, that's what," growled Halvah. "Hair I'd spent years growing out. Melted them right into my scalp, and it all had to be shaved off. I still have the scars."

"Like I said, I was twelve," said Eddy, abashed.

"And I was nineteen and my girlfriend broke up with me. Said she didn't date bald people."

"I'm sorry," said Eddy. "Really, I am. I regretted it the moment I did it."

"Yes, because you got kicked out."

Eddy held out his hand. "No, I deserved it. Can we have a fresh start now?"

Halvah considered this for a moment, his arms still crossed while Eddy's hand hung suspended between them. Finally the beekeeper took it, his eyes calming. "I suppose the past is the past. Anyway, I have much more pressing problems to worry about. Have a nice day." And he stepped out into the alleyway without a backward look.

"Do you think he cut your pipe and graffitied your door?" Spencer asked later that night over steaming mugs of tea.

Eddy plucked a piece of lint from Hamlet's sweater (cream with avocados). "Maybe. But I doubt it. He didn't seem upset enough to do that. Even though ironing those beads into his hair was one of the worst things I've ever done. Really, I was a good kid overall. There was just something about Moose, I mean James. He seems like a fine enough fellow now, but back then he was always looking for a fight. Even with pimply little camp kids."

"Sounds a bit like his stepfather," mused Spencer.

"Who's his stepfather?"

"Foggy Lawson. From the Drunken Warbler? I like him very much, but he used to have quite a violent streak. He's worked on it though. Went to anger management and he's much better now."

"Glad to hear it." Eddy sipped his tea. "I like Foggy too."

Brooke Binder: All I know is James Halvah is a kind man. You know my friend Bobi Pinn? Well, she used to have money problems. She wouldn't want me saying anything about it, of course. But James helped her out.

Harry: I went to Camp Fell, too, though it must've been the year after Eddy, and Moose was still a counselor. He sure had a short fuse then. But he was going through some stuff. I mean, his mother had remarried and he was stuck with a new stepfather. But I'm sure you know about that. Everyone in town knows about Halvah and Foggy. Loved each other one minute, hated each other the next. Halvah was always trying to one-up Foggy.

Bobi Pinn: Money problems, Lieutenant? No, I've had many problems in my life but certainly never financially.

Margaret: Minor lacerations sustained, Lieutenant. I repeat. Minor lacerations sustained.

River Surfing

Two weeks later, I was cloaked in a tapestry of torment. Hunger had snuck up on me—the Prius of feline suffering. There was nothing . . . and then, suddenly, it was there, *the famine.*

If I didn't dine, I'd die. I'd just keel over right there on the floorboards, all four legs shooting up like the pale grass that would cover my grave.

Spencer had gone to pick up a new guest and still hadn't returned. Delirious, I looked at the clock by the front door. It was now fifty-six minutes past my dinnertime.

Stumbling into the kitchen, I slid around the walls in order to keep upright. The fridge wasn't far. I could see it in front of me, a beacon of hope. Sometimes it didn't latch properly, and I prayed this was one of those times.

It wasn't. The portal was firmly shut, and I bit the traitorous shrew right on her drooping door gasket. It didn't matter that I hit sheet metal and battered the enamel on a premolar. What mattered was there was a well-sauced noodle stuck to the gasket—a spill from an era not so long ago.

Wolfing it down whole, I sat back, smacking my sticky lips. Though far from full, I no longer feared imminent expiration. Raising a paw, I used it to wash my face—going up, down, and around in a method that takes years to perfect. In fact, it takes so much skill some cats never perfect this face baptism, no matter how old. Miss Tut, for instance, lacks the elasticity to reach the soft basins at the back of her ears. Other cats miss their inner eyes or the tips of their whiskers.

It was during this ritual that Pete Moss glided in on silent feet. Honestly, the man didn't walk; he hovered. Needless to say, I was unaware of his presence until he placed a calloused hand on my lumbar and I shot straight to the firmament. Now, normally cats don't fly. But at that moment, I swam the paws and flew to the counter, my fur billowed to serve as my parachute. The landing was rough as I came in too fast and slid bum-over-chin across the granite slab. In desperation, I threw out Dewclaw to act as my ice ax, and just as I careened over the edge, it caught. I lurched to a halt, hanging in midair like a listless flea, my heart hammering.

Pete ended what he started by scooping me up and holding me to his chest. Cocooned against it, I felt relief . . . until I felt the unmistakable vibrations of his laugh. I stiffened and prepared to protest. But before I could utter a word, he reached out and unlatched my food cupboard. Immediately all was forgiven, and I looked up at his whiskered face with liquid eyes.

Five minutes later, stuffed with kibble, I waddled to the bay window to watch for Spencer. Outside, a cold spring rain came down in sheets, its tears streaking the glass. Sitting with my tail around my toes, time ticked slowly by, the pale green world turning to mud as night fell.

Spencer was late. She was late, and the raindrops pelting the rooftop reminded me of that fact with every bark and hiss. *She's late, she's late, sheee's late.* Adjusting my position, I watched them spatter into the muddy puddles of the driveway. It was as though tiny cocoa whales lived in a tiny cocoa sea. The raindrops, the umbrella effect of their blowholes. I pondered what it would be like to live in the sea. To be a sea cat.

I was untangling my imaginary sea-self from an imposing clump of seaweed when I saw headlights flash up the drive. Sopping wet shadows of sopping wet town deer leapt out of the way as Spencer's car splashed toward the inn. In the passenger seat, two fluffy ears framed a long snout, and I pictured the new guest registry I'd seen on Spencer's computer that morning. The new arrival's name was Cork. A young border collie who'd failed sheepdog school in Ireland but still enjoyed herding various things like wasps and trout and so forth. He was to be set up in the Shamrock Suite for two months while his humans closed their affairs overseas. They would then join him in Colorado to begin a new life together.

Preparing myself for the mild-to-medium regurgitation that often occurred upon meeting new dogs, I went to the door and took up my welcome stance. Each paw was placed mightily on a knot in the wood flooring, my chest was thrown out, my tail poofed to its fullest setting. As manager, one must offer warmth and hospitality while simultaneously hiding any weakness or flaw.

Spencer turned the knob, but it was the wind that flung the door open with a *bang*. A sheet of icy water hit me square in the face while a set of muddy paws trampled me into the floor. Freeing myself from the tangle of limbs, I rolled to my feet in time to see another set of headlights at the end of the driveway. But these were unmoving. *Watching.* Before I had time to reflect on the matter, however, Spencer shut the door and peeled off her jacket.

Shivering, she rubbed her arms. "These spring rains are going to be the death of me. Is Eddy still at Witching Flour?" I nodded as she grabbed a towel off the hook by the door and knelt to dry Cork's paws.

Wiping droplets of water from my whiskers, I faced the collie, resuming my stance. "Welcome to Fox Burrow Inn. I'm Bijou, your manager."

"Eh? Oh, thanks." Cork glanced down at me incuriously, but then his eyes widened. "Sister," he said, reverently. "Forgive me, I didn't realize. It's an honor to make your acquaintance."

"Sister?" I stepped closer. "What do you mean?"

"Why, your full name must be Sister Mary Bijou. You're Catholic, like me. And a progressive one too. In fact, you're the first nun I've met who shaves her head like a monk."

Catholic? Nun? I stared at him in confusion. But then, suddenly, it clicked. *Shaves her head like a monk.* . . . Red-hot shame bubbled to the surface of my fur. The collie was looking down at my bald spot. My very own Friar Tuck. The fur had grown back some but not all the way, and the remaining crop circle had blinded him with Faith. And yet, while scandalized, I saw an opportunity for prestige instead of solely shame. If I played along, I could forever have the upper hand to this Irish mutt.

Ducking my head piously, I touched him with a gentle paw, performing the Benediction.

"Bijou . . ." said Spencer, looking at me knowingly. "What in the world did you just do?"

Stepping back, I let out a meep of innocence.

"I'm yours," said Cork reverently. "Anything you ask of me, I'll do. Just say the word."

"Guests are not to be toyed with," Spencer reminded me while my snaggletooth performed a rapid bench press of the upper lip. "You know that. Now, would you show him to the Shamrock Suite while I prepare him a warm dinner?"

I have to admit, I really started to like Cork the moment I showed him his outdoor patio and he displayed how he could catch raindrops in his teeth, his jaws snapping loudly. He was a blur of black-and-white agility. A vision of determination and focus. He had a responsibility to Play, and it cloaked him with Burden. As he caught drops, I sat in the doorway and listened as he told me his life story.

"I went to an all-lads' sheepdog school in Galway, and I had a whale of a time," he said. *Snap, snap.* "Just not herding sheep. Thing is, I've got a Distraction deep in my bones, and it calls to me regularly. I've got to Play, see? And not just with sheep. Sheep are too predictable. Not like raindrops and sprinklers and such. Anyway, I failed school and so my family decided to move to the United States for a fresh start."

He paused in order to snap up seven drops in particular, his teeth clacking vigorously with each one. I watched, mesmerized, as he stared upward, waiting for the next set of drops to align, his ears cascading down his neck floof, his eyes immense.

Spencer stepped into the suite just then, carrying a bowl of warm dog food. "Here you go, Cork. Oh, you're sopping wet again, buddy. I'll go get more towels." She glanced at me. "Everything good, Bij?"

I assured her it was. I liked our new guest very much.

She bent to scratch me under the chin. "Eddy and I think it may be warm enough to go to the river and surf tomorrow afternoon. It's supposed to be sunny. Want to come?"

I rubbed against her fingers. Few things were better than basking in Spencer's bike basket, batting at river spray while she surfed. "Yes, I want to come," I chirruped.

Cork turned from the rain, his ears plastered to his head solemnly. "Just as I want to corral everyone in the world into a single room. Alas, some dreams are more achievable than others."

The following afternoon, the clouds had cleared and a choir of chickadees serenaded the inn. Their voices danced through the air, high, then low, spinning and waltzing like dust motes beneath the sun. The birds themselves bounced in the trees like fluffy Ping-Pong balls, full of bluster and bravado.

The squeak of the screen door disrupted me from my post beneath a high-altitude shrubbery, and I turned to see Spencer descend the porch steps. She was adorned in her river gear: turquoise board shorts pulled over a black wet suit, with a helmet and life jacket in hand.

Walking over to her bike, which was propped against one of our two apple trees, she hooked a small trailer to it. Then, retrieving her surfboard, she put it inside the trailer. Spotting me, she waved. "Time to go, Bijou!"

Immediately Skunk galloped out of the house, wafting peach oil everywhere, her black fur glistening. She'd leapt onto the trailer and was performing tippy-taps before I'd managed to extract myself from the shrubbery.

Wet grass squelched between my toes as I trotted toward Spencer, inhaling the fresh petrichor emanating from the soil. Petrichor, I thought, was the most delightful scent in the world—second only to a fat, freshly caught cod.

Reaching the bike, I allowed Spencer to lift me into the basket, where I filled it nigh to overflowing. Then we started off, Skunk on the trailer, Spencer happily pedaling, and me, the proud figurehead, letting my whiskers flutter in the wind.

We stopped at Witching Flour to pick up Eddy. He'd been there since before dawn, coddling numerous high-maintenance macarons. Now he waved at us merrily from the window and yelled that he'd be ready in five minutes.

As Spencer and Skunk trotted through the newly painted, graffiti-free door to assist him, I stayed in the basket, soaking up sun rays and watching Gray Birch ready itself for another summer of tourism. Brightly colored kayaks, SUP boards, and cruiser bikes dotted the lawns of rental businesses. Food trucks had been hauled out of their winter warehouses, and boxes of chips, pickles, and buns were being stuffed inside. Dotting the sidewalks were artful, chalky signboards declaring them *Opening Soon!*

Across the street, a few early bird tourists huddled together, poring over trail maps and looking doubtfully up at the mountains, which still maintained thick frostings of snow. Vikings, I knew, could scale those peaks fearlessly. But these humans, with their canary-yellow gaiters and caramel lattes, were no Vikings.

"Afternoon, Bij." Eddy donned his sunglasses as he came outside, his dimples deepening as he tossed his new river surfer onto the trailer. Scooping up Fennec and Hamlet, he placed the puppy in his Outward Hound backpack before mounting his bike with the piglet still tucked under one arm.

"Um, you okay riding like that?" Spencer stepped out from the bakery with a fat chocolate chip cookie in each hand.

"I ride even better one-handed," he said, winking and performing a perfect circle in the road.

"Impressive."

"I spent most of my childhood riding my bike back and forth from the beach." He grinned. "You should see me do a wheelie."

It was half a mile from Witching Flour to the river, and we stopped by a friendly wave called Midtown. It curled and coiled around itself, waving a frothy hello.

The bike lurched as Skunk bounded off the trailer and her legs split in four directions, each one wanting to chase a different scent. And so she stood, splayed in the path for several seconds before she caught sight of a stick swirling at the water's edge and chased that instead. Hamlet shadowed her every move, his skin thickly frosted with SPF 50.

Agreeing to keep an eye on Fennec, who Eddy removed from his Outward Hound backpack and placed gently in the trailer, I watched Spencer and Eddy rock-hop down the bank and then slither into the water like happy seals. Settling more comfortably into the basket, I observed everything through somnolent lids. The river was high with snowmelt, its waters snapping, sudsing, and spuming. A sunray romped by, and a trout propelled itself from the water to snatch it. River surfing, I thought drowsily, was something the ancestors would greatly approve of. In fact, I was 100 percent certain they did it on their shields, their swords renegade paddles that made fish flee.

In companionable silence, Fennec and I watched Spencer partner with a wave, all power and grace, until she got bucked off and swam, grinning and sputtering for shore. Once there, Eddy gave her a hand out, dapples from the nearby aspen leaves dancing on his face. "Okay, you're going to have to give me some tips," he told her. "This is different from surfing the ocean. The wave here never breaks, and its smaller size doesn't mean it has less power. It's moving fast."

"Hey, if that dog can do it, so can you." Spencer grinned and pointed downriver at the Pocket Wave, where a teenager surfed with his black-and-white mutt. The dog stood at the front of the surfboard, legs deployed, tongue out, waving the flag of joy. I shook my head. Somehow over the years, dogs had lassoed a certain aptitude for balancing on unstable things with nothing more than blunt claws and a blind bliss.

"Right," said Eddy, grabbing his board and slipping back into the water. Immediately, he was swept up in the wave's white-capped boils, and for a moment it looked as though he'd get kicked right back out again. But, summoning his years of experience on the ocean, he paddled to adjust his position and then popped to his feet, riding the wave for several seconds before getting spit out. Spencer's cheer was joined by Foggy's as the bartender walked toward us along the riverpath.

"Oh hey, Foggy," said Spencer, wringing out her pony-tail over the dusty path as Eddy swam for shore.

A smile poked through his gray whiskers. "Beautiful afternoon."

Sleepily, I watched them chat as Eddy challenged another wave. Hamlet, spotting Foggy, left his newly claimed wallowing mud and romped over for attention. Obligingly, Foggy bent to pet "the little chap" and compliment him on his "sun safety" and "thickness of application" before moving on to pet Fennec who, surprisingly, allowed him.

"*Ahem.* Excuse me," said a prim voice. We all turned to see Gray Birch's queen bee, Demelza Corn, standing behind us. Up close, she was a woman with far too much neck and a permanently puckered mouth. Her lashes were spiked with mascara, like some kind of cheval-de-frise for the eyes, and she stared at Fennec, who tried to hide. "Don't tell me that is a *pit bull.*"

"He sure is," said Eddy, climbing the bank and leaving a trail of wet footprints. "His name is Fennec. Oh hello, Bobi. I didn't see you there behind Demelza. I'm enjoying my new haircut and you were right, it does showcase my brows, which were suffocating in darkness."

Peering around Demelza's shoulder, the hairdresser, Bobi Pinn, also stared at Fennec. Lifting her gaze, she nodded at Eddy. "Oh? That's very good news."

"Enough chitchat. The dog is horrifying," said Demelza, turning to Spencer. "How long has your friend had it?"

"Eddy's had Fennec since he moved here, Demelza." Spencer sighed. "And he's a very good puppy. Completely harmless."

Demelza licked her lips, smudging blood-red lipstick outside the natural lip line. "I'll say it again, the dog is a *pit bull*. Everyone who's anyone knows they have violent inclinations. The thing could've tore my leg off just now as I walked by. Or worse, bitten the throat clean out of Chi Chi." Opening the turquoise bag that was slung across her torso, she revealed a shaking, potato-colored rodent creature.

"Demelza, Fennec wouldn't do that." Spencer's tone rose slightly as vexation set in. "Pit bulls aren't violent dogs. It's only some of their owners who train them to be that way, giving the whole breed a bad rap. Fenn here is just about the sweetest, shiest thing alive. I'm sure he'd like Chi Chi."

Demelza flared her nostrils, her salt-and-pepper hair stirring in the breeze. "Chi Chi is a Chihuahua. Sired by champions. Nothing like that . . . that *beast*. I'm sure he'd murder her in seconds if given half a chance."

"Now, now, Demelza," said Foggy. "That's a little extreme. Murders don't happen in this town."

"Do not 'now, now' me, Foggy Lawson," Demelza said coldly. "Murders could absolutely happen in this town if we allow just anyone to move in! This *dog* is against the laws of both the town and nature. You agree with me, don't you, Bobi?"

Bobi gave a start as though she'd been called on by her least favorite teacher. "Oh, well now, I'm not sure. I mean, he doesn't *look* vicious. Actually he looks like he could be quite valuable . . ." She trailed off under Demelza's angry gaze.

In the bike trailer, Fennec tried to bury himself under Eddy's surfboard cover, his little face a tapestry of terror. "It's okay, boy," said Eddy, scooping him up protectively. Immediately, the puppy tucked his head in Eddy's elbow.

"Oh my God, he's *fine*," said Demelza, rolling her eyes. "Just tell him *no* instead of coddling him."

"Fennec can't hear a thing we say, Demelza," said Spencer, her voice coated with frost. "As far as we know, his life was quite difficult up until Eddy rescued him, and you're not helping him at all."

Seeing an opportunity for flight, Chi Chi took this moment to leap from Demelza's bag, and she landed on the riverpath in a poof of dust. Immediately Skunk bounded over, and the two circled each other nose-to-butt in a ritual of salutation I'll never understand nor would ever wish to.

"Chi Chi, *no*." Demelza scurried after her. "Chi Chi, get back here this instant!" Snatching up the Chihuahua, Demelza stuffed the poor thing back into her bag before rounding on Eddy. "Pit bulls are a danger to society. In fact, they're not so unlike Californians that way. The *coastal elite*. Ha! More like the coastal criminals. They should not be allowed within our town limits. In fact, I'm certain there's an ordinance."

"There's not," said Spencer. "There's definitely not."

"Well then, there *should* be." Demelza stuck a witchy finger in Eddy's face. "And I will see to it personally that it is not only established but enforced. You outsiders think you can just move in here and break our laws and change our ways. Well, sir, not on my watch."

"Okay, I've had enough of this," said Spencer. "Such hatred, Demelza! You don't even know Eddy."

Demelza crossed her arms. "I know enough."

"Don't blame Eddy for buying the firehouse, Demelza." Foggy spoke with a much practiced quiet and calm. "It was the seller who chose."

Demelza's eyebrows rose sky-high. "And what would you know about that, Foggy? All you do in this town is pour beer and make toddies."

Foggy smiled. "I was the seller, Demelza. And you love those toddies as far as I can tell. In fact, you'll be at the Drunken Warbler again tonight, won't you? Around seven o'clock with the Toddy Club?"

Everyone took a collective breath and stared at the bartender.

"*You* were the seller?" Demelza said, shocked.

"The building had been in my family for a long time." Foggy smoothed his whiskers, a thinly veiled sorrow behind his eyes. "And I never thought I'd be the one to sell it off. But poor decisions led to poor finances, and well, that's that." He shook his head, and Spencer placed a comforting hand on his shoulder.

"Well, I'm shocked to my very core, Foggy," said Demelza. "*Shocked.* I've never felt so betrayed. This town is supposed to look after its own, and my Toddy Club, *by the way*, provides half your business. You have no right to judge it. We put on fundraisers, and we host the Founder's Festival every fall."

"I never said you didn't do good things, Demelza," said Foggy. "But going after this man and his puppy isn't one of them."

Glaring, Demelza turned to Eddy. "Keep that thing in a cage or throw it in the river. I don't care so long as I don't see it around town. And not only am I going to obtain an ordinance, I'm going to report this dog to the police immediately. Come along, Bobi. We're leaving."

DEMELZA CORN: I *told* you Eddy Line and his dog would bring trouble to this town, Lieutenant. I reported them weeks ago. And Spencer, well, she's nothing like her mother. Mae Bonanno and I didn't always see eye to eye, but she was a Toddy Club member and we could always agree on one thing: Gray Birch comes first. This town . . . we both love it. Well, at least she *did*. Maybe it was all a lie. She and that husband of hers, Richard, deserted us and moved to Florida after all. Got all set up on her brother's horse farm. Guess they like it better than running the Fox Burrow Inn. I mean, they let their daughter turn it into a godforsaken *pet* inn, of all things.

BOBI PINN: Everyone loves Foggy. Sure, he's had a rocky past. Got himself into trouble. Had a short fuse and whatnot. But he's been working on himself a lot. He's a pillar of this town now, no doubt about it.

Monsters at Witching Flour

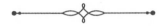

Sometimes I think about Lapland at night. Though from Scandinavia, the ancestors sadly had not resided in Lapland. But I've heard the stories. They say it's the place all Vikings repose after testing their merits. Therefore, it is one of my greatest wishes to visit this magical region of the north.

That night, I eyed Spencer as she bustled around Fox Burrow in her pajamas, feeding our guests. Though the real Lapland was far away, *hers* was right there. It called to me, proffering organic cotton flannel and cherishment. If only she would sit down.

"I just can't believe the *nerve* of Demelza," said Spencer, opening a can of cat food with a loud *pop* and *schwick*. "She actually reported Fenn to the cops. She actually did it."

"Yes, but Lieutenant Tennant was less than impressed," said Eddy, holding out Miss Tut's bowl for Spencer to plop the food in. "He confirmed there's no town ordinance against pit bulls and never will be. This is a dog-friendly place, Spence. Which is one of the many reasons I like it. Practically every trail in Malibu said *No Dogs*. But here there are water bowls on every café patio, two dog parks, and of course, the monthly Pooch Scooch 5K. I mean, half the pups aren't even on leashes most of the time. They get to run and play and have responsibility. The Lieutenant likes Fennec. I've seen him slip treats to him through the hedge."

"Still," said Spencer, taking the bowl and carrying it into Miss Tut's suite, "that woman is a narrow-minded, rubbernecked nark."

"A rubbernecked nark." Eddy laughed and tugged her braid. "Wasn't she a friend of your mother's?"

"Not really. Mom was part of the Toddy Club, so they often saw each other and organized events together. They were friendly, but I wouldn't say they were friends."

"You know," Miss Tut purred, looking at me from the top branches of her carpeted tree, "John Quincy Adams skinny-dipped in the Potomac every day. *And* he wore his own hair instead of a wig to his inauguration. What was left of it anyway."

"Odin has two ravens," I said, again trying to relate. "Huginn and Muninn. And I don't think baldness runs in their family." Hungrily, I watched her descend the tree to eat her wild salmon, and I wondered if there was a wild salmon somewhere out there thinking about me too.

"Ready for your dinner, Bij?" Spencer asked, spotting my salivation.

Popping onto my back legs, I assaulted the doorframe with something akin to a bear hug to show her I was. Then, leading her and Eddy to the kitchen with a prance and a floof, I fantasized about double portions and dessert.

For once my dreams came true.

My normally level-headed Spencer was so scattered filling bowls of food for guests and talking with Eddy that she scooped three times the normal portion into my ceramic bowl. Immediately, my snaggletooth emerged to lead the charge, and with a battle cry I fell face-first into the vessel.

Ten minutes later, I laid supine on the pouf by the fire, wheezing beneath a belly that looked like a molehill. I was the snake who ate the goat. I was the hummingbird who banqueted the square mile of nectar. I'd never been so full.

Fennec scampered into the room and jumped onto the pouf just as I'd sunk into a soothing dream of digestion. With great effort, I cracked open an eyelid. Having recovered from this afternoon's trauma at the river, his eager little face looked down at me while his whole body wriggled with the flag of play. Locked within his boxy puppy jaw was a sock stolen from the laundry room. It hung limply out either side of his mouth, wisely playing dead.

Popping onto his back legs, Fennec bounced his front paws off my bloat, one, two, three times before spinning in a circle. Holding back regurgitation, I pondered the point of puppies. I pondered this while he bounced off my bloat again and then while I booted him off the pouf and fat-chased him down the hall, his face radiating glee.

Skunk, who'd been scream-sneezing every forty seconds due to an unknown allergy, dragged herself downstairs from the oil cabinet. "It's dogbane," she lamented as I waddled speedily by. "It has to be. Spencer must've bought it to kill me. I must've been a bad girl."

"It's not dogbane," I told her impatiently. Anytime Skunk had allergies she thought it was dogbane. But I was fighting a war on two fronts—south I quelled the dinner rebellion while north I rose up against the puppy perpetrator. I had no time for rumors of dogbane.

"You haven't seen any peanut butter lying about, have you?" Skunk called woefully as Fennec and I sped away. "It's nuts, but that's what I want for my last meal."

Her following scream-sneeze blew us out the cat door and onto the soft, infantile lawn that looked purple in the fading light. The ensuing tangle of limbs was padded by both sock and bloat, and when at last we rolled to a stop, I was victorious. My snaggletooth saluted shamelessly while he wriggled on his back, trying to unpin himself. His dog head tattoo snarled up at me, huge, black, and ugly. It was such a strange part of him. Incongruous and loud, while he was everything silent. Even now in his play, he'd uttered no noise.

Stepping ceremoniously off him, I shook my head as he leapt to his feet and stuck his hind end in the air, ready to do it all over again. But a loud crash in the woods nearby resulted in an airborne moment for Bijou. Beside me, Fennec went stiff with terror, his triangular ears flat, his tail stuffed between his legs. Before I'd fully descended, he'd shot back to the inn and disappeared through the cat door, the sock abandoned and strung out along the grass.

The crash sounded again, closer this time, and I unsheathed Dewclaw while donning the imaginary helmet. Facing the woods south of Fox Burrow, I saw a shadow prowling through the trees. Dilating my pupils to better penetrate the darkness, I saw a pair of deciduous horns, early in their growth but destined to be huge.

"Evening, Bijou." A giant buck stepped out of the trees, his coat half-thick, half-shed, giving him a wild appearance.

"Harvey," I said, sheathing the sword. "How are you?" Harvey was the king of the town deer, young and strong and with a mind like Eleanor Roosevelt. At least according to Miss Tut.

"I'm not used to this year's antlers yet," he said, scraping them along the ground and leaving deep furrows in the soil. Perfect for planting catnip, I thought, eyeing them. "They catch on everything. I nearly brought down a young sapling back there. Scarred it for life."

"Speaking of scars . . ." I nodded toward his left shoulder where a line of hair was missing, the skin beneath jagged and raised. "Looks like you're getting a fine one there."

"Oh yeah, this cut's healing up just fine. Artemis, you know Artemis, the real dopey looking buck? Well, he was much worse after our duel for Lottie than me. You remember Lottie, the doe? She's living in Aspen now. Anyway, Artie lost an eye and one antler during that battle, so my scar's nothing in comparison. Actually, I saw him just a few minutes ago. He was very amicable, and we got to chatting about things like the fishiness of the river water and what your friend Eddy is making at the bakery tonight. We're hoping he'll leave us apple cores in the alleyway again."

I cocked my head. "But Eddy's not at the bakery tonight. He's inside the house with Spencer."

"Well, Artie saw a light inside the bakery. Kind of sweeping around."

"What kind of light sweeps?"

"I don't know. A cleanly one, I suppose."

I snorted. "You alfresco beasts don't know anything about the indoors. I suppose it must've been a flashlight. A flashlight sweeps."

"Oh, hello there, pig," Harvey said as Hamlet scampered up to us.

"Bijou, why is Fennec so scared?" the piglet asked after greeting the buck.

But I ignored him. I ignored him because the Gong of Alarm had suddenly struck me between the ears. With a wildly successful inhale, I placed my paws on Hamlet's snout. "We must go."

"Go where?"

"Just don your helmet," I ordered the piglet. "And remember the blood of Hildisvini runs through your veins."

"But where are we going, Bijou?"

"To Witching Flour," I replied. "To capture an intruder."

"Well, then. Happy trails," the buck said. And he disappeared back into the forest.

On the way to the bakery, I stumbled over an ambitious bud of decorative kale and in doing so inhaled a very small rock, which decided to perch halfway down my throat. By the time we arrived at Witching Flour, my breaths rasped so loudly Hamlet shushed me as we looked for signs of intrusion.

The old brick firehouse was silent, roosting like a hen on the street. "I don't see anything," whispered Hamlet doubtfully. Mentally, I slapped him upside the head. Vikings don't shrug off the possibility of Danger without a proper investigation. Unsheathing Dewclaw, it glinted in the moonlight as I summoned the piglet with paw signals.

"Right," he said. "I'll stay here and keep watch."

"No, I'm waving you forward," I hissed, dramatically signaling again. Just then, an arc of yellow light swept across the thinly papered garage windows and disappeared. Trilling identical battle cries, we bolted to the alleyway and through the kitchen window that never quite latched.

I landed softly. Hamlet, however, caught a hoof on an industrial-sized whisk, thus commencing the most furious battle between swine and utensil since 1904. Immediately, the light went out with a *snap*.

In a blind panic, Hamlet searched for his adversary

while I saw everything with a Norse clarity. Reeling the piglet in by his tail, I waited for his eyes to adjust and then pointed to the whisk, which lay defeated on the floor. Victorious, he followed me out of the kitchen.

The main room of the bakery was awash with moonlight, and our shadows slunk along the walls, both spiky with helmets and horns.

It was when I passed the silver fireman's pole that I looked up and saw them. The thick tread of the intruder's boots standing at the edge of the hole cut into the second-story floor. My following battle cry, however, got lodged behind the very small rock still perched in my throat, and Hamlet reacted by thumping me soundly on the lumbar. What came next was a bellow purer than a brass cavalry bugle as the rock sailed through the air to land with a *clack* on the gluten-free pastry case.

Instantly the boots above disappeared, and I spun toward the stairs and charged after them, my whiskers leading the way.

The second floor, that was to be Eddy's apartment, was not nearly so nice as the bakery downstairs. It smelled of mortar dust, and sheets of thick plastic hung from the doorway and walls, leering, ghostly, and silhouetting all manner of shadow and shade.

Stepping over the threshold, I raised my imaginary shield. Rows of boxes were stacked along the walls, and in the center of the room was a jumble of paint cans and tools. A slight breeze rippled the plastic, ushered in by a broken window overlooking the silent, obsidian back alley. And there, just in front of me, were bootprints etched softly in the dust.

Crouching, I stalked them like I'd stalk moles under a membrane of snow. They stopped abruptly at the fireman's pole and then vanished. Swept away like spindrifts of snow. I paused to sniff the air, my nostrils wide enough to envelope a grape and its grown grandchild.

I'd just detected a musty, mannish scent when Hamlet reached the top of the stairs, and I waved him urgently back. The scent came from the darkest corner of the room. The corner shadowed by a sheet of plastic opaque as molten candle wax.

Dropping down, I slithered forward, propelled by my ancestors who were pounding their shields and screaming in my head. The corner, meanwhile, tensed like a monster waiting to pounce.

And pounce it did.

A knife suddenly flashed from behind the molten plastic, sailing through the air so silently I would've missed it had it not kissed my whiskers. With a *thud* and a *thwang* it struck the floorboards inches away, quivering like a doorstop. The wooden handle was carved with something I could've made out had I not been too busy taking to the sky like a maddened bee, the ancestors now caterwauling like banshees.

Midair, the intruder threw aside the plastic and walloped me so hard not even my bloat could absorb the woe. Instead my midriff felt permanently altered, like wet concrete forevermore marked with the imprint of this rabid stranger.

My engines stalled and I crashed to the floor as the heavy boots pounded past me, out the broken window, and down the fire escape. "Who is it, Hamlet?" I bellowed. "Hamlet! Who is it?" But there was only silence, and when my pupils rediscovered sight, they saw the piglet buried headfirst in a box, quivering.

The Question of WC

Did Vikings still hold a place in modern society? I found myself horribly riddled with doubt. All night I pondered this in Skunk's oil cabinet, curled around the intruder's wood-handled knife, nursing my wounds. My bloat was bruised, there was no doubt. But mostly it was my pride that suffered. Not only had my own Vikingness been thrown into question but the piglet's as well. I'd failed him as a teacher. His courage, he'd said, had fled upon seeing the knife, and cowardice had stepped in. He'd told me he hadn't wanted to go from pig to bacon. Knives could do that. He'd seen it on TV.

WC. Those were the letters the wooden handle was carved with. Were they initials? And if so, why had WC been snooping around the bakery? To steal? To hurt Eddy? Was it the same person who'd cut his gas line and graffitied his door?

A knock sounded on the cabinet, and Spencer poked her head in. "Aren't you sick of hiding in here, smelling like a perfume shop?" Her face was sweaty from yoga. "I know Skunk loves it but not you, Bij. You're too outdoorsy."

Quickly, I laid my tail over the knife. Spencer didn't know what had happened. Neither did Eddy. And they never would.

"You should come outside," Spencer said. "It's a beautiful afternoon. It almost feels like summer, and Skunk's on the agility course, despite her allergies. Actually, I think they're helping. She jumps twice as high when she sneezes." Reaching in, she scratched me where the lumbar meets the tail, activating the two-ton jack stand that all kitties have in case of a flat back tire.

Despite my best intentions, despite telling my backside *No*, I was hoisted skyward and the knife was revealed.

"Um, Bijou?"

Yes?

"Why are you incubating a weapon?"

Our gazes locked and we blinked. Once, twice, three times. Then I tapped the initials with a rapid-fire paw. If the blade were mine, *BB* would be carved into the handle, not *WC*.

"Where on earth did you find this?" Spencer asked, grabbing it. "Or, oh God, could someone have broken in and *put* it here? Is this another threat against Eddy?" Cursing, she left the room, holding the wooden handle between two fingers like a moldy sponge.

Listening to her feet thump down the stairs, I decided to follow. Emerging from the cabinet, I stretched creaky limbs. Outside, I could hear the yips of Cork and Widmer as they cheered Skunk around the agility course. Mentally I rapped their noses with a rolled-up newspaper. The Pom would definitely take their applause as declarations of love.

A lovely springtime warmth engulfed me as I stepped outside. Nearby, two yoga mats lay unfurled on the grass. Tahereh sat on one in a deep forward bend, and she looked up as Spencer approached and dropped, cross-legged, onto the other. Wordlessly, Spencer held out the knife. Tahereh studied it while transitioning smoothly into a butterfly pose. "Whose is that?"

"I don't know. Bijou was enveloping it in the oil cabinet."

"Weird." Tahereh's dark eyes found me where I crouched in the grass, and I quickly hid behind a nearby watering can.

"But *how* did it get there?" Spencer said, shaking her head. "Honestly, I'm worried. What if this is another threat or prank against Eddy? What if whoever put it there knows the animals like that cabinet, and they assumed Fennec would go inside?"

Peering at Spencer from beneath the watering can's spout, I thought about my directive for Hamlet to carry the knife home from the bakery. Possibly that had been a poor decision.

Tahereh reached out and took the knife, turning it this way and that, holding it up to the sun, and then sticking it firmly into the ground. "WC," she said. "Are those initials?"

"I think so. Could be a lot of people," said Spencer.

"But let's be honest, you're thinking of the same person I am."

Spencer eyed her askance. "The kid who likes to torture squirrels? The kid whose father is in jail and whose grandmother hates Fennec and Eddy?"

Tahereh nodded. "William Corn the Third. Otherwise known as Pim."

Spencer groaned and twisted her hair into a bun. "Okay, I know that kid has had a rough go with his father in jail and all . . . but if he really broke into my house and put that knife where my animals sleep, he's in big trouble. Do you think I should tell the police?"

"I think you should go to him first. Him and Demelza," said Tahereh. "Try to get some answers before you throw out an official accusation."

Spencer stood and yanked the knife from the ground. "Okay. Let's go then."

"Now? But I haven't laid in Savasana yet. I'm not prepared."

"You don't have to come. But if I don't go now, I'll talk myself out of it. You know me, I hate confrontation."

Sighing, Tahereh scrambled to her feet. "Fine, I'm coming. But all we're doing is asking if the knife belongs to Pim, right? Then we'll go from there. It doesn't have to be a confrontation."

"We'll see. Demelza already hates me, and I'm not exactly a fan of hers either. Let's take our bikes."

"Good idea. Bikes typically aren't very threatening."

Pete Moss agreed to come over and watch the guests while I accompanied Spencer and Tahereh across town. Pete was always very reliable (as the naturally mummified often are), and Spencer told him for the hundredth time that she couldn't run the place without him.

Taking up my position as figurehead in Spencer's bike basket, I vowed to be a better Viking. The ancestors hadn't sailed the sullen seas, their claws digging runes into longships, only for me to be thwarted so easily.

Pedaling past Witching Flour, Tahereh asked Spencer if she wanted to stop and tell Eddy about the knife, to which Spencer said no. She didn't want to "cause crestfallen dough" or "malform a pie," which Tahereh agreed would be unfortunate.

Demelza Corn's house was a massive stucco thing perched on top of a knoll overlooking town. It resembled a flushed apricot in the afternoon sunlight, and we parked our bikes unsteadily in the gravel driveway.

Before we could approach the door, however, it opened and Demelza swooped out. "You *do* realize bikes are gateway vehicles to harder transport like skateboards and scooters, don't you, ladies?" she said, her claws perched on bony hips. Chi Chi, the russet potato dog, shook uncontrollably from the doorway beside a mat that said, *Wipe Your Paws*.

"No, I didn't realize. I suppose I've never thought of them that way," said Spencer agreeably, walking up to her. "It's a lovely afternoon, Demelza. Do you have a moment to chat?"

Demelza ran a suspicious gaze over her and then over Tahereh and me. "I suppose. But I already have guests. It's a Toddy Club biweekly and the ladies are inside making lemonade. We're discussing plans for this year's Founder's Festival. But, seeing as you don't want *anything* to do with the Toddy Club, Spencer, I'll take no offense if you decide to leave."

"Actually, I'd love a glass of lemonade," said Spencer, smiling brightly. "How about you, Tah?"

"Yes, that sounds very refreshing," agreed Tahereh. "It's quite warm today."

"A pint of ale for me," I grunted, unstuffing myself from the basket and landing with a *thump* on the gravel.

"No cats," said Demelza, pointing to a sign that read *Absolutely NO Cats* on the door just above the *Wipe Your Paws* doormat. "The last thing I need is a hair ball ruining my rug."

Annoyed, I informed her I hadn't had a hair ball in five days. Also, her sign said nothing about no Vikings.

"Sorry, Bij," said Spencer, looking at me with sympathy. "Just soak up the sun out here, okay? We won't be long."

"Maybe Chi Chi will keep you company," said Tahereh.

Brows raised, I looked over at Chi Chi and saw only an empty doorway where she'd been, dust motes lingering from her terror-filled flight. "No need. I'll patrol the grounds." Lifting my paw, I pushed off.

"Hold on, Bijou," Spencer called after me. "Just be careful, okay? Don't get into any trouble."

In response, I patted Dewclaw where it hung, wrapped in its imaginary sheath.

Eager to restore confidence in my Vikingness, I circled the house with a long and purposeful stride. But patrolling the grounds proved so dull that ten minutes later I sat on the back patio, tapping the armored plates of a doodlebug while fogging the glass of Demelza's French doors.

Inside, among a frightful number of Monstera plants, I could see Bobi Pinn sneakily adding bourbon to the pitcher of lemonade while Dr. Flora and Brooke Binder gathered around the knife, which had been placed on the kitchen counter. Slightly off to the side, Spencer and Tahereh spoke with Demelza, who looked as though she hadn't smiled since the Cretaceous period.

Seeing me through the window, Chi Chi yelped and crammed herself beneath a paisley armchair. I responded by freeing the snaggletooth, which resulted in even more terror. Refocusing on the women, I saw that Brooke Binder had absentmindedly picked up the knife and was now stirring the lemonade with it. With an exasperated cry, Bobi swapped it for a long wooden spoon. Then, shaking her head, Bobi gathered glasses from the china cabinet—pocketing a rather expensive-looking crystal salt shaker in the process.

Mouth agape, I pointed out the crime. But no one else had seen. Sitting back, I watched Bobi pass glasses of lemonade to everyone (a smug and incriminating bulge in her pocket) and pondered the act of pillaging. I supposed a true Viking wouldn't be against it. But then, a true Viking wouldn't pillage their friends. That was breaking a code.

A moment later, the *stomp, stomp* of footsteps announced I had only seconds to launch myself out of the way before Demelza burst onto the patio.

Spencer followed, regret rumpling her brow. "Oh, come now, Demelza, I'm not accusing Pim of anything. It just made sense to ask if the knife was his, seeing as the initials match. But if you say it isn't, then it isn't. I believe you."

Demelza whirled, her face positively polar. "This is coming from that new boyfriend of yours, isn't it? He sent you to do his dirty work. The pretentiousness of these urban types!"

Each freckle on Spencer's face brightened like a shooting star. "You would know all about pretention, Demelza. Of that, I have no doubt."

The two women stared at each other coldly, the only sound the ring of a Norsecat drawing her sword. But before any more words could be hurled, the hum of a car sounded, crunching and purring its way up the drive.

Turning, Demelza marched around to the front of the house. Spencer and I quickly followed, taking this as our opportunity to exit stage left.

"We shouldn't have come here," Spencer muttered as Tahereh bumped into us on the front lawn. "It's time to leave."

"So soon?" Tahereh replied brightly. "The lemonade is delicious."

Spencer cracked a grin. "The lemonade is spiked."

The car lurched to a stop in front of the house, the engine ticking in an attempt to self-soothe. *Gray Birch Police* was painted on the side, and in the back seat was Pim, his freckled face smashed against the window. Demelza paled.

"Afternoon, Demelza," said Lieutenant Tennant, exiting the driver's seat and doffing his hat. "Ladies." He nodded at Spencer, Tahereh, and the others who'd crowded onto the porch. "Got your boy here."

"I may be getting old, Lieutenant, but I can certainly see that." Demelza stared at Pim, her eyes twin pots of poison.

"Yes, of course," said the Lieutenant. "Anywho, picked him up last night. He and another boy were helping themselves to a buffet of hot dog buns with pickles in them at one of the food trucks downtown. A food truck that wasn't open, I might add."

"He told me he was staying the night at his friend Kyle's." Demelza battled both tooth and lip to get the words out.

"Kyle Winkelmeyer? Yeah, sure. That's the boy I picked him up with."

"Why wasn't I informed of this last night?"

The Lieutenant rubbed a hand over his face, white stubble rasping against his palm. "Both your grandson and I left you several messages, Mrs. Corn. I assumed you got them and simply wanted to leave him overnight to teach him a lesson."

Demelza hesitated. "What time was this exactly?"

"Oh, about nine, I'd say."

"We were at the Warbler at nine, Demelza," said Bobi.

"About three drinks in," offered Brooke.

With a growl, Demelza descended on the police car, yanked open the back door, and dragged William Corn the Third out by his ear. "You listen to me, boy. Just because we received word your father may be getting out of jail soon is no reason to act out. If you think you're showing off for him, you aren't! He won't be proud. Now *get in the house.*"

Spy

Nine o'clock. That was roughly when Hamlet and I had been at Witching Flour the night before, fighting the intruder. Pim, it seemed, had an alibi. Not for breaking into a food truck, of course. But for breaking into the bakery.

"Oh, damn. We left the knife at Demelza's," Spencer said as we pedaled home. "I meant to keep it."

"It's probably best to get rid of it," said Tahereh, her face scrunched in concentration as she wobbled slightly on her bike. "At least now it's away from the animals and Bijou's not going to accidentally stab herself with it."

I took offence to this. A Viking accidentally stabbed herself as many times as a zebra miscounted her stripes. So only once or twice.

"All that confrontation for nothing," Spencer lamented. "We didn't learn anything except that Pim was arrested last night. But I suppose he could've put the knife in the cabinet before then. Honestly, how would I know? I don't look in there every day."

I smooshed myself further into the bike basket, feeling the first flutterings of shame. I'd never meant for Spencer to see the knife, and this was why.

Tahereh's bike wobbled into a ditch and back out again. "I'm ready to lie in Savasana now."

A few days later, I propped on Spencer's knee while she worked on Witching Flour's Facebook page. Specifically, she was creating the announcement for the grand opening party, which had been set for June 1. A date that approached rapidly.

"We need a better photo of the macarons," she told me. "They're so pretty and these pictures don't do them justice. The lighting is horrible. They look like paunchy yo-yos."

I grunted a response but was only half paying attention. Most of my focus was pointed at Dell, Spencer's laptop and my frequent enemy. Currently it took up the lovely, meaty part of Spencer's lap, while I was forced to prop uncomfortably to the side. It would pay for this later.

I only dragged my glare away from it when the front door opened and Eddy entered along with Fennec and Hamlet. All three were dusted in flour. "I think I finally got them right," Eddy announced.

Spencer looked up. "The chocolate soufflés?"

"Yep, they're perfect. Even at this altitude. I'm going to grab some lunch and then head straight back." He plopped on the sofa next to her. "What are you working on?"

"The announcement for the opening, and we need better photos." Spencer shut Dell and I let out a meep of glee. "I need a break. I'll join you for lunch. Though I'm not sure what's in the fridge."

"I went to the store last night," Eddy said, standing and giving her a hand up while I tumbled to the floor. "Oops, sorry, Bij." Eddy immediately scooped me up, and we followed Spencer into the kitchen.

"Chips!" she said. "And potato salad! And sandwich stuff!" She poked her head around the fridge door. "I like you."

We took lunch outside. It was breezy but warm, and from the inn's old picnic table we could see Cork and Widmer lounging on their patios. After eating, I sat like Garfield at the base of the table and mentally thwacked a nearby gopher when he stuck his head out of a hole. Sunwarmed and full, one could nearly forget about intruders and knives, gas pipe cutters and graffiti artists. Skunk came and sat beside me, and I drowsily analyzed the underside of her chin, which looked like whipped cream, and her nose, which looked like two caverns within a mountainside. My own nose looked like the Painted Desert. Each stratum a different color—black blending into brown into pink.

I was ruminating deeply on the Painted Desert (Who painted it? And why?) when something caught my attention at the edge of the forest. I sat forward and peered at the trees, which looked nearly black against the blazing sunlight, and I felt my Viking senses tingle. Something was there. Something was *watching*.

I glanced at the others, but they were oblivious. Spencer and Eddy were discussing wheat versus almond flour, and Fennec and Hamlet had fallen asleep in a pile. "Skunk." I turned to the Pom, who was eyeballing a cloud that looked like a peanut. "*Skunk*."

She snapped to attention. "What?"

"Look into the forest. Do you see anything? Hear anything?"

"No, nothing," she said after a moment.

I frowned. Had I imagined it?

"But I do smell something."

Bench-pressing my recent meal, I rolled upright. "Really? What?"

"I don't know exactly. It's hard to decode. Desperation maybe. Or damp bark."

"You smell desperation." My mood chilled. "Or damp bark. Are you sure you're not smelling yourself?"

"I don't think so. Not this time."

I took a deep breath. Started to draw Dewclaw.

"Oh, I wouldn't bother," said Skunk, her nostrils flaring. "It's moving away."

I started forward. "Even so, the forest must be thoroughly combed."

"Uh-uh, not so fast, young lady," said Spencer, blocking my way. "I don't want you running off right now. We have work to do."

I dragged my paws as we headed back to the inn, stopping every few steps to look suspiciously over my shoulder.

In general, Vikings don't appreciate ill-matched warfare. But that evening ill-matched warfare presented itself, dangling right before my eyes. My opponent was a gutless, brainless shoestring, and I told myself it didn't deserve to die. It was easy prey. Too easy. I almost took pity. *Almost.*

When it skittered through the air to the left, instinct made me dash right. We met halfway around the circle, where I crushed its skull.

"Good girl, Bijou!" Eddy cheered. "You're so quick." He let go of his end of the string and patted me while I vigorously shredded its corpse. Biting and ripping and ripping and biting.

"Um, Spencer? Is it okay that Bijou's hacking like that?" Eddy suddenly crouched over me and attempted to take the string away.

"Is it stuck down her throat?" Spencer rushed into the room, a potato in one hand and a peeler in the other.

"I think it might be."

"God, Bijou." Spencer dropped her cargo and knelt beside me, taking my face between her hands. "Okay, girl, open up. *Bijou* . . . open your mouth right now." I loosened my jaw and felt a familiar burn as she tugged the string from my throat. "Eddy, call Dr. Flora, would you? I think I can get this out, but if not, tell her we're rushing over for emergency services."

The string chafed on the dangly thing at the back of my throat as Eddy dialed. "No one's answering at her office."

"That's weird. She should still be open. Did you try her cell?"

"I don't have the number."

"Use my phone." Spencer jerked her chin toward the table by the door. "It should be in there."

"She's not answering that either," Eddy said a moment later, kneeling beside my head. "But I left a message. Do you want me to try getting it out?"

"I think I'm getting it. Yeah, here we go. Almost there, Bij . . ." And with a final tug, the string left my throat and I performed an outstanding inhale.

"Better?" Spencer asked, petting me.

"So," said Eddy ruefully, "I'm guessing strings aren't the best toy for her then?"

Leaning forward, Spencer planted a kiss between my ears. "Let's just say this isn't the first time this has happened. It's a good thing cats have nine lives."

While Spencer and Eddy finished making dinner, I sat in the bay window and cried "lunge" and "riposte" to Hamlet, who was sword fighting a rubber plant. He sprang at it with unencumbered glee, his jowls flapping, his imaginary sword still unnamed.

"Take a short break," I instructed when he won the battle, his sides heaving.

Sheathing his sword, he moved off for a drink of water while I gazed out the window. It was dusk, and I watched the sky weave a tapestry of color. No one possessed a loom quite like the sky, I thought. She was the most bewitching. The ultimate Viking queen.

As the sun disappeared, I noted the first far-off stars, clustered like grapes. Then I noted that two of the stars had fallen very close to the ground. Squinting, I watched them hover, motionless, their lights making the bumps and shadows of the driveway lunar and otherworldly.

Those aren't stars, I realized. They were headlights. Sitting at the end of our driveway. Watching.

A shudder crawled coldly up my spine, kicking away my earlier doubt. A spy was definitely out there, lurking in the forest, lurking now. But why? Questions swirling between my ears, I watched the headlights turn and drive silently away, leaving the driveway ink-black and alone.

The Call of the North

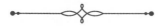

"**S**pencer, wake up."

Something shook Spencer, which in turn shook me where I lay curled on Freyja.

"Spencer! Wake up, honey."

"What's going on?" Spencer groaned and cracked open her eyes the same time I did. Eddy's face loomed over ours in the murk, his eyes deep, dark pools.

"Fennec is gone."

Spencer sat up so quickly the bedcover was yanked out from under me. "What? What do you mean, he's gone?"

"It's five o'clock, Spence. I woke up to go to the bakery and he's not anywhere. Also, the door to the mudroom is open and one of its glass panes is smashed."

Spencer held a hand to her mouth. "Someone broke in?"

"It looks that way."

"Oh my God." Swinging her legs over the side of the bed, she pulled on a robe. "I'm calling the police."

"Okay. I'm going to search for him outside." But instead of moving away, Eddy looked helplessly at Spencer, his hands clenched. "He can't hear me when I call him. He can't even whimper or bark to let me know where he is. I'm worried, Spencer. What if we never find him?"

"We'll find him," Spencer said, firmly. "And we need to see if anything else was taken. The thief may not have stolen him at all. Maybe he just slipped out the door."

Pounding my imaginary helmet into place, I didn't hear the rest of the conversation as I was too busy bolting down the stairs, Skunk and Hamlet hot on my heels. "Spread out," I ordered when we reached the first floor. "Skunk, you stay here and search the entire house. Hamlet, you check the barn. I'll search the grounds. We'll regroup under the picnic table at zero six hundred hours."

Their faces blanked.

"That's six o'clock."

Their faces cleared.

"If you find him, trumpet the call of the north and I will hear it, no matter how far away."

"But I'm not northern," protested Skunk.

"You don't have to be."

"Still, I'd rather trill the song of the south."

"Fine, Skunk. You trill, Hamlet and I will trumpet."

Outside, Spencer's and Eddy's cars both sat in the driveway. I searched them thoroughly, but no puppy was hidden underneath or within. As well, theirs were the only tire tracks, meaning the thief had snuck in on foot.

"Bloody wonderful," I muttered, turning toward the forest. A doe with a prominent black chin strap paused her stroll across the yard to look at me. "Have you seen any prowlers about?" I inquired.

She thought for a moment. "I saw a coyote a moment ago."

"Are you sure it wasn't a pit bull puppy?"

"It was a coyote," she assured me, sashaying toward the forest.

A *thump* reached my ears then, and I looked over to see Eddy forcing open the door to the gardening shed. "Fennec?" he called, clapping his hands, stomping his feet. "Fenn?" He disappeared inside, his headlamp battling the gloomy predawn.

Setting my jaw, I faced the forest and followed the doe's tracks to its edge. Eddy would search the whole Fox Burrow property. *I* would search all that was unknown beyond.

A cold fog blanketed the forest floor as I crept through the trees. The wood was still hushed with sleep. Even the birds slept, their beaks tucked into their chests, their eyelids fluttering with dreams. There was something about being in a dark forest that made me feel close to the ancestors. That made me hunger for battle.

Ahead, a shadow moved from behind a small aspen and I shot toward it, Dewclaw extended. But it was just the doe, chewing her cud. Screeching to a halt, I tipped my helmet. "Morning."

Her startled gaze followed me as I slunk deeper into the trees. I was pondering the pros and cons of deer when I crested a hill and saw headlights below. Two vehicles sat facing each other on a rutted-out old fire road, and two men stood between them, hunched in the cold. As I watched, something small and boxy was passed from one to the other.

Instantly, I launched myself downhill in a squall of pine needles. The two men looked at me in shock as I charged between them, swatting the small and boxy to freedom. "Fennec!" I cried in triumph.

But it wasn't Fennec. It was an actual box, and it clattered disappointingly across the ground.

"Bijou?" Pete Moss hovered over me, emitting the first word I'd heard him say in months.

"Okay, you got what you wanted, Moss," the other man said, eyeing me doubtfully and jumping into his truck. "The deal's done and I'm outta here." Starting the engine, he roared down the fire road.

When the dust cleared, Pete was nowhere in sight. The man dissipated like mist over a lava field, and I spun three circles before spotting him. He stood where the box had been, now clutching it in his gnarled hands.

"What's gotten into you, girl? You shouldn't be out here." He formed the words slowly, his mouth unused to the exercise. "It's not safe." Using a corner of his worn flannel jacket, he gently wiped forest debris from the box.

What was inside that thing? I had to know.

"Come on, Bijou. I'll take you home. Spencer will be worried." Opening the passenger door to his truck, he gestured for me to jump inside.

I tried to explain about Fennec. That *he* was the one we should worry about. Not me.

"Come on now." He bent to scoop me up, but I backed rapidly away.

"Bijou . . ." His voice frosted with disapproval. Clearly he didn't like having to speak so much, and he flapped his hands toward the truck impatiently.

What kind of transaction had I stumbled upon in the woods? What could a bog body like Pete possibly want? To walk across a sodden field without fear? To no longer be waterlogged? Really, what was inside that box?

Meeting his gaze, I demanded to see the box's contents. But with a shake of his head, he packed the box behind the truck seat and scuttled toward me. His face dappled in shadow, he looked terrifying. Nearly as terrifying as the famous Viking, Eric Bloodaxe, though perhaps 5 percent less likely to make his peers soil their breeches. Before I could say *Freyja*, he'd stuffed me into the truck and shut the door. Inside, a John Wayne bobblehead tipped his hat from the dash.

The driver's-side door opened with a loud creak and Pete climbed in. Again, I explained about Fennec. But he just insisted on taking me home, and we bumped down the fire road, a carpet of brittle overgrowth snapping beneath the tires.

When we arrived back at Fox Burrow, a police car squatted in the driveway, its hood streaked with the fire colors of dawn.

"See? They're looking for you," Pete said, parking several yards away. He reached over and opened my door. "Out you go, Bijou. Quickly now. I'm not coming in."

Turning, I dropped from the truck to the chilled gravel below. As soon as my paws touched the ground, Pete drove off, leaving me with a faceful of exhaust and strange misgivings about the man I thought I knew.

"Bijou!" Skunk trilled the song of the south, and I turned just in time to be bowled over.

"What's the news?" I asked, spitting out a mouthful of her black fur.

"We found him."

"Where?"

"Hamlet found him by the barn. He was caught on a nail sticking out of some old wood."

"How was he caught? His collar?"

"No, he had a rope tied to him. Bijou, whoever broke into the house tried to take him. They must've panicked when we woke up. Hamlet cut him loose."

"What else did they take?"

"They didn't take anything as far as Spencer and Eddy can tell."

Hamlet joined us then, looking extremely proud of himself beneath his sweater (gray with clementines). Unsheathing his sword, he held it out for us to imagine.

"I named it Snip," he stated, looking at me for approval. "Snip freed Fennec." Ever since the piglet had hidden from the intruder at Witching Flour, he'd been working to redeem himself. And tonight I congratulated him, saying Snip was a brave and fitting name.

Spencer, Eddy, and Lieutenant Tennant strode from the house then, and Eddy's face was pale and somber as he held Fennec against his chest. Even from here I could see the fear that glossed the puppy's eyes.

"He must have been downstairs drinking water or something when the intruder came in," said Eddy as he and Spencer walked the Lieutenant to his car. "He no longer stays in his puppy pen at night. He has free range of the house."

"We'll find out who did this, Eddy," replied the Lieutenant. "Don't you worry. And I'll have my deputies keep an eye on the inn and the bakery." He got into his car but kept the door open, eyeing Fennec. "I just don't know why anyone would steal a puppy. Makes no sense to me, and I can't help but think there's got to be something personal behind it. Same with the cut gas pipe and the bullying messages you just told me about."

Shaking his head, he slammed the door shut, and Skunk, who'd been blinking sleepily at a tuft of yellow grass, promptly leapt in a northwesterly direction and fell into a ditch.

"You two keep that puppy close," the Lieutenant said, rolling down the window an inch. "And call me if anything else happens. Anything at all."

While Spencer, Eddy, and Hamlet took Fennec to the kitchen to make him a warm and comforting breakfast, Skunk and I decided to interview the cats upstairs. They may have seen the prowler. After all, their windows looked directly over the backyard.

First up was Miss Tut, who said she hadn't seen a thing. Not with her cataracts and not with the extra glass of meowsling she'd ordered before bed. "Sorry, dears, I slept like a youth on holiday." Dots of fuzz from her blanket balanced sleepily on her whiskers. "But check with Betty next door. She's much more nocturnal."

Betty, who'd come to the inn two nights ago, was just getting ready to sleep the morning away when we knocked. A fluffy ginger with white paws, she looked at us with annoyance. "Yes, I was awake all night. I find I sleep much better during the day. But I didn't see anything unusual."

"And you didn't hear anything unusual either?" Skunk asked.

Betty yawned. "Sorry, no. Try Minerva next door."

Minerva was a no-nonsense tabby with markings around her eyes resembling glasses. She took the whole affair very seriously and apologized profusely for hearing and seeing nothing. "I will meditate on how I can do better," she said somberly before suggesting we visit her neighbor, the young Fuzz Aldrin.

Fuzz was peering out the window at a milky morning cloud when we entered his suite. "So it *was* a break-in," he said when we told him what had happened. "I thought I saw a shadow tiptoeing across the yard. Now I know it was real."

"You saw the prowler?" I thumped him between the ears in celebration.

"Fuzz," said Skunk, "what did the prowler look like?"

He thought for a moment, his jet-black fur made all the more handsome by his bright yellow eyes. "Like a human, I suppose. I was juggling four toy mice at the time, so I didn't really pay attention."

"That's okay," I encouraged. "What else can you remember?"

"Well, it had something in its hand."

"A rope?"

"Yeah, maybe. But I couldn't see much more than that."

"Thank you, Fuzz," I said. "As your manager, I'm grateful and I'll be sure to send up some freshly laundered mice. Report to me immediately if you remember anything else."

Downstairs, in the kitchen that now smelled of freshly ground coffee, I went to Fennec. He was huddled on a kitchen chair, on top of Eddy's jacket, and he burrowed in further, disappearing but for one sandy ear flopped over the zipper. "Why would someone do this?" I whispered to him. "And who were they?" He shivered, and I placed a paw gently on the tip of his ear. "I wish you could tell me."

Grand Opening

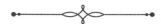

The next two weeks were filled with hefty managerial loads and long hours of helping Spencer and Eddy prepare for the bakery's grand opening. When not working, quick trips were taken to the river to surf, and Tahereh and Harry (and sometimes Delphiki) were met for drinks and chitchat.

All the while, I carried the weighty responsibility of Hamlet's education, and together we'd made it nearly halfway through *Magnum Vikus*. He now knew dozens of runes and could follow me around the yard, reading them as I scratched them into trees. At night my eyes itched for sleep as I read well past my bedtime, determined to keep my knowledge one step ahead of his.

June 1 approached with still no leads into the crimes that had been committed. But no *new* crimes were committed either. Everything pointed to the promise of a successful grand opening and a busy summer. As the mountain snows melted and the river swelled, flocks of tourists descended upon the town and delicious scents filled the streets as the food trucks pronounced themselves *OPEN!* in multihued chalk.

Demelza Corn and Spencer found themselves in a fragile truce when Lieutenant Tennant informed them that Pim had a solid alibi for the night of Fox Burrow's break-in. As well, Pete Moss and I were back to our old selves. So I'd seen him in the forest with a strange box. So what? I knew Pete. He was harmless. Bog bodies seldom committed crimes.

The morning of June 1 dawned bright and clear, with not a cloud in the sky. A perfect day for Witching Flour's grand opening party. The whole town had been buzzing about it for the past two weeks, as had Spencer and Eddy, who rushed about everywhere with pink cheeks and checklists.

Curled on Freyja, I opened my eyes and stretched. "Skunk," I said, flicking my tail at her where she laid upside down on the foot of the bed. "Skunk, wake up."

"Yes, I'm single," the Pom murmured, her eyelids fluttering in her sleep.

Beside me, Spencer woke up and ran a hand through her tangled hair. "Today's the day," she said, petting me.

"The day for what?" Eddy teased, entering the room with two steaming mugs of coffee.

Fennec and Hamlet looked up from their places on the bed next to Skunk. With love and treats, Fennec had overcome the "Incident of Scariness," and now he rolled onto his back, his legs sticking straight into the air, exposing the ugly dog head tattoo for pets. Leaning over me and covering my face with a sheet of blond hair, Spencer obliged.

Sinking to the edge of the bed, Eddy handed Spencer her coffee before setting his on the bedside table with a loud *thump*.

"Yes, you can court me!" Skunk bellowed, shooting awake with wild eyes and a string of drool rappelling from her mouth to the quilt.

All of us looked at her, our brows raised.

Her eyes clearing, she let out a howl of lament. "He was an Australian shepherd, Bijou," she said, her fur deflating. "With blue eyes and an accent."

I extended a paw and patted her on the snout. Skunk often dreamed of her future husbands. "Was his name Armand again?"

"No, Orville."

"God, this coffee is good," said Spencer, sipping it while sinking back into the pillows. "You make it better than I do." She smiled as Eddy sank in beside her. "How are you feeling about the party? Ready? Excited?"

"Ready enough." He kissed her forehead before removing his glasses and polishing them with the hem of his shirt. "And excited enough." Reaching out, he threw open the window and the cool morning air drifted in, scented with wildflowers and grass and dark, wormy earth and—something else too. Something that chilled the backs of my nostrils as I inhaled. I glanced at Skunk to see if she noticed it too, but all she said was "Orville" and rested her chin sadly on top of her paws.

The grand opening party was to begin at six o'clock that evening, and we knew there would be an excellent turnout. Spencer's flyers had been posted all over town. The *Gray Birch Gazette* had written an in-depth article on Eddy and Witching Flour. The bakery's social media accounts had quickly gained strong followings, and people had been trying to peer inside the old firehouse all week. Eddy, however, had kept the windows covered, stoking curiosity, as he worked ceaselessly on his doughy, sugary creations.

The week before, he'd finally hired an employee. Lo was a plump, red-haired woman in her middle years with a hundred-watt smile. She'd previously worked at the food mart, making cheap birthday and graduation cakes, and so was incredibly pleased with the upward move to Witching Flour.

Everything had come together. All of the remodeling for the bakery was finished, the tables and chairs were set in place, and the display cases and floorboards had been polished until they gleamed.

Eddy was to spend the morning baking fresh goodies for the party while Spencer managed the drink deliveries, put up the giant banner over the garage doors, strung lights overhead, and helped the band set up in the corner. "The band" being just one man, an old friend of Harry's from law school named Homer who played a mean guitar and sang mostly on key.

"We aren't going to have nearly enough chairs," said Spencer, her hands on her hips as she eyed the space. "People are going to have to mill."

"Milling is good," said Eddy. "Milling is what we want. It may even be warm enough to open the garage doors, then we'd have that nice indoor/outdoor mix." He paused as a gust of wind suddenly blew past, shaking the windows. "Then again, maybe not . . ."

Spencer and I went to the door and peered outside, where we could clearly see gothic clouds gathering over the mountains. "It's getting cloudy," Spencer announced. "But hopefully nothing comes of it. It's not supposed to rain. Colorado is just being Colorado, moody and capricious."

I turned as Fennec, Skunk, and Hamlet came tumbling down the stairs. They'd been napping in Eddy's apartment, which was getting close to being finished. They raced into the kitchen, drooling over the maple bourbon cupcakes Eddy had just pulled from the oven.

"Nope, these aren't for you," Eddy said, chasing them away.

Skunk snapped up a fallen crumb anyway.

"Bijou?" said Spencer. "Can you please take these three outside to play for a while? We'll all go home for lunch in a little bit."

Assuring her I would be the epitome of responsibility, I ushered the others through the kitchen door, snapping up three maple bourbon crumbs on the way.

Outside, the wind still blew and it flapped our lips as we rounded the corner. Crossing the street, we stepped onto the thick carpet of grass that made up the town square. Perched in the middle was a lacy white gazebo, and within it sat a few tourists eating falafel from a nearby food truck. One of these tourists was a huge, woodsy-looking man dressed in a turtleneck. A massive black beard covered most of his face, and when he saw us he spilled a glob of tzatziki sauce on his shirt. I figured the sight of the four of us together could be strange to some people—especially now that we were engaged in an epic sword fight.

"En garde!" brayed Hamlet.

"Allez!" Skunk cried.

"Coming through, coming through. *Oops*, oh dear," said Bobi Pinn, stumbling through our mayhem with a falafel in one hand and a bag of groceries in the other. I lowered Dewclaw so it wouldn't slice her pants, the pockets of which had several suspicious bulges.

My snaggletooth emerged. *Ha! What have you stolen this time, Bobi?*

"Just have to get my frozens into the freezer, you know," she said, slipping by. "It's supposed to be a very warm weekend. Though looking at those clouds, you wouldn't know it. And of course, after sorting groceries, I have to prepare for the party . . . *Excuse me.*" She lifted a leg high over Fennec, who'd ducked in terror as soon as she'd arrived. He now lay frozen on the grass as she gave him a look of cold irritation. "Nothing but trouble, are you?" she muttered. Then, looking quickly around, she hurried away.

It took ten minutes to bring the puppy back to life, and all the while I felt eyes on me, watching. But every time I turned, I saw only tourists, milling about.

"For Hildisvini!" Hamlet bugled, encouraging the puppy to play. His big paws clumsy, Fennec bravely recovered from his scare and he came at me. I parried with an easy flick of the paw, and the sound of our swords rang out across the square.

"Well," said Spencer, staring out of Fox Burrow's kitchen window during lunch, "it looks like it's going to rain after all."

"It'll make the party cozy," said Eddy, ever positive. "Hygge even." He winked at her.

Finishing her sandwich, Spencer piled the dishes in the sink. "Okay, so I'm going to take care of all of our guests here, shower, change, and then get back to the bakery around five."

"Sounds good." Eddy stood and pulled on his rain jacket. "I have a few more things to make, but we're nearing the finish line." He caught her hand as she headed for the feed room down the hall. "Thank you, Spencer. I couldn't have done this without you."

"You could have." She smiled. "But it wouldn't have been nearly as much fun."

"*Snow?*" Spencer cried a few hours later, opening the inn's front door and staring out at the giant flakes. "You've got to be kidding me!"

Quickly, she shut the door, worry lines etching her forehead as she tugged the delicate gold chain around her neck.

The necklace had belonged to her grandmother, and she only wore it for special occasions. Wrapping a sweater around her cream-colored blouse, she looked down at Skunk, whose great mane loudly promised to umbrella her face from the storm. "And of course I already took the snow tires off the car. Well done, Spencer. Letting Colorado fool you into thinking it was actually summer. I guess we walk." Grumbling, she went to the coat closet and rummaged around for her winter coat and snow boots. Finding them, she then dug out two dog jackets, one for Skunk and one for me, both size small.

"I don't need it," I protested. "I'm a Viking." But she'd already stuffed me in it up to the armpits.

As we strode stiffly down the drive, I heard a *clack*, *clack*, *clack* and looked back to see Cork out on his patio, blissfully snapping up snowflakes.

"At least someone's enjoying the snow," muttered Spencer.

Walking through town, I saw countless shocked faces peering out of windows as the massive wet flakes covered the ground. Main Street had emptied, and a hush cloaked the town as we trudged toward Witching Flour. Passing by the Drunken Warbler, however, we discovered where many people had taken cover. Inside, Foggy served drink after drink, frenzied by the sudden crowd.

"See? Isn't it hygge?" Eddy said when we entered the bakery and shook off the snow.

"Oh my God," Spencer said. "Eddy, this is beautiful."

The lights she'd hung earlier were now lit, casting a fairyland glow over the bakery and illuminating the snowflakes piling up on the windowpanes. The tables had all been covered in cream-colored cloths with lanterns and sprigs of lavender in the center. Spiraling out from these were plate after plate of Eddy's creations. Cupcakes and brownies, cinnamon rolls and Danishes (chocolate, cherry, and almond), éclairs and monkey bread, Bavarian pretzels and baguettes, macarons and chocolate soufflés . . . all of this and more.

"You've outdone yourself," Spencer said. "No one could possibly want a Monstera shop over this."

Eddy ducked his head, but his smile betrayed pride as he bent to help me out of my jacket and wipe up the snowmelt beneath.

"You don't think the snow will keep people from coming, do you?" Spencer asked.

"I don't know. But it'll be good no matter what." He kissed her cheek. "My most important guests are already here."

With no work to do, I accompanied Skunk upstairs while Spencer assisted Eddy and Lo (who'd just arrived with a loud proclamation of "Snow!") with last-minute details. The scent of all the homemade goodies infusing the bakery was so delicious my stomach growled, and Homer, who'd also arrived and was unpacking his guitar in the corner, jerked his head up in fright.

Upstairs, the apartment was no longer filled with mortar dust and plastic. And praise Freyja, because I *still* had a flashback of that knife tumbling through the air. But the place was clean now and fresh, with newly painted brick walls and the same lovely hardwood floor as below. Perched on the dog bed overlooking Main Street, Hamlet and Fennec sat together, waiting for the first guests to arrive.

"We aren't allowed downstairs once people show up," Hamlet informed us. "Eddy said."

"Maybe *you* aren't," I replied, settling on the window-sill above them. "I doubt that rule applies to me."

"Scoot over," said Skunk, wedging herself between the piglet and the puppy. "Oh, Bijou, it's so warm right here. You have to join."

"You know, I don't mind if I do." I stepped down from

the windowsill as they made room for me, and together we looked out at the snow and awaited the town.

I woke with a jerk.

Stuffed between Skunk and Fennec, I'd fallen asleep. We'd all fallen asleep. And by the boisterous noise below, the guests had arrived and Witching Flour's opening party was in full swing. Scrambling off the dog bed, I headed for the stairs, not wanting to miss any more of the action than I already had. Behind me, the others still snored.

On the first step, I stopped. The party sounded much more wild than anticipated, but that wasn't why. No, I stopped because a few steps below two people stood in the shadows, arguing. Their hands waved about, and their hoarse whispers rose straight to my ears.

"But why lie?"

Foggy. That was Foggy. He must've taken a break from the Warbler to come over.

"How could I possibly tell you the truth? We were *engaged*, remember? And you know how angry you can get."

That was Dr. Flora. I adjusted my pupils to see better.

"I've worked hard on controlling my anger. You know that." Foggy shifted and the step beneath him creaked. "Is this why you're never at home or in your office anymore?"

Dr. Flora threw up her arms. "Don't exaggerate, Foggy. You make it sound like I'm ditching my duties."

"Well, I know a few animals who could've used your help recently, Flora. You're the only vet this town has. You have to be there for them. Instead you're off . . . *galavanting* with your new beau."

In the dim light of the stairway, she paled. "Well, I'm sorry if that's true. But I have a life to live, too, you know."

"But not at the expense of others."

"No, Foggy, *no*. You forced me to tell you the truth, and so I did. The rest of my life is none of your business. Honestly, I shouldn't have even come here tonight. I'm going home."

"Flora." Foggy reached out and grabbed her arm. "Don't go. I'm not upset."

She glared at him. "You *are* upset and you're hurting me." Yanking her arm from his grip, she rushed down the stairs.

His heavy footfalls followed her, along with the light *clink* of something falling from his neck to the floor.

Snow Madness

I didn't know what to make of what I'd just witnessed. But a spat between ex-lovers was hardly what I wanted to think about. What I *wanted* was a maple bourbon cupcake. Or seven.

Downstairs, the bakery was packed. Everyone who'd taken cover from the snow in the Drunken Warbler had migrated to Witching Flour. And they were drunk. And what do drunk people enjoy? Carbs and sugar. Eddy was killing it.

Everyone loved his confections, and they oohed and aahed over the beautiful transformation of the old firehouse. Everyone also loved that champagne was flowing freely, and every bit of the space was filled with people toasting and laughing and thumping each other's lumbars while Homer played madly in the corner, his toupee slightly askew.

"Bijou Bedelia Bonanno!"

I froze as Spencer caught me with my whiskers dipped to their roots in a dewy champagne flute.

"What are you doing down here? I thought Eddy told you to stay upstairs."

"That rule doesn't apply to me," I assured her, licking fizz from my chin.

"I suppose you think that rule doesn't apply to you." Spencer sighed and took a sip from her own flute. "Okay, fine, you can stay. Just don't get into any trouble, Bijou. And stay away from the food, all right? No one wants to ingest a cat hair."

"I, too, find them dry and flavorless," I said. Kissing me between the ears, she threaded her way through the crowd to a guest who was exuberantly calling her name.

A few moments later, I was interrupted again. This time by a horribly rude, horribly condescending *"Ahem."* I knew who it was without even looking up from my rapidly emptying flute.

"And what, may I ask, are *you* doing here?" Demelza Corn said. "Eddy Line allows *cats* in this bakery of his? Around all this food?" She adjusted the scarf condemned to hang around her bony neck. "That just goes to show what kind of establishment this is. No animals would ever be allowed in my Monstera shop. Only Chi Chi, of course, whose hygiene I oversee personally."

"Why hello, Demelza." Eddy approached with a plate stacked high with colorful macarons. "I'm delighted you came. Have you eaten anything yet?"

"No, I have not," she said shrilly. "I was too busy watching your *cat* drink champagne."

"Ah, I see." Eddy looked at me, his brows arched. "Well, I'm afraid Bijou does what she wishes, Demelza. Macaron? They're fairly delicious."

Demelza narrowed spiky eyelashes. "No, thank you. I don't eat foreign cuisine. I simply wanted to see what you had done with our lovely, *historic* firehouse. Now, if you'll excuse me . . ." And she turned and marched toward Pim, who was amusing himself by throwing brownies at Homer.

"Help yourself to a swag bag by the door!" Eddy called after her, grinning at me. Then, lowering his voice, he said, "She'll just love the Witching Flour T-shirt inside, huh, Bij? Oh, I see Harry and Tahereh. I'm off to say hello." He ruffled my tail. "Just stay away from the food, okay, girl?"

As he left, he swiped my flute of champagne. Naturally, I went in search of another. Many had been left unattended, sitting haphazardly on tables and chairs, and I had no problem spotting a likely candidate.

This candidate was nearly full and had been left perched on the precarious edge of an underage fig plant. Upon seeing my approach, it threw itself into the soil, and I had no choice but to chase it into the maze of stalks and stems. Now, normally I don't enjoy the taste of dirt. But Temptation is not a coy mistress. Unhinging my jaw, I reared back my head and then plunged it into the earth like a furry excavator. I spent a blissful moment crunching well-fermented rock and soil.

"Bijou?"

I halted midchew, my nose filthy with unrestraint.

"Bijou? Where are you?" Spencer's voice was laced with worry.

Dishonorably discharged from the fig plant, I meowed around a thick coating of dirt on the incisors.

"Oh, thank God." She plucked me from the floor. "I need you. The others followed you downstairs and now Demelza's spotted Fennec. Needless to say, it's a problem. She's also not thrilled about Hamlet." She carried me through the crowd toward the base of the stairs, where I spotted a rift in the flow of happy people. "I need you to go back upstairs, Bijou, and take the others with you. They do what you do. Be a good example."

Floating in Spencer's arms, I reached out and snagged a half-eaten cupcake from an abandoned napkin. By the time we crossed the room, it'd slipped agreeably down my gullet, and I washed dollops of frosting from my whiskers.

"Oh, no," Spencer murmured in my ear as we stopped beside Demelza and Eddy. "It's gotten worse."

I blinked at Demelza, who was gesticulating wildly, and Eddy, who was standing stoically, and then looked down at Skunk, Hamlet, and Fennec, who were cowering behind Eddy's legs.

Between the noise inside the bakery and the loud babble of the ancestors complimenting both food and drink in my head, I heard nothing of what they were saying. I only knew I wanted to save Eddy from the sorrowful look on his face and Fennec from the growing terror behind his eyes.

Wiggling from Spencer's arms, I darted behind Eddy's legs and hefted my imaginary shield to block Demelza's vitriol. "Bijou!" Skunk whispered, her tongue lolling anxiously out the side of her mouth. "There you are."

"Come on," I said. "Let's get out of here." But our pathway to the stairs was blocked. Too many legs encircled us, and we were pushed farther and farther into the corner. Terrified, Fennec froze.

"He won't move, Bijou," Hamlet said, trying to scoop the puppy up from where he'd curled into a tight ball on the floor.

"We've got a code dog situation," Skunk announced, flinching as Demelza let loose another insult. I took the hit square on my shield and looked up to see a smile spread across her face, thick as sunbutter. She was enjoying her cruelty, and Eddy's restraint was wearing thin.

Eddy had just opened his mouth to reply to this insult when a scream swept through the room.

Jumping, everyone looked over to see Bobi Pinn fall

headfirst into Homer's guitar, spilling her champagne onto herself. Laughing, she clapped a hand over her mouth and let a huge, black-bearded man help her unsteadily to her feet. Tilting my head, I realized he was the man from the gazebo. The one who'd spilled tzatziki sauce on his shirt.

"This party has gotten rather out of control, hasn't it?" Spencer said, looking around. "I wasn't expecting it to be like this."

"It's the snow," said Eddy, turning his back to Demelza, who'd fallen silent at Bobi's scream. "It seems to have sparked a bit of madness."

It was true, everywhere I looked it seemed the bakery had turned into a frat house of sugared, champagned fools. Summer fever had taken hold and was now in full revolt against the snow. Dozens of underdressed bipeds boiled together, trapped in the unsuspecting snow globe of Witching Flour.

"*Mr.* Line," Demelza said, startling her neck scarf. "I expect you to remove these animals at once or I will call the health inspector."

Eddy turned back to her, his lips frozen in a polite smile. "And I expect you to remove that drink from your grandson's hand, Demelza. We don't serve minors here."

Demelza whirled, her eyes searching for Pim, who now wore Homer's toupee while choking down a flute of champagne. With a groan, she started for him, a blossom of red spreading up her neck and across her cheeks. Digging her claws into Pim's ear, she dragged him out the door. Before exiting, however, she threw a look of pure malice over her shoulder at Eddy.

"Bijou, we've got a code dog situation," Skunk said again, her hot breaths puffing into my face like tiny blacksmith bellows.

"Right." I turned back to Fennec, all business, despite the slosh in my stomach.

Spotting the puppy, Eddy dropped to his knees beside him. "I shouldn't have brought him here tonight." He shook his head sadly. "But I couldn't have left him alone at the inn either. Not after what happened with the break-in . . ."

Spencer crouched down and stroked the puppy's tawny fur. "He'll be all right, Eddy. We just need to get him back upstairs."

I patted the puppy with my tail while Skunk revived him with her breath. Eddy and Spencer had stayed as long as they could, but ultimately they'd returned downstairs to assist a completely overwhelmed Lo.

"He's coming around now," said Hamlet, raising his voice over Homer's tinny guitar riff.

He was. The puppy's eyelids fluttered as I kneaded his soft fur. Then he stared up at us, and for a moment fear flickered. It dissipated quickly, however, when he realized he was safely upstairs. Letting out a great sigh, he burrowed more deeply into the dog bed, pulling my tail over him like a heavy, northern quilt.

"Yes, you rest," I encouraged as Skunk and Hamlet sandwiched him on either side. Not very tired myself, I propped on the windowsill to look out into the night, careful to keep my tail over Fennec.

Outside, the flakes came down in a thick blur and several people ventured about, breathing in the cold air. I watched them with interest, swiveling my ears to pick up their voices through the closed window. "Beautiful night," said Brooke Binder, floating from person to person, her giant spectacles coated white. "Just wonderful. Hello. Hello." She paused to let Dirk Square Jaw serenade her with Sir Mix-a-Lot's most famous song.

My snaggletooth pinged against the windowpane. Middle-aged, the man still lived with his mother, Sue, who owned Gray Birch's "humans only" inn, the Doe. He'd never *not* lived with her, and he spent most of his time coming up with ways to woo those he called the "weaker sex."

A slow clap followed the rendition, and I looked over to see James Halvah leaning against the brick wall. Dirk bowed and then quickly steered Brooke away from him. Shaking his head, the beekeeper said something to the person next to him. (Harry maybe? It was difficult to tell beneath his hat.) The streetlight flicked on then, illuminating the other man's face. Not Harry. Foggy.

And Foggy's face was a dark, expressionless canvas.

Foggy said something too softly to hear, and Halvah jerked his head up, coughing out a white cloud of breath.

Raising his hands, Halvah said something back, and I watched with wide eyes as Foggy suddenly tore his hat off and stamped it into the snow.

"I didn't think you'd want to know about me and Flora!" Halvah's voice rose. "I knew it would only hurt you. I can't believe she told you."

"I'm your stepfather!" cried Foggy. "How could you keep this from me?"

"She's better off with me," said Halvah. "You're not good for her. Just like you weren't good for my mother."

Clenching his fist, Foggy looked for a moment like he was going to punch Halvah, and I felt a surge of excitement at the idea of imminent battle. But, restraining himself, Foggy kept his fist at his side. Then, without a word, he turned and reentered the bakery, leaving Halvah red-faced and puffing in the snow.

"Of course you may rest up here for a while," said Spencer, leading Foggy into the upstairs apartment. "Eddy and I are trying to bring the party downstairs to a close. I mean, good Lord, was this opening a success or a colossal failure? I don't even know."

"It was a success," said Foggy. "You both did well." He smiled, but it didn't reach the pinch around his eyes.

Spencer looked at him with concern. "Are you sure I can't bring you anything? A glass of water? Some more food?"

"No, no. I just need to lie down in the quiet for a moment. I'm sure I'll feel better in a little while."

"Well, you can cuddle with the animals," said Spencer. "In fact, Fennec could use some extra love. Demelza scared the bejesus out of him earlier."

"Demelza scares the bejesus out of us all," said Foggy.

Resting his fingers between my ears, I felt their gnarled tips tremble slightly as we looked out the window at his half-buried hat below.

Too Soft to Be a Rock

This time I didn't jerk awake.

This time I drifted slowly out of a velvet darkness only to realize it was because wakefulness was quieter than sleep.

The party was over. Everyone had left and I felt a swoop of panic, fearing I'd been abandoned. It was short-lived, however, because looking to my right, I saw a sweatered ham hock and to my left, a bushy black bustle. Both Hamlet and Skunk still slept, and I stretched my legs out, bracing against their snouts.

Wildly comfortable on the flat of my back, I swiveled my neck to look at Foggy and Fennec where they had fallen asleep on Eddy's bed in the middle of the apartment.

But Foggy wasn't there. I looked for lumps beneath the covers. "Fenn?" But the little pit bull had disappeared as well. I yawned. They must've gone below.

Lying there, I pondered going below as well because the longer I lounged, the more I realized I was drifting timelessly in the black haze of Hunger. The ceiling fan suddenly looked like a school of mackerel, the bedposts, stacked cans of pâté.

Wedged as I was between Skunk and Hamlet, I would need an extraordinary amount of momentum to free myself from the dog bed. I looked down expectantly at my bloat, and obediently it began to sway left and right, slowly at first and then faster. Soon I was vacillating like a warship in a storm surge.

With a soft fur-on-fur *pop*, I launched from the bed like a stone from a siege weapon. But instead of flying heroically over a castle wall, I flew assbackwards down the staircase, my claws extended but finding no purchase.

I landed in a heap at the bottom, my claws worn down to nubs. Looking up the stairs, I saw long, thin marks now carved into each and every step. The only thing that softened the blow was the cupcake I'd landed on.

Hearing voices in the kitchen, I made my way through the cluttered aftermath of the party to find Spencer and Lo washing a mountain of dishes. Soap bubbles floated through the air, and I popped one with Dewclaw.

"I told Foggy he could stay the night," Spencer was saying. "I mean, Eddy doesn't live here yet, so no one's using the apartment. But he insisted on going home."

"I'm sure he'll be fine," said Lo, dipping her purple dish gloves into the soapy water and coming up with an iPhone. She frowned at it. "How in the world did this end up here?"

Spencer snorted and dried it with her cloth. "Someone is going to be unhappy when they wake up tomorrow and discover that it's missing. Oh hi, Bijou." She smiled at me. "Did you have a nice nap?"

Weaving between her legs, I assured her I did. Looking up, I noticed that her grandmother's gold necklace was missing from her neck.

"I know," she said sadly when I pointed this out. "I lost it somehow. The clasp must've broke."

"Hey, do you mind if I call my babysitter?" Lo asked, checking the clock on the wall. "It's already after eleven, and I told her I'd be home by now." Lo had a ten-year-old son she raised on her own.

"Sure thing," Spencer said, taking over the purple gloves. "You don't have to ask me, I'm not your boss."

"Speaking of the boss . . . Eddy's been gone awhile, and it's pretty cold out there." Lo nodded at the thermometer hanging just outside the window, illuminated by the alley light.

Spencer groaned. "It's June now. *June*. Sometimes living in the mountains is just too unpredictable. Maybe I should follow my parents to Florida." Dipping her hands into the hot water, she sighed. "That's better. Anyway, I'm sure he and Fenn will be back soon."

"I don't know why they needed to walk all the way to the river in this weather," said Lo.

"It's Fennec's favorite place. I think the river soothes him."

"The poor puppy was so scared when he came running downstairs. I wonder what spooked him."

"He probably had a nightmare about Demelza Corn," muttered Spencer. She flapped soapy hands at Lo. "Never mind her. Go call your babysitter."

Roosting on Spencer's toes, I stared up at her as she washed a plate. Fennec had come downstairs scared? He'd seemed fine when we'd fallen asleep. Needy, but fine. What had changed? He must've been in quite a state for Eddy to take him all the way to the river in this weather.

Standing, I circled twice before returning to the exact same position.

They would be back soon. I cocked one ear at each door. Yes, surely they'd return any minute now.

But as time ticked by, something cold and uncomfortable tickled the back of my mind. A whisper from a wizened ancestor perhaps. Or a blood memory of plunging through the ice into the black waters of a fjord. I didn't know for sure, but *something* made me leave Spencer's toes and dart outside when Lo stuck her head out the front door, her phone pressed to her ear.

"Yes, Karen, it's *still* snowing," she said, shutting it quickly behind me.

Blinking against the sudden onslaught of wet, icy flakes, I looked up and down the street for signs of Eddy and Fennec. But the only thing I saw was Foggy's truck still parked across from the Drunken Warbler. I studied it with downturned whiskers. Perhaps he hadn't gone home after all and was instead curled up in one of his own corner booths. Well, at least he was warm. My own pelt was growing frigid, despite my orders.

Reluctantly, I started down the empty street toward the river. It was my duty as manager to make certain my guests remained unharmed and de-iced at all times. Also, Fennec and Eddy were no longer simply guests. They were members of my clan.

Using my paw like a wiper blade, I brushed a layer of snow off my face, leaving wet streaks across my vision. And so, with blurred eyes, I didn't see the vehicle parked ahead of me until I walked directly beneath its tailpipe. When the engine coughed to life, I nearly shot clean through the rusted metal.

"Ah, *there* we go. See? I told you we could get her started."

Eddy? Stumbling from beneath the tailpipe, my ears ringing and marginally poisoned with carbon monoxide, I saw him exit the car. It was a beige Buick LeSabre, parked in front of the Doe.

Tinkering about beneath the hood was Sue, the tiny owner of the Doe and the unfortunate mother of Dirk. "Yes, indeed!" She cackled, slamming the hood and retying her headscarf. "Thank you, young man. Now I can get home to my nightcap and novel."

Eddy smiled. "You did all the work. I just turned the key when you told me to."

Patting his cheek, Sue slid into the driver's seat. "You rest up after that big party now. I could hear it all the way from the Doe. Sounded like a rowdy one."

"More than expected," Eddy admitted. "Drive home safe."

As she drove away, I trilled a greeting and asked about Fennec, but Eddy didn't hear me. Nor did he see me with his feeble night vision. Instead he trotted to the nearest stop sign, where the Buick had once again choked and died. Popping out of the driver's seat, Sue lamented that the car was "in a mood" and that it "needed a change in attitude."

I searched for signs of Fennec as Eddy and Sue busied themselves beneath the hood again. But I couldn't find him. He wasn't inside Eddy's jacket or in the car or waiting anywhere nearby. Why wasn't Eddy worried?

Eddy answered this question a moment later when the snowflakes thickened. "I'm worried I did the wrong thing sending Fennec to the river," he told Sue. "The weather is getting steadily worse."

"Ah, they'll be fine," she grunted, smashing the skull of a piston with her wrench. "He'll be happier down there away from me. He didn't like me at all."

"He just has stranger danger," said Eddy. "It's nothing personal."

They? Who had Eddy sent Fennec with?

Eddy didn't say anything more, but I could tell from his expression that he was feeling guilty, like he should've taken the puppy himself. But he couldn't have left Sue stranded in the storm either. He was a man torn.

Turning, I completed my walk down Main Street and then swung south where the riverpath began. Walking along the water's edge, I felt its spray, warmer than the snow. In the dim light it looked like a silver belt on a white dress, raised with stitches of cataracts and boulders of beaded ivory. I paused at its beauty—it would've been barbaric not to.

Remembering my mission, I pressed on, my paws *whisk whisking* softly in the snow. Mine weren't the only tracks. I followed others, some human, some pooch, and they stretched ever onward with no sign of return. Why had they gone so far? And why were they suddenly zigzagged and frenzied?

Breaking into a trot, I swallowed down my growing apprehension. I'd earned 103 tabby stripes for bravery after all, and I wasn't about to have them revoked now.

Rounding a bend in the riverpath, I summoned a more speedy gait, hoping to warm myself against the brumal night.

And I stumbled.

On what I couldn't immediately say. Rising from where I'd fallen, I shook the snow from my eyes and searched for the obstruction. It had felt odd. Too soft to be a rock. Too hard to be much else.

And that's when I saw it in all its gruesome horror. The Crime of Awfulness. Only then I didn't know it *was* a Crime of Awfulness but thought perhaps a human had made the offbeat decision to doze in the snow, propped up by an unenthusiastic shrubbery.

It was the human's arm I'd stumbled upon—flung out and frozen. Perfect for tripping up the rare hare-footed Norsecat. Reaching out, I tap-tapped the arm with a rapid-fire paw. But nothing happened. It didn't wake, it didn't move, and the snow fell in a vexing hush.

I was a splat in the snow. A gray-and-black-striped mop, wrung out and left to dry under the watchful eye of a blizzard.

Ten dark, horrible minutes had floated by since I'd faced the corpse head-on, since I'd identified it as my poor friend Foggy Lawson. Ten slow, tedious minutes since I'd found Fennec's empty collar with no sign of the puppy himself. What had happened? I couldn't believe it. It simply couldn't be true. I laid there and waited for Trauma to vacate the system. But I couldn't wait forever. I needed to sound the alarm.

Slowly, I flexed one paw. Then the other. One front, the other back, prepping both engines. Vikings didn't fall apart. They *couldn't*. Not fully. Vikings were blocks of muscle and mettle. One did not simply allow incidents like cold-blooded Crime to debilitate one's baser instinct. And baser instinct right then was advocating for me to gallop in a northwesterly direction posthaste.

Muscles burning, mettle fusing, I obeyed—feeling Foggy's poor, vacant stare on my tail all the way back to Witching Flour.

JAMES HALVAH: My God. Oh my God.

POLICE LIEUTENANT LOU TENNANT: I'm so very sorry. I know it must be a shock.

DR. FLORA: Foggy? No. That's not possible. You've made a mistake, Lieutenant. It can't be him. Let me just give him a ring. I'm sure he'll answer and clear up any confusion.

Police Lieutenant Lou Tennant: I'm sorry, Flora, but there's no confusion. Foggy has been murdered.

Bobi Pinn: I'm too shocked for words. But I must insist I don't know anything. Not a thing!

Dirk Square Jaw: Well, I can tell you one thing, Lieutenant. I'm not dying cold and alone like Foggy. Real men don't get murdered.

Police Lieutenant Lou Tennant: Thank you, Dirk. You may leave.

18

The Very Dead and Disappeared

I rammed my shoulder into the back door of the bakery—
six, seven, eight times until I felt it bruise. Unhinging
my jaw, I bellowed for Spencer. She was right there on the
other side of the wall; I could hear her clinking plates and
laughing with Lo.

Unsheathing Dewclaw, I scratched a deep fissure into
the door, clumps of wood pulp falling dead at my feet. Surely
she would hear those brittle screams. But nothing happened.
No footsteps sounded coming toward the door, and no concerned cries of "Bijou?!" rang out. Only another carefree
peal of laughter.

I was about to climb the slippery, snow-laden fire escape
to bang on the upstairs window and alert Skunk when Eddy
came sprinting up the alleyway. His tortured face was a Ror-
schach mask as he passed from shadow to light under the
streetlamps, and it was clear that he knew. He must've gone
to the river directly after me.

"Spencer!" He pounded on the door, his legs planted on either side of me.

Immediately hurried footsteps sounded, and the door unlocked and swung open to reveal Spencer's worried face. "What is it? Are you okay?"

"No." He pushed past her into the kitchen, and I followed as she closed the door. "I need your phone, Spencer. I tried to use mine, but it got too cold out there and died."

Wordlessly, she pulled it from her pocket and handed it to him.

"What happened?" asked Lo, water dripping from her gloves to the floor.

He held up a hand. "Hold on, I have to make this call."

"Eddy," Spencer said, her voice hollow as she took a step backward into Lo, who steadied her. "Where's Fennec?"

Eddy's eyes pinched, but, pressing the phone to his ear, he turned away. "Yes, hello? I'm calling to report a death. Possibly a murder. That's right, a murder. You heard me correctly."

"A *murder*?" Spencer gasped, and Lo jumped, knocking a plate off the counter.

"No, *no*," Eddy snapped. "I know what I saw. I was just there. Yes, down on the south riverpath about a half mile from where it begins at Main Street. Yes, the victim is a man. About fifty." Closing his eyes, Eddy pinched the bridge of his nose beneath his glasses. "I know him. His name is Foggy Lawson."

Spencer let out a strangled cry and clutched Lo, who clutched her.

"There's more too," Eddy continued. "Foggy had a dog with him. My dog, Fennec. Foggy was walking him for me and now he's missing. *No*, I'm going to assume he's alive. Uh-huh, right—a puppy, four months old. Pit bull. Yes, *pit bull*. You heard me right."

Her hand to her mouth, Spencer sank to the kitchen floor.

"Right. I'm currently at Witching Flour—yes, the old firehouse. My name is Eddy Line. Okay, I'll remain here until an officer comes by." Slowly he lowered the phone from his ear and pressed *End Call*.

I knew he wouldn't be there as I raced upstairs to the apartment. But there was a part of me that had to make sure. That had to know he hadn't run back here, somehow slipped inside and buried himself back between Skunk and Hamlet.

"Fennec!" I yelled, summiting the stairs. "Fennec Wolfric Ollivander Line!" I used his full name, as once overheard from Eddy.

"I'm Skunk," said Skunk, baffled. She looked over from where she vacuumed up crumbs from beneath a workman's forgotten cooler. "Skunk Anita Estelle Bonanno."

"Skunk, where's Fennec? Is he here?"

"No, he's downstairs." She accordianed herself in order to better reach a wizened chickpea.

"No, he's not. Skunk, listen to me." I grabbed her tail with both paws and unraveled her. "I just found Foggy and he's not well."

Skunk shrugged. "Probably a stomachache from too many sweets. That's why he went home."

"Not a stomachache. And he didn't go home." I looked sadly into her cocoa bean eyes. "Foggy is dead, Skunk. I found him just now on the riverbank. And Fennec is gone."

"Dead." She blinked.

"Yes, dead."

"Dead?"

"Dead."

"Dead?"

"Dead."

She was silent for a long moment, and I watched the chickpea make its way down her throat. Then another blink. "Gone?"

"Gone."

"Gone?"

"*Skunk.*" I batted the knoll between her ears with impatient paws, aiding in Comprehension.

"What's going on?" Hamlet stretched from his position on the bed, his eyes muddled with sleep.

Skunk's voice was hollow as it crept between her lips. "Death has struck. And it becomes me."

"*You* didn't die, Skunk," I said.

"Then why does it feel like I did?"

"That's called grief." I dragged her to her feet as she slumped. "But we don't yet know what's happened to Fennec. We need to find him."

"Wait, what happened to Fennec?" The piglet was wide-awake now, and he scrambled off the bed. "Bijou, tell me."

"We need to go to Fox Burrow immediately," I said, leading them toward the window overlooking the fire escape. "I'll explain everything on the way."

Galloping up Fox Burrow's drive, I was all too aware of the drumbeat of my own heart. The notes pulsed loudly like I was headed for battle, each beat a perfect copy of the last. My tail, too, twitched in rhythm. *Beat, twitch, beat, twitch.* Unbidden, Foggy's gray beard floated into my mind's eye—a bristly perimeter to a kind and worn face. With gusto, I batted it away. Now was not the time to mourn.

Fennec had to be at Fox Burrow. That's where he would run if he escaped the violence. The inn was actually closer to the river than Witching Flour was. The words *IF HE ESCAPED* loomed large in my mind's eye as I ran, snow filling my tracks almost as quickly as I made them.

As Fox Burrow came into view, my internal temperature inflamed and any snowflakes that hit the bald spot melted with a hiss. Every minute with the knowledge of Foggy's death and every minute without the knowledge of Fennec's added more fuel to the fire.

"Rouse all the guests," I instructed Hamlet and Skunk, who panted beside me. "Inform them of what happened and then question them. See if there's even been a *hint* of the puppy's arrival."

"Where are you going?" asked Skunk, her fur sopping wet.

"To search the area between here and the river. Remember, we found him before. Go to Cork first. Tell him what happened and tell him I need his help. He'll do anything you ask."

"Sister, I found nothing," said Cork solemnly. "There is no sign of the puppy. I've failed you."

We all sat, exhausted, under an apricot sunrise, and I laid a paw on the border collie's wet, rubbery nose. "We all failed."

The snowfall had stopped, and the trees and shrubs surrounding Fox Burrow drowned within their own whitecaps and cornices. Summer, it seemed, would never be. *Could* never be. Witching Flour's grand opening was a distant memory, something that had happened long ago in a different world under a different sky. This new world was bleak and horrible. Full of the problems of the very dead and disappeared.

Bone-weary, I turned my attention back to the little group crowded on Fox Burrow's porch. Eddy and Spencer had at last come home from the bakery, escorted by Lieutenant Tennant.

"What a night." The Lieutenant doffed his hat and ran a hand over his eyes.

"I can't believe Foggy's gone," Spencer whispered. "I just don't understand it. I don't understand what happened."

"Don't you worry, Spencer," said the Lieutenant, placing a hand on her shoulder. "We'll get to the bottom of this. We will." He turned to Eddy. "And your puppy. We'll find him. I'd call every shelter within a hundred miles if I were you. And put up missing dog flyers too. Anything to spread the word and get folks looking for him."

Eddy nodded, his face heartsick. "I will. I'll do whatever it takes to get him back."

"Just so long as you keep it on the legal side of things."

"I'll do whatever it takes to get him back," Eddy repeated.

"Okay, we're going inside," said Spencer, taking Eddy's arm and steering him toward the door. "Thank you, Lou. Please keep us updated as much as possible."

I bathed with a bitter disquietude as the sun continued its upward slope and Spencer made tea. Obviously my search of the grounds had proved fruitless. As had Skunk and Hamlet's questioning of the guests. They'd seen nothing and knew nothing. Fennec hadn't returned. It seemed more and more evident that whoever had killed Foggy had taken Fennec. This was the second time now Fennec had been snatched. Only this time we hadn't been able to save him. Angrily, I plucked twigs from my underbelly. I needed Sleep, the great healer.

A knock sounded on Fox Burrow's front door, and I watched Spencer hurry to answer it. "Pete," she said, giving him a hug. "Thanks for coming. Come in and have some tea." She ushered him into the dining room where I could see Eddy staring out the window, his hair disheveled, his face gray.

"I'm afraid I don't know anything helpful," said Pete slowly, dusting off his words. "I was only at the party for a few minutes last night. You know I'm not keen on crowds."

"I know." Spencer sighed. "But maybe if we can all just put our heads together and *think*. There's got to be something . . ."

"I should've been with him at the river," said Eddy quietly.

I got up and entered the dining room, settling on Eddy's lap, where he laid a hand on my head. "I should be the one who's dead, not Foggy."

Spencer shook her head. "Don't say that, Eddy. No one should be dead."

"They came for him before, Spencer." Eddy turned shadowed eyes up to her. "Think about it. Someone broke into this very inn and took Fennec, but their plan was thwarted by a rusty barn nail and my alarm clock. This time they weren't going to let anything get in the way. Not even Foggy."

"But *why?*" Spencer picked up her teacup and then set it back down again without drinking.

Eddy stared outside at the snow. "I don't know."

"The night of the inn's break-in," said Pete, clearing his throat. "The first time they tried to take Fennec, well, I think I saw someone in the forest."

"Our forest?" Spencer asked, her brows rising. "Here?"

Pete nodded. "I think it was a woman. But it was late; I don't know why she'd be there."

Spencer picked up her tea again, cupping it between her hands. "What woman?"

"Why were *you* in Fox Burrow's forest if the hour was so late?" Eddy asked, frowning.

Jumping onto the table, I sat in front of Pete, curling my tail around my toes. I wanted to know too. It was time to learn the truth about that mysterious box.

Pete lifted pale, probably waterlogged, hands. "I was there to meet a man. Specifically the man who sells me Cohibas."

Eddy's eyes widened. "The cigars? Aren't they illegal?"

Pete rubbed the back of his neck and shrugged.

"But you don't smoke," said Spencer.

"I don't smoke them," said Pete. "I resell them. Fetch a pretty good price too."

A rumble of relief grew in my throat. The mystery box was full of illegal cigars? How boring and how Pete. Of course he'd had nothing to do with Fennec.

Her eyebrows drawing together, Spencer walked to the window and sipped her tea. "So this woman . . . what did she look like?"

"I suppose she was of average height and average weight. I didn't see her face, Spencer."

"Well, what do you bet it's a face soured with wrinkles and rimmed with spiky eyelashes?"

"You really think Demelza's capable of murder, Spencer?" asked Eddy. "I know she doesn't like Fennec, but that's extreme. Besides, there's no way she could overpower Foggy."

Spencer looked deep into her tea, as though the answer lurked somewhere beneath its sorrel surface. "Maybe not, but she's got a grandson who probably could."

19

The Inglorious Pim

A t that moment the doorbell rang, and everyone looked at each other with confusion. "Who's here at seven in the morning?" asked Spencer, setting down her tea and heading for the door. "Maybe Lou's found something."

I jumped off the table to follow, and together our feet padded quickly along the creaky floorboards, our toes curling as the door opened to reveal Demelza Corn in all her odium, standing there as though summoned.

"I didn't do it," she said, pushing her way inside. "I assume you think I did, so I'm here to set the record straight."

Startled, Spencer closed the door behind her. "You already know about Foggy and Fennec?"

"News travels quickly in this town." She looked around the inn with distaste. "Lieutenant Tennant was at Cocoa Pod the moment it opened, and he let the news slip to everyone there, including me. You really need to water your house-plants more, Spencer. They're dying."

Hearing Demelza's voice, Eddy and Pete strode into the foyer, Eddy's jaw clenched, a vein throbbing in the middle of his forehead.

"Ah, see? I knew it. You've all decided it was me," said Demelza. "That's why I'm here to tell you it wasn't. Really, the fact that this town has a murderer in it just goes to show its recent decay. Outsiders really *do* bring crime." She shuddered, her lashes thickly coated and lips blood-red even though the sun was barely up.

Spencer crossed her arms. "Where did Pim go after you both left the bakery last night?"

"You really think my grandson had something to do with this?" Demelza's voice went dead cold.

"Well, I believe that's my cue to leave," said Pete, zipping up his jacket and filling the icy silence. "I'll do another sweep by the river for the dog." Exchanging a meaningful look with Eddy, he slipped out the door.

That look. *A sweep by the river.* No, Pete was up to something else entirely. "I'll go help him," I announced, pushing through the maze of ankles and calves and leaping through the doorway.

"Bijou!" Spencer called. "Don't go out there. You'll freeze!"

I assured her I would do no such thing by puffing out an expanse of boreal floof.

Pete grunted when I caught up to him by his truck. "Coming with me, are you?" With a resigned sigh, he waved at Spencer to let her know I was accompanying him before opening the door and ushering me inside.

With a victory pound on my imaginary shield, I leapt onto the ripped passenger seat and exchanged nods with John Wayne. Pete slid into the driver's seat (with a squelch I doubted very much could be attributed to the snow) and turned on the engine.

I knew where we were going as soon as we rounded a corner and headed up the knoll overlooking town. And it certainly wasn't the river.

We parked just below Demelza Corn's apricot house, hidden behind a copse of snow-laden trees. This was a stakeout, I realized, and from our position we could just see the inglorious Pim through the window. He sat cross-legged on the kitchen counter, using a pocket knife to carve sweet nothings into his slingshot. The blood of countless squirrels and bunnies had stained that slingshot red, but did it seem even more vivid and carnal than usual? Could it possibly have been used on Foggy?

Chi Chi, the russet potato dog, sat at Pim's feet, begging as he ate from a bag of corn chips. Did she know what he did with that thing? Was she aware that she was no bigger than a rabbit herself? She quivered with excitement as he dropped her a chip. Apparently she led a life of willful ignorance.

Glancing at Pete, I noticed his gaze wasn't on Pim or Chi Chi. It was on the shed in the backyard, its metal siding just visible behind the house. Could Fennec be in there? Tapering my own eyes to tiny knife points, I tried to pierce the metal to see inside and failed.

Pete drummed his fingers on the steering wheel, and I could see cogs turning behind his eyes. He was calculating the risk versus reward of breaking into that shed and of doing so while Pim was home. While he calculated, I exited the vehicle, rappelling through the open window and landing with a muffled *thump* inside a prosperous snowbank.

Before I could reorient myself, Pete pulled me out by the tail, and I swung Dewclaw fruitlessly at his kneecaps. He refused, however, to release his hold and insisted that I wait in the truck while he investigated.

"Vikings don't wait in trucks," I told him as he plopped me back on the seat, rolled up the windows, and shut the door. "Vikings who wait in trucks destroy trucks." I pounded my paws on the window as he floated from shrubbery to shrubbery up the drive and then slipped around the house.

Entombed in a frosty silence, I stared at John Wayne, who stared back before politely bobbing his head.

I was contemplating the merits of furthering the seat's wretched state when Pim stepped out of the house, his slingshot in one hand, a phone in the other. Forgetting the seat, I watched him saunter to his snow-covered bike and brush it off, talking on the phone as he did. A moment later, he shoved the phone into his pocket and rode off.

Jumping onto the dash, I smooshed myself against the windshield in an effort to see where he was going. But as he disappeared around the corner, I found myself instead staring at the same doe with the prominent black chin strap I'd seen in the woods two weeks earlier. From the look on her face, it seemed she didn't appreciate the bulging, watery eyes of a Norsecat boring into her from behind cracked glass.

De-smooshing myself, I tipped the imaginary helmet. "Morning."

She didn't respond, and I felt her judgy gaze on me while I began to gallop like a hamster in a ball around and around the cab, looking for a way out. I needed to follow Pim. For all I knew, he could be on his way to kill and kidnap again.

I found my exit through the driver's-side door where the handle was loose and kindly toward the thumbless. Shooting from the truck like a caffeinated moose, I zoomed right past the doe, kicking puffs of snow in her face as I chased Pim's tire tracks down the knoll.

At first I thought he was going to the river, and I was shocked that even he, dumb as he was, would return to the scene of the crime. But instead his tracks veered onto Sourdough Drive, and I found myself puffing and heaving right back to Fox Burrow.

Demelza's car was still there, parked next to Spencer's and Eddy's, but Pim's bike was nowhere to be seen. Narrowing my eyes, I followed his tracks around to the back of the house where I spotted it leaning against a snow-shocked lilac. Why was he sneaking around the inn like a little villain? If he'd been talking to Demelza on the phone earlier, why not just go to the front door and announce his arrival? Instead I watched him slowly open the door to the mudroom and slip inside. Horrified, I bellowed a grand warning and received an instant bray from Widmer on his patio around the corner. But there was no time to go to the Lab for help. Darting inside, I followed Pim down the dim, cold hall.

Up ahead I could hear the voices of Spencer, Eddy, and Demelza, and they'd risen considerably since I'd left. Insults poured from Demelza's mouth while Eddy and Spencer attempted to fend them off. But lost within their anger over Foggy and their worry over Fennec they'd allowed themselves to be dragged into Demelza's dirty fighting pit, and there she beat them with experience.

Crouching behind a bookshelf, Pim watched the four of them while I watched him. He seemed interested for a time . . . until he spotted one of Spencer's hygge books and quietly began to flip through it, pulling swaths of pages from the binding and letting them flutter to the floor.

A growl built deep in my throat and I prepared to pounce.

But then Pim abruptly let the book drop from his fingers. Eddy had taken several steps toward Demelza, his eyes flashing with rage, and everyone, including me, inhaled collectively— waiting for an impossibly possible blow.

But with a huge exhale, he stepped back. "I'm sorry." He cleared his throat, anger and embarrassment fisticuffing for top emotion. "Really, Demelza, I don't know why I did that. I don't think I've ever been this angry." He ran a hand down his face and it softened like butter. "But no one should come between a man and his dog. Not like this. Not ever."

Trembling with the much-hated adrenaline that accompanied confrontation, Spencer reached out and touched his arm. At the same time, Pim found one of Skunk's tiny tennis balls loitering by the bookshelf and loaded it into his slingshot. Before I could react, before I could blink or meow a warning, he'd taken aim at Eddy's face and released the weapon.

Highly motivated, the ball sped through the air in a beautiful arc, and I watched Skunk tear into the room from wherever she'd been hiding and launch at it like a tiny hippo, her mouth wide enough to swallow a ship bow. With a *snap*, her teeth closed on nothing but air, and together we watched, wide-eyed, as the ball smashed not into Eddy's face but Demelza's. She'd stepped forward and Eddy had stepped backward at just the right moment, and now Demelza's nose gushed blood.

A shocked sizzle befell the room.

Before any of us could regain our wits, red and blue lights flashed outside and three police cars snaked their way up the drive. Eddy and Spencer exchanged horrified looks as Demelza cupped her face and collapsed. The cars stopped, their doors slammed, and multiple boots crunched quickly across the snow.

Thump, thump, thump. "Spencer Bonanno! This is the police! Open up!"

Confessions

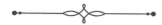

Lieutenant Lou Tennant and his coterie of policemen entered Fox Burrow in two blinks and a tail swish. With locked jaws and quick eyes they took in the scene: Demelza writhing on the floor with blood pouring from her nose, a pale-faced Eddy looming over her, and Pim . . . well, *Pim* had turned tail and fled as soon as the ball had hit, and no one had seen him but me.

Skunk was back in hiding, either under the stairs or in the oil cabinet, and she'd taken her ball with her. In fact, I realized, it looked very much like Eddy *had* punched Demelza.

Lieutenant Tennant shook his head and let out a great sigh. "Well, this is very disappointing."

Spencer spoke from Eddy's elbow. "Eddy didn't do this, Lou. Someone threw something from over there and it hit her." She pointed to where I was sitting, and I raised a paw in solidarity.

"Who?" asked the Lieutenant. "Who else is in the house?"

"I don't know. But there must've been someone. They must've fled through the back door."

Immediately, Lieutenant Tennant ordered two police-women to search the woods behind the house. Then he turned back to Spencer. "You and Eddy both have Demelza's blood on you. See there on your shirt? I'm sorry, but I'm afraid I'm going to have to take all three of you into the station for questioning now. Not just Demelza as initially planned."

"What? You came here for me?" Demelza's voice was thick from behind the cloth she now pressed to her nose. Two officers had helped her to a chair where she'd folded in on herself, acting every bit the frail, old lady. "Why? I certainly had nothing to do with Foggy."

"No?" said the Lieutenant tiredly. "Then why did we find threatening letters in Foggy's house? They were very clearly written and signed by you."

Demelza's eyes widened from their perch above the cloth.

"It seems he told you he was the owner of the firehouse. That he was the one who chose to sell it to Eddy instead of you. So you decided to punish him for it. There were some nasty things written in those letters, Demelza."

"I have nothing to say about those letters, and if I did, I'd say they were harmless. I only wanted him to know how I felt. Letters certainly don't kill people. Anyway, how did you know I was here? Am I being followed, Lieutenant?"

"You're not being followed. The waitress at Cocoa Pod told us you were on your way here. Come along now, we'll discuss this more at the station."

I watched with horror as Eddy and Spencer were rounded up alongside Demelza and ushered out the door.

Making myself as big as possible, I followed them onto the porch. Strutting up to Lieutenant Tennant, I informed him I was a witness and could corroborate their innocence.

But the Lieutenant didn't see me. It was as though he were blind to Scandinavians. I was about to jab him with Dewclaw when Eddy spoke to me softly. "Bijou, I need your help, girl. I need you to keep looking for Fennec. Will you do that for me?"

Lowering Dewclaw, I looked up and met his dark, anguished gaze.

"Don't worry about us," he said as the Lieutenant led him and Spencer away. "Save Fennec." Throwing back my shoulders, I promised him I would. And so my honor was bound.

I trotted through endless slushy, melting snow. My imaginary armor rested heavily on my shoulders, and ice balls formed painfully between my toes as I made my way across town. I was headed to Dr. Flora's vet clinic and Skunk and Hamlet followed a few paces behind, their bravery sputtering about like candle flames in the wind. Watching Spencer and Eddy be led away by the police had rattled them immensely.

Pete Moss had arrived back at Fox Burrow just as we'd left, and he'd been empty-handed. Fennec hadn't been in Demelza's shed or anywhere on her property then. And so, as the sun warmed and snow streamed from the trees, we searched.

Dr. Flora seemed like a good person to investigate. And then, after her, I wanted to investigate James Halvah. After all, they'd both argued with Foggy right before his death.

The vet clinic was housed in a small, two-room brick building that should've been open. The hours listed on the door stated as much, yet the place was locked and dark. Staring up at the *Closed* sign, knowing I couldn't receive help if I needed it, I began to feel ill with multiple deadly afflictions.

Skunk and Hamlet were taking turns pounding my lumbar as I hacked up a particularly speedy strain of the

Black Plague when Dirk Square Jaw sauntered up the sidewalk. Ignoring us completely, he paused to catcall Brooke Binder as she clopped down the sidewalk from the opposite direction. Rolling my eyes, I froze as my gaze swept across his boots.

Those were the boots I'd seen in Witching Flour. On the night of the bakery's break-in. I recognized them immediately. There was no mistaking that thick, bombastic tread.

Without a second thought, I unsheathed Dewclaw and stabbed him in the shin.

"Ow!" he cried, hopping on one foot, his round, piggy eyes discovering me as I lunged toward him again. "Crazy cat! What's wrong with you?"

He kicked at me and I riposted like a boss.

His following bellow only made me run faster as I chased him up the street, Skunk bounding after me and dragging Hamlet by his sweater while he struggled to brandish Snip.

"Oh! Oh my. Have a pleasant morning!" Brooke exclaimed as we tore past her, Dirk shrieking as I hacked at his ankles.

We destroyed four pots of frostbitten flowers, three cruiser bikes, and a little free library before cornering him in the alleyway behind Witching Flour.

Planting our paws as wide as they would go, we blocked his escape, a snow/mud slop squelching between our toes.

As a man who prided himself on being all things Man, Dirk was certainly having a difficult time upholding any of his Manly Ideals while experiencing the pure terror of facing a battle-distended Viking cat and two of her warriors. Licking thin lips, his gaze darted about in search of an escape. Finding none, he moved sideways toward Witching Flour and tried the back door, which was locked.

"Don't tell me you're going to break in again," I said.

"Go back to the abyss!" he screamed.

Exposing the snaggletooth, I stepped forward and he took a pen from his pocket and plunged it into the slop. "You shall not pass!"

I continued forward, flanked on either side by Skunk and Hamlet, who were siphoning many gallons from their pools of bravery.

"Okay! I'm sorry I threw that knife at you," Dirk squawked like a hen. "You surprised me and anyway, it's not *my* knife. It belongs to William Corn the Second. He gave it to me for safekeeping when he went to jail. He didn't want his delinquent son, Pim, to find it."

I kept our line moving steadily forward, squeezing out his confession.

"I wasn't doing any harm at the bakery that night either," Dirk gushed, stumbling backward. "I didn't break in to steal anything. I had a date the following evening, see? And I didn't want to disturb Mother at home. Mother is very fussy about my dates. The firehouse was always my old standby before it was sold, and now it's even better because it has a kitchen where my date could cook me a romantic meal. Anyway, I was scouting it out that night to make sure Eddy hadn't moved in yet."

The pure stupidity of this man's crime brought our forward march to a halt. He'd broken into Witching Flour and thrown the knife at me all in the name of an unchaperoned date? The man was too dim-witted and watered-down to have committed the crimes I actually cared about. It was time to move on.

Scoffing in his general direction, I turned tail and summoned Skunk and Hamlet with paw signals. "Do we all agree this man-child is not the murderer of Foggy nor the dognapper of Fennec?" I asked formally.

"We do."

"Then we must point our investigation in another direction."

"South?" asked Skunk.

"No, north. But first we must find food to keep up our strength. Then we're going to visit James Halvah, and if we're lucky, Dr. Flora will be with him."

Now, normally cats named Bijou don't dumpster dive. But desperate times and all. A few minutes after leaving a very unnerved Dirk Square Jaw alone in the alleyway, I found myself fishing from a stenchy garbage bin. Reeling in a sizable medley of what was once a vegetable stir-fry, I took care to avoid the onions and garlic and then gagged loudly as it slid down my throat. As a non-meat eater, Spencer would love it. I, however, only managed another bite by tricking myself into thinking it was a nice Icelandic cod. Yet it *did* boost my energy, and I dropped the rest for Skunk and Hamlet, who waited eagerly below.

We were on our way to James Halvah's house when we saw James Halvah himself pull up to the police station in a police car. Sliding from the back seat, he looked at the officer who'd driven him with a sad gaze. "I can't believe he's gone," he said. "This just doesn't make any sense. Foggy and I had our differences, yes, but I never wanted him dead." He ran a hand down his face. "I know people saw us argue at the party last night, but I can explain that."

"Well, that's why you're here," said the officer. "To explain."

"Investigation redirect!" I announced. Extending a paw at Halvah, who was disappearing into the station, I informed Skunk and Hamlet that we were going to follow him inside. In reply, Skunk promptly pointed out the *No Dogs* sign on the door.

"No matter," I told her. "*I'm* not a dog, so I'll go in alone. You two go get Cork and maybe Widmer or Fuzz Aldrin. Whoever wants to help. Take them to James Halvah's house and see what you can find. Report back to Fox Burrow at seventeen hundred hours. That's five, Skunk." Understanding flooded the Pom's face, and it looked like constipation.

Slipping into the police station, I spent the rest of the day listening to the rather dull testimonies of dozens of townspeople—all the while dodging the creative capture tactics of a certain secretary named Margaret.

POLICE LIEUTENANT LOU TENNANT: James Halvah, did you have an argument with your stepfather, Foggy Lawson, last night at Witching Flour's grand opening? And after this fight, several witnesses said you left the party. Where did you go?

HALVAH: Unfortunately yes, I did have an argument with him. And I regret it immensely. Those were our last words, Lou . . . and I feel wretched. Afterward, I went to a prearranged destination with Dr. Flora. The Do Si Do Barn over in Cherrytown. You know it? I suppose it's time to confess. We like to square-dance, Flora and I. And I'm afraid we're quite in love, despite her previous engagement to my stepfather, Foggy. It's time for people to know.

POLICE LIEUTENANT LOU TENNANT: Demelza Corn, you found out that Foggy Lawson owned and sold the firehouse to Eddy Line some weeks ago, and this made you so angry you wrote him threatening letters. Do you dispute this? And your grandson, William the Third, better known as Pim. Where was he last night during the time of the murder?

DEMELZA: Yes, I found out some weeks ago that Foggy was the owner of the old firehouse. And how could I not be angry? Foggy Lawson betrayed me, one of his own people, by selling the historical old place to an outsider. Yes, I wrote him letters, but I certainly didn't kill him, Lou. After the party I went home and indulged in a nightcap with Bobi Pinn and Brooke Binder. We were nowhere near the river, and neither was Pim. He was in his room the whole night.

POLICE LIEUTENANT LOU TENNANT: Brooke Binder, where did you go after the party last night? And can you corroborate the whereabouts of both Demelza and Pim Corn?

BROOKE: I went to Demelza's house along with Bobi Pinn after the party. We were there when poor Foggy died. And Pim was in his room. I could hear him stomping around up there all night. But, oh dear, they really shouldn't have graffitied *Die, Jerk* on the firehouse door last month, and Demelza shouldn't have had Pim cut Eddy's gas pipe. And *I* shouldn't have left the cardboard note on the pipe for Eddy to find. I only wanted to run him out of town so that Demelza could get the firehouse and finally be happy. Leave the rest of us in peace. But none of us wanted to hurt anyone. Not Eddy, not his dog, and *certainly* not Foggy. Celery, Lou? I always keep an extra stick in my purse for hydration purposes.

POLICE LIEUTENANT LOU TENNANT: Eddy Line, Demelza Corn has informed me that you did not, in fact, assault her. She said the object that hit her most likely came from her grandson's slingshot. Most assuredly it was meant for you. She said she called him to come to her aid because she felt outnumbered by you and Spencer and was fearful you thought her capable of murder and dognapping. Therefore, I am releasing both you and Spencer Bonanno.

EDDY: Demelza told you that? Well, that's a relief. I suppose people can surprise you in the end. I'll be glad to get home and begin the search for Fennec. I must find him, Lou.

POLICE LIEUTENANT LOU TENNANT: Margaret? What do you mean you're still trying to capture that damn cat? Forget it, we must now focus our very limited resources on finding something, *anything*, that leads to an answer in this case.

MARGARET: I hear you, sir. Though I'm ashamed of my failure. The beast has completely avoided capture, and I have stretched my considerable skills to their utmost. I suppose, however, that one of life's lesser skills is knowing when to wave the white flag.

Perched high on a rafter above the interrogation room, I sneezed and wished I could seal my nostrils with a strong Norse clay. Instead I succumbed to a prodigious cough attack. The dust was thick and irritating as I watched the townspeople enter and leave that room. And, one by one, my tenuous leads crumbled away.

Later that night, back at Fox Burrow, Skunk told me she and Hamlet had found nothing at James Halvah's home. Not Dr. Flora, not even a single hair from a sand-colored dog. Unlike Margaret though, I neither possessed, nor wished to possess, life's lesser skill of knowing when to wave the white flag.

Life on the Chain

The next day dawned pale and wet with rain. A crowd gathered on the town square to lay flowers for Foggy. Church bells rang, and my own northern dirge rose and fell on the backs of fat drops. Everyone wanted to know the details of all that had happened, and rumors drifted about like smoke, cloaking Gray Birch in dark speculation.

Everyone knew the police were searching for a murderer that couldn't be found. And everyone wanted to know when the police would release Foggy's body so a date could be set for the funeral. I thought the old bartender deserved a highly respectable one. A cremation in a ship perhaps. Despite the snow, the river hadn't frozen, and it would whisk him to Valhalla in a manner befitting such a master of ale.

Two days later, I gnashed my teeth together as I walked endless loops around the soggy agility course, wracking my brain and feeling the burden of broken honor. I'd promised Eddy I would find Fennec, and yet I was no closer to doing so.

"Bijou Bonanno!"

I paused my loop as Spencer waved at me from the porch, a blanket wrapped around her, a disheveled ponytail hanging lopsided over one shoulder. "Come inside and dry off please. You'll catch your death."

I assured her I was water-and-death-repellent.

"Also," she said, luring me with magical words, "it's dinnertime."

Immediately, I speed-marched from the agility course into the foyer, bringing muddy paw prints with me. Kneeling, Spencer rubbed me dry with a soft towel. My eyes bulged and the snaggletooth was forcefully exposed as she paid rigorous attention to the semi-bald spot. "There, that's better." Rising, she tossed the dirty towel over a hook by the door. "Skunk and Hamlet are already eating in the kitchen."

On the way there, we passed the living room where Eddy sat on the floor surrounded by dozens of papers. Most were printed news articles; some were pages of his own hand-scribbled notes. The majority of these notes had been crossed out, great swaths of black ink angrily outing them as dead-end clues that pointed nowhere. But one page, the one Eddy held in his hands now, remained clean, whole, and unredacted as he studied it, the words *Fennec-Pre-Adoption* scrawled across the top.

"You want pâté or chunky?" Spencer asked, picking me up and whisking me past.

"Chunky," I replied, craning my neck back toward Eddy. "No, pâté." Passing a window, I saw three town deer outside plucking at sodden grass with nimble lips.

In the kitchen, Skunk and Hamlet solemnly stared at their food. In fact, they'd barely eaten anything since Fennec's disappearance, and I was forced to lead by example, eating their meals as well as my own. It was vital at least one of us kept up our strength.

Eddy's phone rang just as I polished off Skunk's dog food, and I waddled down the hall to eavesdrop.

"Officer Pemberton," Eddy said, pacing about the living room. "Thank you for calling me back. I was told you are the officer who rescued the pit bull puppy I adopted?" Picking up a throw pillow, he plumped it before setting it back on the sofa. "Yes, that's right. Uh-huh. Just over two months ago. Near downtown Denver. I believe you arrested the man who had him. He was beating him." Plumping another pillow, he glanced over as Spencer entered the room. "No, they told me you arrested him for drug possession. You couldn't make the animal cruelty charge stick. I agree, it is unfortunate." The bags under Eddy's eyes darkened as he paced to the bay window and looked out. "What do you mean it wasn't fully investigated like you'd advised?"

Spencer came to stand beside me, and I leaned heavily against her socks.

Eddy listened for a long time before finally turning away from the window. "Well, this is very disturbing information. I had no idea. Seriously, none whatsoever. That explains a lot about his behavior."

Pacing back to the window, he told Pemberton all about the Crime of Awfulness. Then, after listening for a while, he said, "Thank you, Officer. You've been incredibly helpful. Best of luck to you, too, and I will call the ASPCA directly as you suggested."

"Well?" said Spencer when he hung up. "What did he say?"

Collapsing on the sofa, Eddy deflated the throw pillows. "You were right that I should call him, Spence. And he honestly wasn't surprised. I mean, he was surprised about Foggy's murder, but he wasn't surprised about Fennec."

"He wasn't?"

"No. He said pit bulls are particularly prone to theft. Sometimes they're even snatched right out of people's yards. Especially the puppies. It seems they're very profitable." Leaning forward, he let his head drop toward the floor. "You know when you think something awful has been lost to the annals of history, but then you find out it's still right here, staring you in the face?"

I nodded and my Viking helmet slipped to one side. My eyes had grown dry from staring and I blinked.

"That's what this is." Eddy looked up with hooded eyes. "Dogfighting, Spencer. It's more popular today than ever, despite its illegality. Officer Pemberton said huge fighting rings still exist throughout the country, some containing hundreds of dogs, and as soon as one is toppled another one pops up to take its place. The fights happen everywhere, and they tempt gamblers with hundreds of thousands of dollars exchanging hands in a single night. School teachers participate. Vets participate. All kinds of ordinary people participate. And, obviously, it's the perfect blood sport for criminals."

Blood sport? Fennec? I felt a horrible tightening in my chest. *No.*

"What's a blood sport?" asked Hamlet, coming into the room with Skunk. "Bijou?"

I didn't have the heart to tell him, and I moved to sit on Eddy's feet as he continued.

"Pemberton said they've attempted to shut down the fighting rings in Denver for years but can never seem to bite the head off the snake. He said he's almost positive Fennec was born into one. What did he call it . . . a life on the chain. That's what it was. He was born into life on the chain."

"So what about the guy he arrested?" Spencer's face was sheet-white. "Can't they get information out of him about the ring?"

"Nope," said Eddy. "Apparently he died in prison his first night there. Two other inmates attacked him. Allegedly they tried to peel a tattoo right off his neck and pierced an artery."

I looked up. A tattoo? Was that why Fennec had his horrid geometric dog head tattoo? Because it marked him as part of a dogfighting ring? Could it be that *all* members of this ring were marked with the same tattoo? Including the humans?

"My God," said Spencer, coming to the same realization. "Eddy, you have to call Officer Pemberton back."

"Why? What have you thought of?"

"His mug shots. We need to see the dead man's mug shots. Eddy, we need to see his tattoos."

"I knew it," Spencer said, looking over Eddy's shoulder at the computer screen. "That tattoo must mark all the members of that particular dogfighting ring. Thank God mug shots are public record. Maybe it can lead us to the ring itself."

"I'm forwarding this to Lieutenant Tennant," said Eddy, typing rapidly on the keyboard. "Then we need to call the ASPCA."

I moved closer to the screen, scowling at the man's sneering face until it shimmered and swam before me. There, on the left side of his neck, was the geometric dog head tattoo. Only his wasn't so crude as Fennec's but had been etched by a steady hand with a fine needle. Officer Pemberton had said it was definitely the tattoo they'd tried to cut off.

Sliding from the sofa like a bulbous toboggan, I summoned Skunk and Hamlet to the other room. Skunk had explained to the piglet the ins and outs of blood sports and now he brandished Snip, his skin flush with Viking Rage.

"Now, don't go destroying anything just yet," I told

him, batting his imaginary blade away from a horrified houseplant. "We still don't know exactly who to destroy. That's what we need to figure out."

Skunk, who'd been staring aimlessly at the wall, suddenly announced, "Fuzz Aldrin is calling."

"What?"

"Fuzz Aldrin. You know, our young feline guest with the black fur—"

"I know who he *is*, Skunk."

"Yes, well, he's calling from the vent just there." The Pom pointed her snout at a rectangular grate in the wall near the ceiling.

"How in Odin's beard?" Lifting my paw, I pushed off, stopping when I was perched on top of the shelf right beneath the vent. "Fuzz?"

The dark-furred youth blinked eager yellow eyes at me from behind intersecting metal. "Bijou! Hello. I'm here to relay a message."

"How are you in the vent?"

"Oh, I've got the whole ventilation system figured out. I can reach any part of Fox Burrow I want from in here."

I felt a swoop of admiration. The youth had just achieved one of my lifelong aspirations. "Fuzz, tell me *how*—"

"I've been going all over the inn relaying the news about the dogfighting ring to the other guests," he continued. "Everyone is worried and everyone wants to help, which is why we've all been putting our heads together, so to speak."

"That's excellent. If you could first just answer my first question—"

"We were thinking about that dog head tattoo just now, and Widmer remembered talking to a town deer the night of the murder. This deer, Bijou, well, he said he saw a man at the gas station that very night with the very same tattoo, right on his neck. He thought it was a weird place for it. And ugly too."

I leaned forward, smooshing my whiskers into the vent. "Really? You don't say. What else did this deer say to Widmer?"

"He said that the man was very large with a very thick black beard. He was filling up his tank in order to leave town. Apparently he told the woman at the pump next to him that he was heading home. Said he got what he came for."

Suddenly I had a vision of the black-bearded tourist I'd seen in the gazebo. He'd also been at the grand opening, helping a tipsy Bobi Pinn to her feet after she'd crashed into Homer. "Did he say where he was going?"

"No." Fuzz's yellow eyes bulged as he pushed them up against the vent.

"What about his car? Was there anything telling about the car?"

"Widmer didn't say. Be right back."

Fuzz scampered off, his claws ringing on metal. Before long, he was back again, breathless. "It was a truck," he said. "Black with tinted windows, and it had Colorado plates and an *I Heart Denver* bumper sticker."

I bristled. "Well, I'd bet my third life that truck was taking Fennec right back to the fighting ring."

Fuzz Aldrin lifted a paw, rudely shushing me, his elder. "Hold on. Miss Tut just rang."

"Rang? What do you mean, *rang*?"

But he'd already disappeared down the duct.

While he was gone, I used Dewclaw to pick a remnant of Skunk's dinner from between my teeth.

"Well?" I asked when his yellow orbs again bulged through the vent.

"Miss Tut just heard Widmer bark four times."

"Ah, yes," I remembered. "Three barks inform us there are no bears. Two barks means there are, and one bark means the javelin has already been thrown and we'd best move aside. But what does four mean?"

"That he has retrieved a memory."

"What memory?"

"An important one."

"Go on."

"Widmer remembered that the deer saw a bandage on the forearm of the black-bearded man at the gas station."

"Let's just call him Blackbeard," I said.

Fuzz nodded. "Okay, Blackbeard. But there was no scent of blood on the bandage. Instead the deer said it smelled like titanium dioxide, lead, nickel, iron oxides, and ash."

I blinked. Who knew town deer had such a prodigious sense of smell?

"What smells like all that?" asked Hamlet from below.

"Ink," I said, slowly. "The man had a fresh tattoo."

"And there's only one place in Gray Birch to get a tattoo . . ." said Skunk.

I nodded. "The Stygian. On Princeton Street."

"Ah, Sister. I was hoping you'd come out. It's such a nice evening. Looky here, I can catch 257 raindrops in a row. Been practicing all day." Cork was out on his patio, his eyes turned up, his ears running down his neck floof, water droplets shimmering in his black-and-white fur.

"Sorry, no time to chat," I said, trotting past.

With a flourish, he snapped up three drops in order from smallest to fattest. "Yes, you'd best crack on then. But where are you off to?"

"I'm just chasing a lead," I said, lengthening my stride.

"Chasing?" Cork turned his long muzzle away from the heavens to look at me, a quiver of excitement taking hold. "Did you say *chasing*?"

A groan speedbagged my throat. There was simply no time to deal with a border collie who suffered from Distraction deep in his bones. "Not *chasing* a lead, no. Stalking? No. Trailing . . ."

"Excuse me, Sister, but I must come." Hot breath washed over my tail, and I turned to see him looming inches behind me, his black-and-white face awash with earnestness. Behind him was the lofty fence surrounding his patio, supposedly unjumpable.

"How did you jump that?" I asked, impressed.

"Belief, Sister."

"We're going to the tattoo parlor," said Skunk, trotting up to us importantly, Hamlet at her side.

"Very good," said Cork. "I've always wanted a tattoo. What are we getting? Perhaps a four-leaf clover."

"Wait! I'm coming too," said a buoyant voice.

Skunk, Hamlet, Cork, and I all turned to see Fuzz Aldrin bounding toward us, his tail straight as a flagpole.

"Oh, fine then," I said. There was simply no time to argue about it. "Everyone, to the Stygian."

Tattoos and Ducts

Though closed, the Stygian's sign still flickered in the front window, coloring the mud below it orange. Together, we sat before it in a row, catching our breath.

"Why aren't we going in?" asked Hamlet, shivering profusely beneath his sweater (this one burgundy with hashtags).

I clapped him on the lumbar. "Oh, we're going in. I'm just searching for the best way. Perhaps the roof . . . or maybe I can slip Dewclaw under a window and unlatch it—"

"The best way in is there," said Skunk.

"Where?"

"Just *there*."

"Skunk, that's a wall."

"Yes." She blinked rain from roving eyes.

"Walls do not usually allow for entry."

"That one does."

Cork stepped forward then, his nostrils flared, his back end waving the flag of purpose. "She's right," he said. "There *is* an entry here." He moved forward to infiltrate when suddenly his head snapped to the left as a twig despaired and flung itself from the gutter above. For a moment the world stilled as the collie froze, his right front leg up, his long nose pointed where the twig had drowned within a pile of its kith and kin.

"*Cork*," I warned, sensing a massive Distraction coming on. But it was too late. Performing an impressively gymnastic move, the collie placed himself beneath the gutter exactly where the twig had fallen. Now he waited, his eyes turned up, his ears once more running down his neck floof. I sighed. That this canine had failed sheepdog school was certainly no surprise.

I turned to Skunk. "We've lost him. Show me this entryway."

But the Pom was no longer there. Nor was Hamlet or Fuzz. Naturally, my eyes turned mudward to see if they'd sunk in.

"Bijou!" I looked up to see Hamlet's thick nose beckoning me from a dog door installed into the wall of the shop. Before, it had blended seamlessly with the pale vinyl siding. How Skunk had detected it was a mystery to all non-Poms.

With a last glance at Cork (who was three feet in the air, his jaws snapping around a twig), I pushed through the flap and into the Stygian, which reeked of dog. Not just a regular dog. But *dog* dog.

Attaching the imaginary nose clamp, I searched for the perpetrator. But each of the three rooms making up the tattoo parlor was empty (though I did find the stinky dog's daybed under the front desk, upon which Skunk now scribbled a love note).

Across from the front desk, Hamlet stared longingly at a wall full of sample tattoos, his gaze lingering on one of a sweater-clad hog.

Sighing, I joined Fuzz Aldrin where he opened the desk drawers. Blackbeard's information was here somewhere, and I was determined to find it. Awash in the neon glow of the window sign, my paws dug rapidly through various stacks and files and odds and ends. After a few minutes, Fuzz and I had unearthed several letters of encouragement to the owner of the tattoo parlor, *Peanut*, from his *loving mother, Doris*, half a moldy sandwich, and a large notepad filled with rough sketches. There was nothing, however, about a certain murderous customer.

Moving away from the desk, I inhaled a critical surplus of slightly fresher air. Head cleared, I spotted the computer sitting on top of the desk. The answers I searched for most likely lived in there. Though, looking at the flat-faced intellect, it didn't *seem* very intellectual. Not perched on the desk, humming to itself with a blank eye.

Propelling myself onto the desk, I sat and gave the computer a lengthy stare. But when I tapped the spurious mouse with a rapid-fire paw, the screen demanded a password. I responded to the demand by brandishing Dewclaw. As with most things in life, this could be settled with a duel.

"The password is *PeanutRules1*," chirped Fuzz Aldrin, joining me on the desk with a shell-pink sticky note between his teeth.

"Eh?" I lined up Dewclaw with the thumping heart of the computer. It was an odd heart, too, only a single black line palpitating within the password box. *So vulnerable*, I thought, preparing for a magnificent plunge. *So feeble.*

Just as I was drawing back in order to hurtle forth, Fuzz shouldered me aside and began tapping the keyboard. Momentum muddled, Dewclaw and I plunged right off the desk and shot pointy-end first into a trash can, but not before I'd seen *PeanutRules1* clearly written on the sticky note beneath *PASSWORD*. Cursing youths worldwide and their affinity for technology, I made a hasty exit from the trash can.

"Bijou, I want this." Hamlet's breath was sweltry with Need as he held up the drawing of the sweater-clad hog in front of me.

"And I want this." Skunk's voice came from beneath the desk where she sat on the stenchy dog bed, staring at a tropical beach drawing. "Hamlet found it for me. He thought it would match my innermost self. And Bijou, it *does*."

"You're not getting tattoos," I said crossly.

Leaping onto the desk again, I pushed Fuzz aside, taking control of the computer. Playing masterfully with the mouse, I soon unearthed a folder labeled *Consent Forms*.

And this was where we found Blackbeard.

We knew it was him because it seemed one geometric dog head wasn't enough. He'd wanted another, this one extra large and on his forearm. His name, it seemed, was John Smith, and his address was indeed in Denver.

"121 Puck Street," read Skunk. Joining us from below, her nose smudged the screen.

121 Puck Street. What a vile place that must be.

Looking outside, I saw a shadow jumping up and down beneath the gutter—its teeth clacking loudly enough to be heard through the window. It was so loud, in fact, I envisioned those teeth bared and biting. Ripping into flesh and cartilage. A thousand sandy hairs filling the air like dust motes, twirling with violence.

Shaking my head, I wiped away the terrible image and quelled my stomach, which now roiled like a kicked anthill.

Back at Fox Burrow that night, Spencer rounded on me furiously. "Not only did you, Skunk, and Hamlet go, you took Cork and Fuzz Aldrin with you! Our *guests*, Bijou. They were entrusted to our care! Not to mention someone just *stole*

Fennec and killed Foggy—" She broke off, tears making little runnels down her cheeks. "How could you do that to me?"

Eddy came up and put his arms around her while I sat miserably at her feet. She was scared. I'd scared her. I was a litter clump.

She looked down at me over Eddy's arm. "You can't keep taking off like that, Bijou. I was worried sick. If anything ever happened to you . . . *any* of you, I don't know what I'd do."

"They're all home now, Spence," Eddy said, brushing back her hair. "Safe and sound."

I nodded, meeting her gaze with sorrowful eyes.

Letting go of Eddy, she knelt with a sigh. "Okay, I'm not mad anymore. But can I please have a hug?"

Immediately, I bowled her over with a Viking's embrace, and she squeezed me tightly beneath her chin. We stayed like that for a long time, our eyes closed, blocking out the rest of the world in favor of our cocoon.

At last she pulled back with a watery smile and stroked my ears. "Be good tomorrow while Eddy and I are gone, you hear? No more running off. Promise me you'll stay in the house, okay? Bijou?"

I worked my jaw, but it was locked with surprise. Gone? What did she mean, *gone?*

It was Miss Tut who enlightened me when I entered her suite later to perform her turndown. "They're going to Denver," she purred, watching me knead her pillow to a state of plump perfection. "Ack! Careful!" she said as I spun, nearly knocking over her glass of purrgundy.

"They're going to Denver?"

The elderly Siamese nodded before taking a sip. "They were discussing it while plating my salmon. Apparently Denver is home to a small branch of the ASPCA, and they've been invited down to discuss dogfighting as it pertains to Fennec's case."

My snaggletooth emerged for the first time since leaving the Stygian. We'd known we needed to get to Denver. To John Smith and 121 Puck Street. But we'd had no idea how to do so. Now the solution had landed in my lap. "Excellent," I said, accepting Miss Tut's offer of purrgundy. "Spencer won't mind if we carpool."

The next morning I finished breakfast in a rush. Spencer and Eddy were already standing out by Spencer's car talking to Tahereh, who'd insisted on going along.

Washing down a clingy bit of kibble with a large gulp of water, I bellowed for Skunk and Hamlet. It was time for the three of us to get ourselves into the car. Startled, they looked up from where they ate less than a man's length away, Hamlet with a piece of lettuce clinging to his nose. At least they were finally eating again.

Beyond the windows, the sky was gray as we marched toward the cat door. Reaching it, I prepared to push through. Only I didn't push it, *it* pushed *me*, and for a horrible second I stood, shocked, as my nose morphed into a homely, smooshed shape.

Extending both paws, I pushed again, but it didn't budge. *No.* Had Spencer locked us in? For the first time I could remember, the cat door was sealed.

Outside, a *beep beep* sounded as Spencer unlocked her car. In two bounds, I was at the bay window, rapping the glass with steely knuckles. From the driver's seat, Spencer gave me a guilty but resolute wave and mouthed, *Be good.*

I mouthed something decidedly bad in return, but she was already swinging the car snoutfirst down the driveway.

Horrified, I watched its back end disappear, my heart turning sideways as my brain shouted *121 Puck Street* over and over again. After a while, I realized it wasn't my brain shouting the address but Skunk in a clear soprano.

She continued to bray as I left the window and raced to check all other possible exits, Hamlet hot on my heels. But not only were they all firmly fastened, they seemed entirely too smug about it. Enraged, I speedbagged a crew sock that was hopelessly lost in the mudroom.

Hamlet dragged me away right as I was on the verge of murdering the thing. Dropping to my haunches, I breathed for a moment, trying to restore order. Never had I been locked in like this before. Not once. I swallowed and found my throat claustrophobic.

They're going to Denver and they're not going to save Fennec. They don't know how. The puppy is going to be lost forever. Hope had all but left me when Hamlet tapped me on the shoulder with a cloven hoof.

"Bijou?" he said. "I was just thinking . . . Fuzz Aldrin got out to come with us to the Stygian. Fuzz Aldrin knows how to escape."

I raised my head and gave him a watery smile. "That's true. Good thinking. But I'm afraid it's too late. Spencer's car has already rumbled down the road."

"Freyja wouldn't want us to give up," said Hamlet. "Maybe we can still catch it."

"Bijou, I think they're coming back," Skunk whispered, her breath as pungent as a dead otter in the cramped ventilation duct.

"What?" I inched along in front of her, right behind Fuzz Aldrin, my bloat smooshed up around my ears.

"I think I hear Spencer's car."

I stopped moving long enough to hear the familiar rumble of the engine. Yes, it was coming back up the drive! "How much farther to the roof?" I asked Fuzz.

"Not far," he said, looking over his shoulder. "We just have to go around a couple more bends and then get out of the vent."

"My sweater is unraveling." Hamlet's voice came from behind Skunk. "I think it got caught on something."

"Forget your sweater," I said. "Lead the way, Fuzz. And hurry!"

"Yes, sir!" Fuzz cried, leaping ahead. I opened my mouth to tell him *never* to call me sir, but I couldn't push the words *out* while at the same time pushing the body *through*. The duct had tightened even more, squeezing my bloat like a boa constrictor. My body was now like a tissue box, my ears, the tiny tips of tissue barely peeking out. I could no longer see.

"Skunk, I can no longer see!" I bellowed, starting to panic.

Her reply was muffled as my bloat overtook me like quicksand. Lost within the dark places of myself, I flailed. Then the cold finger of Death pushed me from behind.

"Back, you mangy mongrel! Back!" But I was too confined to unsheath Dewclaw, and it pushed me again, and again, and *again*. I began to prepare myself for the long trip to Valhalla. Perhaps I would return as Bijou the White.

A cool breeze suddenly ruffled my fur, alerting me to the nearness of the vent. And with one final push from the cold finger of Death, I popped out of it straight into Fuzz Aldrin, who kept me from hurtling off the roof. Bloat deflating, I took a wildly successful inhale and looked back at Skunk, who emerged with tufts of Bijou hair on her nose. Filled with sudden understanding, I nodded my thanks.

Hamlet emerged next, and his sweater had unraveled so much only a thin band remained around his chest. I watched as the breeze raised goose bumps all over his pink skin.

The roof shingles pressed roughly into my paws as far below, Spencer's car pulled up to Fox Burrow and stopped. Engine running, the passenger door opened and Eddy hurried across the gravel.

"I can't believe I left my wallet," he grumbled. "It must be in my other pants."

"I'll help you look," said Spencer, exiting the driver's side and trotting after him.

"I'll just take a quick nap," said Tahereh, closing her eyes and using her foot to prop open the back door.

High on the rooftop, I praised Freyja for granting us this opportunity.

And then I pushed Skunk off the edge.

121 Puck Street

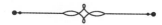

The scents of the city made my head spin. Vikings didn't much like such sewage, slop, and swill. I turned to Skunk. "Doesn't it smell like swill?"

"Who cares about swill when that gutter full of nasty liquid smells so bad?" she replied, her thick mane wilting. "Besides, I'm not talking to you."

"Oh, don't be mad. Pushing you off the roof was the only way. Blunty dog claws and cloven pig hooves don't do well downclimbing trellises."

Sniffing, she turned her head away, her fur shiny and scented with that morning's spritzing of ylang-ylang. She hadn't said a word to me the whole two-hour drive from Gray Birch to Denver.

Encouraged that she'd spoken to me now, I continued, "Anyway, I made sure you landed in the lilac."

"I thought it was fun," said Hamlet, trotting beside me. "So did Fuzz. He wanted you to push him too."

"Yes, well, unfortunately I had to send Fuzz back to his suite." Despite *us* breaking Spencer's stay-at-home orders, I wasn't about to break them even further by bringing a guest along again.

Looking around, I upped my walk from slow to speedy. We'd rounded a corner into a dangerous-looking neighborhood, and while Vikings often invite Danger over for cards and cake, this *particular* danger felt as though it wouldn't enjoy cards and cake but rather the sluggish digestion of an ample house cat.

Overhead, greenish-gray clouds hung low, and I feared we would soon be spat upon. Sure enough, a snappy wind blew in fat raindrops, which splattered all over the sidewalk. "Oh, *drat!*" Skunk yelped as a flapping newspaper unsighted her with today's tornado warning.

Spencer, Eddy, and Tahereh suddenly felt far away, tucked in their comfortable corner of the ASPCA. We'd bailed from the car as soon as they'd pulled into the ASPCA parking lot. Now, an hour later, we wandered aimlessly, unsure exactly where we were or just how far away Puck Street was. Denver, I was starting to realize, was like a huge, cosmopolitan snake, endlessly uncoiling along the foothills.

The streets in this neighborhood were cluttered and dirty, and I leapt over a fallen garbage bin before slithering under a tattered tarp. Skunk and Hamlet followed me bravely. A few minutes later, a raindrop similar in size to a nine-by-twelve koi pond landed on my semi-bald spot, shocking my snaggletooth into view. "Nice grillz," said a mutt from behind his chain link. Having previously not seen the mutt, I didn't reply, as I was too busy removing myself from Skunk's shoulder blades as she bolted up the street.

I'd just touched ground and was stepping into a crosswalk when a purple car with orange flames screeched around the corner, narrowly missing my midsection. Smelling hot rubber and the recooking of my last meal, I lurched dizzily back onto the curb.

"121 Yuck Street. 121 Yuck Street," Skunk intoned, her hair frazzled as she blinked up at the corner street sign.

"It's *Puck* Street," I corrected, regaining my bearings and checking that Hamlet was unharmed as he caught up to us.

"Well, which street is this?" Skunk asked, unsighted again as another gust of wind came along. "I can't see beyond my hair."

I peered up at the sign. "51st Avenue."

"It's not a street?"

"It's an avenue."

"Where are the streets?"

I furrowed my brow in Thought. "They must cross. I think avenues go east/west and streets go north/south. Yes, look. If we go that way, we're on Huckleberry Street."

"Is it close to Puck Street?" Hamlet asked hopefully.

"I don't know. But maybe the street names are in alphabetical order. If they are, we're not too far away. "

Just as Skunk opened her mouth to respond, a huge gust of wind replaced her words with debris. Instantly, she and Hamlet rolled down the sidewalk like tumbleweeds while I skidded behind them, all eighteen claws punishing the concrete.

We rolled and skidded right back past the mutt behind his chain link, our lips flapping an exuberant hello, and came to rest within a mountain of broken crates beneath an overpass.

My legs rigid, I stared up at the concrete undercarriage, listening to the whoosh and rumble of cars overhead. Dazed, I thought the graffiti around me looked like packages of treats, the concrete, an ocean of gravy. But I couldn't think about food now. If my theory was right, Fennec was only eight streets away. Most likely chained up in some bleak warehouse, spikes around his baby neck, his eyes liquid with terror. Had his ears been cropped? His tail docked? Had steroids been injected? Spencer and Eddy had talked about these galling aspects of dogfighting during the car ride.

I turned to Skunk, whose back legs were slung over her head in a perfect plow pose. "Are you alive?" I asked. She nodded the affirmative, as did Hamlet, who was unfurling himself from a crate several yards away.

"Should we ask those gentlemen for directions?" Skunk asked, righting herself.

"What gentlemen?"

"Those, just there." She pointed toward a cluster of bipeds huddled in the corner.

They were bearded and dirty. Their hands rested in fingerless gloves, and their torsos shivered beneath threadbare blankets. Wary, I backed away. But each of them gave me a small, toothless smile. One of them reached into his pocket and proffered a handful of crumbs. Immediately, Hamlet rushed forward and smacked them up, shivering while the man petted him gently.

On either side of the bridge the rain came down so violently the sound was deafening, and I flattened my ears to mute it. We needed to go. Fennec wasn't far. I turned to Skunk. "We don't need directions. I can find him."

As we headed out from beneath the overpass, the men looked at us with concern and shook their heads, telling us it was unsafe. I assured them we'd be fine. But, before we left, the man who'd given Hamlet his crumbs took his tattered hat and placed it on the shivering piglet, tying the earflaps carefully beneath the potbellied's pink double chin.

My theory was right. The street names were in alphabetical order. But the closer we got to P, the less warehouses there seemed to be. Brick replaced rusted metal. Thick grass carpets replaced weeds and dirt. Storehouses turned into small homes, and small homes turned into large homes, and then large homes turned into mansions. Gentrification, it seemed, had reached Puck Street. But according to *Magnum Vikus*, outward beauty can sometimes hide the ugliest inner secrets.

A blast of wind flattened several blooming pink-and-white trees as we turned onto Puck Street, and a flock of debris from Huckleberry Street followed us, littering the manicured yards.

Like the rest of the neighborhoods we'd traveled through, this one was virtually empty of life. Everyone was hiding from the storm. No people walked the sidewalks, no cars were left outside the garages, no animals occupied any of the yards, and every window shade was drawn. Fennec, it seemed, was certainly not locked in a warehouse. But which of these imposing mansions was The One?

"92 Puck Street," Skunk panted, the whites of her eyes showing as she was blown off course again. Detangling herself from a traumatized hedge, she continued, "97 Puck Street. 101 Puck Street . . ."

My heart pounded as we pushed forward, sodden with rain, our veins hot fjords of determination. I unsheathed Dewclaw as Skunk called out, "119 Puck Street! Next one is it!"

The next one was surrounded by a ten-foot hedge so thick an ant couldn't squeeze through without sucking in its sections. We stopped and stared at it, our paws and hooves drowning in two inches of swirling gray water. "121 Puck

Street," Hamlet breathed, reading the black-and-gold address plaque on the solid iron gate, his tattered hat completely soaked through.

Spiraling above the hedge were three white chimneys and two turrets. No lights shone from the turret windows. In fact, the only lights within the darkening sky came from across the street, beaming from the window of a single-story stucco (the only modest home on the block). Glancing at it, I saw a curtain move as a wrinkled face stared out at us. For a moment, we locked eyes, me and this old face that looked as though it'd lived through multiple tornadoes and quelled them all. Lightning sizzled across the sky then, and with a snap, the curtain shut.

"How do we get in?" Hamlet's teeth clacked so violently it seemed he typed out his words rather than spoke them.

"We explore the perimeter," I said. "Look for a weak point. Unsheath your weapons and keep a sharp eye."

Following the green barricade around back, we looked for any opening big enough for a Viking, a dog, and a pig of roughly equal size.

We found it on the southern side of the mansion. A patch of hedge slightly above nose height, burned brittle by the sun.

"I'll go first," I announced.

"But what about the guard?" Skunk asked, water streaming off her nose in a magnificent cascade.

"What guard?"

"That one, just there."

I looked where she pointed, blinking rapidly against the torrent. At first I couldn't spot him through the patchwork hedge. But then there he was, hunkered down beneath a garden statue, miserably hiding from the storm. The statue, meanwhile, met the storm head-on. Nude and glorious and unsympathetic to its missing left arm. My heart swelled with admiration.

"See the gun in his pants?" Skunk panted nervously.

"It's a Smith and Wesson 442," said Hamlet, pressing his snout through stalk and stem.

Disturbed that he knew that, I pulled him hastily back. "Vikings like an honest fight," I reminded him. "It takes no strength and very little thought to pull a trigger. We need to remain unseen. Follow me carefully."

Pushing into the hedge, I immediately hacked on a truculent sprig. My throat burning, I shredded the thing while the guard resettled with his back to the rain. Spitting out pulp, I realized I now had a full view of the back garden.

It was marvelous beneath the dappled black-and-gray sky. Everywhere flowers bloomed, ferns embraced, and vines climbed in an orderly manner. Weeds, having traveled miles beneath the concrete to inspect this fabled beauty, cried out final commendations and died.

Shifting my gaze to the mansion windows overlooking the garden, I noted they were awash with light. And within them flashed the fabulous silhouettes of a fabulous crowd. Snifters swirled and clinked; gowns floated and fedoras dipped. This crowd held no trepidation for the raging storm.

But where were the cars for these people? I wondered. They weren't parked out front. In fact, one wouldn't even know a party was occurring in this home if one wasn't spying through a hole in the hedge. The scent of secrecy made my nose twitch.

I refocused my gaze on the bountiful butt cheeks of the garden statue where the guard shivered and hunched his shoulders against the wind. Wet, frigid misery, I knew, was the perfect cocktail for a blind eye.

"Now's our chance," I said, glancing over my shoulder at the other two.

They were wedged within the hedge, Skunk's great swath of mane covering her nose and forcing her breaths to come and go in shallow whistles. "I'm going to drown in my own fur," she whined. Using my tail, I pushed her mane away from her nostrils, and she sucked in copious amounts of ozone.

"We need to get past the guard and find a way inside," I said.

Their eyes widened three sizes at the word *inside*, and I returned to analyzing the yard. After a moment, I spotted a brick-covered mound squatting on the far side of the garden. A door sat in the middle of this mound, and I felt a surge of hope. Could this be a cellar? And could it connect to the main house?

I summoned the others with paw signals, and together we slunk from the hedge, Skunk sucking air with nostrils as wide as soup bowls.

The garden statue watched us with all-knowing eyes as we slithered around the edges of things, keeping cover while the wind attempted to push us off course. Once, a gust pushed Hamlet so close to the guard his curly tail nearly brushed the man's boot.

"He has a dog head tattoo," Hamlet whispered in my ear when he regained cover with Skunk and I behind a planter box. "On the back of his neck. Same as Fennec's."

I clanged my imaginary sword hilt against my imaginary shield in triumph. There was no doubt we were in the right place now. Fennec had to be here. This was it, the lair of the fighting ring.

Suddenly, Skunk pooled on the grass like spilled ink. Before I could question her lucidity, Hamlet pooled next to her, and the *squelch, squelch* of heavy boots sounded close by. By the time the guard stopped directly over the planter box, I was pooled too. The man was so close I could smell the tic tac on his breath and hear the metallic *ping* of raindrops bouncing off his Smith and Wesson. All he had to do was flick his gaze slightly downward and he would spot us.

Instead he stood, staring longingly at the mansion, looking every bit like a troll with his globular muscles and very little hair. The dog head tattoo stood out like a beacon on the back of his neck, and a growl vibrated the puddle I incubated.

Suddenly, he took a rattling Darth Vader breath. Sorely startled, I was relieved when he pulled out a radio and I realized the sound had come from it, not him. "What?" he grunted.

A voice on the other end spit out a slew of unintelligible words.

"The puppy? The one that just came back?" He paused as my heart hammered. "Right. Yes, sir. Yes, I'll bring him now."

Looking exceedingly happy (for a troll) at being ordered inside, the guard lumbered toward the very same cellar door we were aiming for. Immediately I followed, vaulting the planter box with an agility seldom seen this far south.

The storm drowned out our squelches and splashes, but there, just beyond the corner of my eye, were my black and pink shadows, and I knew Skunk and Hamlet were with me.

Taking a ring of keys from his pocket, the guard opened the thick cellar door with a loud creak. From our positions behind two boxwoods (mine shaped like a duck, Skunk and Hamlet's a goose) we prepped our upcoming entry maneuvers. Two backflips and a pirouette should do the trick, I thought. Just enough to get a Viking through the door but not enough to scream *notice me*!

I performed my maneuvers spectacularly, slipping through the door while staying below the guard's line of sight and missing his boots by a centimeter.

My ensuing celebration didn't last. Just as I'd finished my pirouette, the door slammed shut, and a resounding *thunk, thunk* from the outside betrayed Skunk and Hamlet's fate.

Above, the guard frowned. But, shaking his head, he proceeded down the stone stairway, muttering about the wind.

I sat still for a moment, dazed and thrown by my sudden solitude. From the other side of the door I thought I heard Skunk whine. *Go back*, I silently ordered her. *Go back through the hedge and wait for me.* Surely they wouldn't do anything stupid.

With a deep breath, I gathered my bravery and pushed off down the stairway. I had expected darkness in this cellar, but instead it was filled with golden light. It was also startlingly quiet, the storm melting away beneath thick spans of earth. This was certainly no potato-filled, spiders-and-filth kind of cellar. Instead, it was a wine cellar with arched ceilings, stone walls, and a smooth stone floor. Lanterns hung from the walls, lighting the way back beyond the racks of wine and into a narrow passageway.

The guard ambled down this passageway, but not before he'd paused to sneak a few gulps from an uncorked bottle of Grüner Veltliner hidden within a shadow.

On silent paws, I followed, filling the dark spaces between the light, my shadow on the opposite wall fully horned and armored. Keys jangling, the guard stopped as the passageway abruptly ended at a wooden door. Faint sounds came from the other side, and I knew without a doubt those were the yelps and whines of miserable dogs.

Custer's Last Son

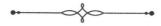

"Come on now, shut yer bark holes!" the guard shouted, swinging open the door and striding into the clamor.

Ugly wire cages lined the circular stone room, and a solitary light bulb hung from a cord in the ceiling. Boxy, bristly dog faces looked out from inside the cages, many with bloody gums from trying to gnaw their way free. No blankets padded these cells. No toys and no food bowls. Only water was provided and most of the bowls were knocked over, any remaining liquid seeping through the web of cracks in the stone floor.

The cages were placed mere inches apart, far enough away so the dogs couldn't reach each other for comfort and companionship, but close enough to antagonize. To make each one feel like they had to protect their limited space and limited food when it arrived. The cages were also badly in need of a cleaning, and the smell of urine and feces emanating from the airless space made my stomach flip.

"Get back, you mongrel," spat the guard as a massive white Bully Kutta lunged at him. She had scars raked across her face, one ear was missing, and slat ribs poked through her ratty coat like tentpoles. He kicked her cage with his boot. "You just can't wait to fight, eh? Don't worry, your time's coming tonight. In fact . . ." He stuck the toe of his boot through the wire and knocked over her upright water bowl. "No water for you. Boss needs you nice and dry so you won't bleed so much."

The Bully Kutta lunged at him again, snapping her teeth right into the wire. "Stupid cur," he said, tapping the pistol in his pants. "Save that energy for the fight, or it's a bullet in the head tonight."

My bloat now rolling like the North Sea, I slunk behind a metal bin labeled *Dog Slop*. From this vantage point I studied the room. There were nineteen dogs in all. Each one was tattooed with the geometric dog head. I could see the crude ink on their bellies when they lunged up, snapping at the guard. Each one was also so skinny that their ribs showed and their spines were bumpy despite overgrown, steroid-injected shoulder and neck muscles. I knew they could all smell the food inside the bin I hid behind because I could. Yet it was obvious they were rarely given any. The torture of that knowledge was so great, I immediately experienced sympathy hunger pains.

But where was Fennec? All of the dogs in the cages were fully grown and battle-scarred.

The guard moved past the Bully Kutta, and I watched him with narrowed eyes, my tail swishing, my sword at the ready. He stopped at a tall red locker on wheels and shoved it aside so roughly the door swung open. Inside were whips, chains, and massive weighted collars. Also, bottles and bottles of orange-and-blue pills, shiny like candy. Steroids.

These dogs were slaves. I tasted blood and realized I'd bitten my own lip.

"Get over here, you little runt," the guard muttered, bending over something previously hidden behind the locker. Squinting, I saw another cage between the guard's legs. This one small enough to house shoes. Fear rolled through my body and spiraled out with my next exhale. I could practically see it, white like vapor.

A twentieth dog emerged. This one colored like sand with huge paws and triangular ears that flopped forward. His were the only ears in the whole room that hadn't been cropped, and he used them to hide terrified eyes.

Fennec. *My* Fennec.

The guard turned, clutching the puppy by the scruff of his neck, and strode from the room, kicking the Bully Kutta's cage again on the way out. I flinched as the massive white dog roared, spittle flying from her jaws.

As I left the cover of the bin and started to follow, a silence hit the room so fast it left my ears ringing.

That's when I realized every canine gaze had latched onto me.

Feeling not a small amount of alarm, I looked back with what I imagined to be a very warm and inspiriting smile.

Snarls rumbled in response, softly at first and then louder.

"*Bait*," the Bully Kutta hissed.

"*Bait*." The chant was taken up around the circle of cages. "*Bait, bait, bait*."

A chill crept up my spine. It felt as though a spell was being cast on me.

Leaping into the passageway, I hid within a shadow just as the guard looked back and yelled, "Shut yer bark holes!" before slamming the door.

The cellar, apparently, didn't connect to the main house, and we traveled back the way we came. Fennec, who'd been roughly stuffed inside the guard's jacket while crossing the garden, was dry upon entering the music-filled mansion. I was not. I was slick as a seal, my bald spot pruny. Outside, the storm still raged and howled, and I shivered beneath an umbrella rack in the entryway. The guard and Fennec stood nearby, looking completely out of place within the flash and sparkle of the party.

Baser Instinct told me to bathe. That bathing, right then and there, was the single most important thing a sodden Norsecat could do. Ignoring it, I instead watched a woman in a long red gown approach, wagging lacquered nails in Fennec's face. Her lips stretched into a penguin-like smile. "Don't tell me this is him?"

The guard nodded. "It's him."

"I mean, *of course* it's him," she trilled. "You can see Custer's Last Stand in him clear as day. Same strong neck, same perfect jaw, same shoulders. You look just like your grand champion daddy, don't you?" She made kissy lips at Fennec, who shrank away. "Ooh, you're going to have to beat that fear right out of him, aren't you?" She laughed, now wagging lacquered nails at the guard.

"Ah, *there* he is," said a nasal voice. "Custer's Last Son." A heavyset young man with a carpet of pale hair approached through the crowd. He paused along the way to share a few jazzy hip thrusts to the music with a couple of women whose startled faces morphed into tinkling laughs of "Oh, *Chauncey*. You devil."

"Ladies." He smiled, and there was something distasteful about the way it stretched . . . like it was a string of cheese melted between two stale cheeks of bread.

Reaching the entryway, he stopped and nodded to the woman in red. "Cousin Agnes."

"Chauncey." Agnes hardly glanced at him, her attention still hovering on Fennec. "My, *my*, just look at the size of his paws. What an absolute *prince*. Except those ears. He can't be a five-time winner like his daddy without cropping those things. Or his tail. Why haven't you docked the tail yet?" She turned to her much shorter, much thicker cousin with a frown.

"I simply haven't had the time yet, Agnes. He's only been returned to me four days. Plus I've been sailing. My *God*, the best sailing. World class. Really, really tremendous—"

"Sailing." Agnes curled her lip. "Yes. I saw your latest wreck on the news."

Beneath the umbrella rack, I tensed as a memory was sparked. *That's right.* I'd seen this man, Chauncey Kane, on the news the night I'd gone to the Drunken Warbler. The night Fennec and Hamlet had first arrived at the inn.

He shrugged. "An unfortunate event. Certainly not my fault. I take no responsibility."

Agnes rolled her eyes and turned back to Fennec. "You're giving the other dog an advantage. Without cropping your dog's ears and docking its tail the opponent will have something to grab onto."

Chauncey folded plump hands. "No one knows that better than me, dear cousin. This dog will be fully cropped and docked by the time he grows into those paws and has his first fight."

"I'm just here to make sure you *win*, Chauncey." Agnes smiled sweetly, caking the makeup around her eyes. "Speaking of, I've got a lot of money riding on this fight tonight. You know I can't buy that house in Lanai without a win. How is the Bully?"

"She's raring to go, right, Ulrick? She'll definitely beat Montgomery's loser pit bull."

The guard grunted. "Yes, Boss."

"You made sure she doesn't have water, yes?"

"Yes, Boss."

"And the bait? It's ready?"

"Yes, Boss. I just got word it'll be slightly different tonight. The bait, that is."

"Outstanding. I expect people will love it."

"Speaking of Montgomery . . ." said Agnes, "isn't that why you brought Custer's Last Son up from the cellar? To show him off?"

"Ah, yes," said Chauncey. "You're a peach for reminding me, Agnes. A real peach. Ulrick?" He extended doughy arms, and Ulrick placed a horrified Fennec into them.

"He doesn't have a clue I'm his master, does he?" Chauncey frowned and shook Fennec by his scruff. "Stop wiggling. Stop it." Fennec, his eyes huge, lashed about wildly while I unsheathed Dewclaw. "Oh, how *boring*." Chauncey thrust the puppy back to Ulrick. Turning, he made his way toward a presumptuous stairway. "Bring him," he ordered.

Determined to stay close, I sheathed Dewclaw and belly-crawled from the umbrella stand to an imposing snake plant. From there, I slithered to the huge built-in bar by the stairway. Afraid they'd take Fennec all the way upstairs and disappear behind closed doors, I leapt stealthily onto the shelf full of bottles when the bartender wasn't looking and prepared to follow.

But Chauncey stopped on the first landing, halting Ulrick, too, and yelled for the music to be cut. "Gentlemen. *Ladies* . . ." He winked. "I have a tremendous announcement. Yes, that's right. Gather round, gather round."

Caught on the shelf as the bartender and everyone else turned toward the stairway, I cut the engines and sat rigidly between two grenade-shaped bottles of bourbon. I would be the one shaped like a cat.

Chauncey threw his arms out wide. "People tell me I have the best dogs, which is true. They tell me I'm the best trainer, which is also true. I've dreamed of fighting dogs since I was a boy, and when I die I will be remembered as the champion of this sport." He smiled down at the small crowd below him.

"When I was twelve I bought my first champion fighter with just a small loan from my father. I fought it and found great success. Winning came easily and that's what fighting is about, isn't it? Winning. It's not about money. It's about the thrill you feel when they tear each other apart, willing to fight to the death, for *you*." He smiled at Fennec, who withered in Ulrick's arms. "Loyal little beasts, aren't they? Fighting is all they know and they love it."

"Tonight's honey pot is up to a quarter million, dear cousin, so I'd say it's a *bit* about the money too," Agnes tittered, and a number of clinks sounded as snifter met snifter.

Chauncey ignored her, continuing with great fanfare. "I know everyone remembers my late grand champion, Custer's Last Stand."

A murmur of acknowledgment and appreciation swept through the room.

"And I'm sure you know he has only one remaining pup. This one, right here. Custer's Last Son."

Like a billow of fleas, every gaze in the room settled on Fennec.

"Priceless, isn't he?" Chauncey said, while Ulrick held him aloft, Simba style, for all to see. "And you may recall he was stolen from me by the police under false claims of abuse!"

"Boo!" The crowd laughed.

"Well, I'm here to announce that I stole him back! He's my prize, and you should all place your bets on him now.

He'll be fighting in no time, and when he does, he'll win. Every. Single. Time!"

A roar of applause sounded and my stomach curdled.

"Impressive," a bored voice drawled. All noise in the room screeched to a halt as a mousy-looking man in a pinstriped suit stepped forward. "But tonight isn't about this pup of yours, Chauncey, it's about my pit and your Bully. And I think it's time to go down and get this thing started while the storm is still raging outside, don't you?"

Chauncey focused watery eyes on the man. Stretched his cheese smile. "Why yes, Montgomery," he said. "It *is* that time, isn't it? I just wanted you to see your future competition first."

"Of course," Montgomery said. "And I shall enjoy watching him die later on. But for now . . ." He tossed back his drink and set it on the bar top with a *bang*. "Shall we?"

Chauncey puffed out his less-than-impressive chest. "Everyone to the fighting pit!" He clapped his hands. "And Ulrick, send for the Bully Kutta!"

Fennec searched about wildly as the crowd shifted, his too-big paws rigid with terror. He needed to know I was there.

Extending both paws, I sent the bottles of bourbon on either side of me crashing to the floor. Dismayed, the bartender spun, her ice-blue gaze landing on me. But not before Fennec's. His gaze had darted to me like a baby deer, helpless and wobbly, and I comforted it with a Viking's assurance— the silver flash of Dewclaw reflecting in his dark eyes.

The Bully and the Bait

The fighting pit was in the basement of the mansion. Not a yellow-carpet-and-must kind of basement, but a fully finished, stone-walls-and-humidor basement with a crystal chandelier the size of Odin overhead. The windows had been boarded over, giving the huge space a rather cloak-and-dagger feel.

The pit itself was so simple one could almost think it innocent. It was nothing more than a square in the middle of the room made of thick wooden boards, three feet high. Yet as I got closer I saw crusty plum-colored stains splashed all over the boards, and Cruelty itself jumped out and smacked me across the whiskers.

Feeling rather ill and off-kilter, I hid in the understory of the moving crowd, swept up in the flood of hems and oxfords until I found refuge beneath a fat claw-foot chair. Raising my shield to fend off any curious looks, I took a moment to catch my breath, which had succumbed to a hysterical walloping the lungs.

When my breath was sufficiently caught and calmed, I looked for Fennec. Chauncey had announced that it was high time for the puppy to watch his first fight, and I spotted him beside the fighting pit, now clutched in the lacquered claws of Agnes, a soft mound of shifting, shivering sand.

I ground my teeth and clenched my claws. It was well past the time to get him out of here, and yet I couldn't think of a single way to do so.

Commotion suddenly stirred the far side of the room, and a door opened to reveal the massive white Bully Kutta, an ugly black muzzle now imprisoning her face. At the end of her chain, his muscles flexed with the effort of holding her back, was Blackbeard. He looked the same as he had in Gray Birch, though now he wore no turtleneck to cover his dog head tattoo.

A sort of shriek-growl hybrid shot from my mouth before I could cage it, but it was drowned out by the cheers of the crowd. The Bully Kutta, however, had heard. Her red-rimmed gaze immediately snapped to me under the chair, and she lunged. "Ha!" laughed Chauncey. "See that, Montgomery? She'd rip the skin right off a chair. Your dog has no chance."

"We'll see about that," said Montgomery coldly. "Weigh her. She looks underfed."

"Her weight couldn't be more perfect," snapped Chauncey. "But yes. John, take her to the scale."

John? Blackbeard really *was* named John? How seemingly, wrongfully benign.

While the Bully was being weighed, a second dog was brought in, and he was the biggest, burliest pit bull I'd ever laid eyes on. "Long live the King!" cried half the crowd from their snifters.

"Ah, King George," said Montgomery, approaching the black-as-night pit with his hands steepled as though in prayer. "My champion." He smiled when the pit bared his teeth.

"Bully's weight is good, Boss," Blackbeard grunted.

Montgomery quickly walked over to check the numbers himself. Then, wordlessly, he summoned King George to the scale. "Perfect," he said after a moment. "Both of their weights are perfect. It will be a fair fight."

"Now then," said Chauncey, nodding, "where is Ulrick with my bait? I assume you have yours here already, Montgomery?"

Brushing a speck off his pinstripe, Montgomery assured him that he did.

"Tremendous. As my guest, please go ahead and present yours first."

The crowd craned their necks in anticipation, and I crouched, my tail swishing, my claws digging into the rug as King George was dragged into the pit. Once there, he waited, his muscles trembling and his jaw rigid.

At the crook of Montgomery's finger, a muscled minion stepped forward holding a caged squirrel the color of asphalt, its tail a dark plume, wispy as smoke. Terrified, the squirrel chattered incessantly, explaining how he'd just been trying to cross the road to get to his mother's house. She was expecting him for dinner, see. And he was already late.

Montgomery, an impatient showman, got right to the point. "Ladies and gentlemen, let this bait animal demonstrate to you the ferocity of my beast. Afterward, place your last-minute bets as you will."

I watched, horrified, as the King's muzzle and chain were removed and the squirrel was dropped into the pit.

Wild snarls and cheers ensued.

When it was over I was left staring at the insides of my eyelids, wondering how nature had gone so wrong. There was nothing, *nothing* natural about this.

"Attaboy, George," said Montgomery. "You do that in the fight and you get dinner tonight." The crowd laughed—Chauncey too high, Agnes too loud.

I forced my lids open and looked at Fennec. He was still imprisoned in Agnes's claws, his face hidden between his paws. Maybe he hadn't seen it. Was it possible he hadn't seen it?

With a heavy fist, I pounded down my helmet and roared a battle cry loud enough to ruffle all the patchwork quilts in Northern Europe.

A blur of rageful floof, I launched from beneath the claw-foot and commenced a perfectly mad swing of the sword. Cries rang out and an abundance of shoes and napkins were thrown as I struck, parried, and feinted.

Then, from the corner of my eye, something lurched at me. Something white, frothing, and snapping. The jaws of the Bully Kutta were still muzzled, but up close they were terrifying just the same. Lifting the paws, I pushed off, skidding the opposite direction. She wasn't the enemy.

A snifter was launched at me, and, successfully parrying the blow, I found myself thrust upward, onto the edge of the wooden pit. Directly below was the King, red-eyed and midway through a snap. I achieved liftoff just as his blocky head bounced off my shield, sending me spinning through the air.

And, in the mirror on the opposite wall, I saw myself flap gracefully into the outstretched tentacles of Chauncey Kane.

"What," said Chauncey, ignoring the dozens of guests who'd sustained injuries, "is this spectacular *thing*?" Holding me by the scruff, he dangled me at Blackbeard, who shrugged. "Not our bait, I presume?" Blackbeard shook his head. "Agnes? Does this belong to you?"

Her batwing brows rose sharply. "Of course not. I *detest* felines."

Suspended like a pelt on a hanger, I felt like a helpless kitten again—stuffed in that cold box in that cold alleyway, dreaming of organic cotton flannel and cherishment. With my scruff in Chauncey's vice-like grip, my cheeks pulled back and a droplet of drool shouldered its way out into the world.

Agnes sniffed with disgust. "Chauncey, it looks rabid. See? It's practically foaming at the mouth."

"Rabid, huh?" He rotated his wrist, and I spun slowly until our eyes met. There was no understanding there. No morsel of empathy I could appeal to. Only flat gray eyes, the left iris scribbling an *M* and the right iris an *E*.

Still stuck between Agnes's claws, Fennec looked at me with terrified eyes while the crowd dabbed fearfully at their wounds and refilled their drinks.

"How long are you going to make my dog wait, Chauncey?" asked Montgomery. He'd ordered his minion to muzzle King George and drag him from the pit. "If that's your bait, go on and throw it in there with your dog."

"Here's your bait now, Boss," said Ulrick, appearing suddenly through the crowd, a cage in hand.

"Excellent. About time." Letting out a high-pitched laugh, Chauncey turned and stuffed me inside the squirrel's now-empty cage. Slamming the door shut, he set it on the claw-foot chair. "We'll deal with you later, yes? Put the Bully in the pit, John!"

Dragged into the pit and released from her muzzle, the Bully Kutta looked dreadfully, horribly beautiful. She was like a great white shark released into a kiddie pool, and she wanted *out*. Immediately she tried to climb the walls but was shoved back down. Her flanks quaked and quivered with growls, and her eyes roved, searching for an escape.

Ever the patient showman, Chauncey began a long speech about his dog's ferocity and worth and how she was the dog to bet on and so forth, but a growing hum in my ears drowned him out.

There was something black inside Ulrick's cage. Something made of floof and plume and scented with ylang-ylang. A tiny muzzle poked from between the wires, surrounded by a hefty mane. "Bijou?" Cocoa-brown eyes searched and found me in my own prison. "Bijou, is that you?"

Skunk.

Without delay, the whole world rollicked and crashed around my ears.

The Sprightly Dialer

Norsecats were never meant for cages, and within the blackness of my shock, I realized the door to mine was not latched all the way. Chauncey had slammed it so hard it was now jammed. But jammed was better than latched. I rammed my shoulder into the stalwart shrew, but it remained shut, quivering with mirth.

"Bijou?" Skunk called again, her voice wobbly with uncertainty as Chauncey completed his speech and she was pulled from her cage.

Seeing the Pomeranian, the audience clapped and collectively stretched their necks over the pit like cobras. My eyes glazed with panic, and for a moment I saw nothing but Skunk's paws as they traveled through the air, carried toward the pit by Ulrick. Her toes were spread wide as though trying to brake. Her paw pads were muddy, the fuzz between them matted and dreadlocked. It would take Spencer forever to clean them. But that would be okay, I reasoned. Skunk loved pedicures.

I felt all hot and woozy. It wouldn't even be wrong to say I felt a bit nutty-like. Panic, I learned in that moment, was a ruthless and debilitating little shrew.

My eyes bulged unbecomingly as Skunk crossed the lip of the pit, and she looked back at me once more with a doggedness seldom seen in a non-Viking.

As she disappeared from sight, my panic snapped, giving me clarity and throwing me into action. Summoning an ice-cold northern power, I rammed my shoulder into the cage again and again until it finally burst open.

My resulting flight path resembled a 747 on its way to Pluto by way of Chicago, and I came to land on a woman's massive yolk-colored hat.

Shrieking, she bucked me off, and I crashed into the middle of the fighting pit, Skunk breaking my fall. Spitting out tufts of black fur, I pulled the Pom to her feet. "You're not dead!" I informed her helpfully.

"Poms never perish." She knocked a paw rapidly on bloodstained wood.

"And the dog?" I searched for the Bully Kutta, Dewclaw raised, expecting an attack any second.

But the Bully wasn't paying any attention to us. She was huddled in the far corner of the pit, making herself as small as possible, while the crowd (some laughing, most angry) kept her trapped with no way to escape.

"I think she's partial to ylang-ylang," Skunk whispered hoarsely in my ear. "That's why she didn't attack me. That and she *hates* violence. I mean, look at her."

"Make her kill the bait, Chauncey!" the crowd roared. "We didn't bet on a skulking coward!"

My throat tightened like I'd just swallowed a green strawberry.

Standing just outside the pit, Montgomery smugly smoothed his pinstripe. "It seems the fight is over before it's even begun, Chauncey. If a dog doesn't kill its bait, the fight is immediately forfeited. But I'm sure you know the rules as well as anyone."

"This is . . . NOT GOOD!" Chauncey screeched, looking like a red-faced little boy.

Still clutching Fennec, Agnes swooped over and stuck a witchy finger in his face. "This is *outrageous*, Cousin. I will not lose Lanai because of your incompetent mongrel." Spinning, she pointed at Ulrick. "Shoot her!" she demanded. "Shoot that Bully Kutta in the leg and *make* her angry. Make her fight for her life and put the King in there this instant!"

"Yes," said Chauncey, suddenly mollified. "Yes, *tremendous* idea, Agnes! Do it. Shoot the dog, Ulrick."

Immediately Ulrick's trollish face loomed over the pit, a gun in his trollish hand. It leered down at us, ugly and brumal, cocked and ready, and I threw my shield over Skunk. As it swung to find the Bully, she shrank back, terrified, and I shot toward her. "What is *with* this cat?" someone cried.

Pushing off, I reached Ulrick's face just as the gun went off. The sound was deafening, and everyone screamed as the chandelier overhead shattered, veiling the scene in darkness.

Now, I've never ridden an angry bull before. But keeping my seat on Ulrick's face was exactly how I imagined it. Everything went by in a dark blur, and all I could think about was that I couldn't let go. But, little by little, no matter how tightly I held on, Ulrick was unseating me.

I was nearly thrown, when—*bang!* The basement door leading outside crashed open, ushering in the fury of the storm.

Wind howled through the room, upheaving gowns, toupees, and napkins, while sheets of rain gleefully soaked the carpets and pounded the walls.

Ulrick flung me back into the pit just as a newspaper flapped in and unsighted Skunk once again. Unable to detach it, I boosted her over the wooden boards, wincing at her resulting crash on the other side. Leaping after her, I spared a glance for the Bully Kutta and saw her disappearing over the boards in the opposite direction.

Dozens of flashlights swirled into the room along with shouts of *Halt! Police!*

Within this sudden flurry, I saw a bevy of blue-uniformed bipeds adorned with black helmets, guns, and vests. Beneath them, flinging themselves to the floor, were Chauncey's guests—hands raised, snifters abandoned, faces squished into the floor as metal cuffs encircled their wrists.

Then, like a tawny, tiny, *heavenly* ghost, Fennec was there, scampering toward me on wobbly legs, his tail tucked firmly between his legs. I raced toward him and we bumped heads just as Skunk rid herself of the newspaper, shouting a dire tornado warning. Spinning, she saw Fennec, and that warning morphed into yips of glee.

But before she could run to greet him, horror swept across her face, and I turned to see Chauncey stumbling toward us with the red eyes of a madman. His arms hung low, his fingers spread wide like talons as he swooped for Fennec.

Hefting Dewclaw, I bellowed a mad call to arms.

But his talons never made it. They swooped right past us and crashed to the floor, crushed by the rest of his body as he fell. Behind him stood a cop, baton out, the name *Pemberton* stitched in white thread on his vest. And behind him, her body tensely framed in the open doorway, stood Spencer. Her blond hair whipped in the wind, and her blue eyes searched frantically until, at last, they found me.

With a cry, she shrugged off the officer who attempted to hold her back and ran into the fray. Sliding on her knees, she gathered Skunk, Fennec, and me into her arms, and there we stayed, inhaling her sweet Spencer scent, until the last of the cuffs clicked shut.

"Eighteen more dogs were found in the cellar, sir," Pemberton reported to his captain. His boots splashed through the swamp that was now the back garden. Thankfully the storm had quieted to a drizzle, though it was now streaked with police lights. "We're bringing them up now, and they don't look well. Definitely malnourished. Most likely subject to steroids and a whole lot of abuse." Spotting a few other officers descending into the cellar, he trotted off to join them.

Before the Captain could follow, a compact woman with close-cropped, curly black hair approached him. "We'll take the dogs from here." She zipped up her official ASPCA jacket, and I noticed dozens of other rescue workers swarming the scene. She stuck out her hand. "Mariam Short, humane law enforcement liaison."

The Captain shook her hand, squinting through the drizzle. "I'm Captain Garcia, and I'd feel better if you let us handle the dogs first. They're most likely very violent due to their abuse."

The woman shook her head. "No, sir. They may be scared, but they're not dumb. They know a rescue when they see one. My team is trained *specifically* for these circumstances, Captain. Much more so than your officers. I really must insist that you let us do our jobs."

The Captain studied her for a moment, his gray eyes unreadable. Finally, he nodded. "All right then. The dogs are your responsibility." Pulling out a radio, he ordered his officers to move aside. Order received, he lowered the radio and turned back to Mariam. "We've got enough arrests to deal with tonight anyway. The paperwork alone is going to take days. You have somewhere to take all of these dogs?"

"Yes, sir. The ASPCA has a rehab facility across the city where they'll be cared for, evaluated, and hopefully healed from their trauma. Our goal is to have every one of them placed in a loving home just as soon as they're ready."

Captain Garcia raised a brow. "And people are willing to adopt animals like these?"

"Absolutely. Ninety-nine percent of dogs like these transform into loving family members."

"And the other one percent?"

"We still care for, evaluate, and hope to heal."

The Captain shook her hand again. "Well then, good luck to you."

As he and Mariam Short moved off to attend to their respective duties, I looked at Skunk, who was slung across a planter box, her nose resting on her forepaws. "I still can't believe Hamlet saved us," she said.

Sitting beneath the left buttock of the magnificent garden statue, I curled my tail around my toes. "I can. After all, not only does he have the blood of Hildisvini running through his veins, he studied *Magnum Vikus* with an amazing teacher."

"You?"

I licked a damp paw. "Of course."

Skunk adjusted her position as the wind shifted. "I told him not to do anything stupid when I decided to find another way into the mansion. I told him to wait in the garden."

"Good thing he didn't." I picked up the other paw. Licked it. "Anyway, you were very brave for coming after me."

"Stupid more like."

"No, brave. Thank you, Skunk."

She lifted her wet muzzle, her cocoa eyes bright. "You're welcome."

We both looked over at the cellar then as the white Bully Kutta was led gently from it. Terrified after escaping the fighting pit, she'd run right back to the safest place she knew—her cage. Now she trailed an ASPCA worker, meek as a sheep, her nostrils widening as she was offered a bowl filled to the brim with food.

Nearby, Hamlet and Fennec had fallen asleep in Eddy's arms, and his eyes shone as he looked down at the two of them. Hamlet's tattered hat was still on, and it worked very hard to keep his ears warm. Spencer, meanwhile, floated about like a mother hen, tucking blankets more tightly around them while Tahereh went to fetch three paper cups of hot tea that the ASPCA had provided.

"Skunk?" I murmured, drowsy with heroism.

She blinked sleepily. "Yes?"

"How did you get caught and become bait?"

"Dogbane," she said glumly. "I must've passed some as soon as I'd snuck through the doors because I sneezed. Chauncey's henchmen spotted me right away. I think they thought I was a stray, trying to escape the storm."

Boots squelched, and we looked up to see Officer Pemberton approaching Eddy and Spencer. "You see that old lady across the street?" he asked, pointing.

We all looked through the mansion's open gate at the single-story stucco across the street. Standing on the stoop, wrapped in a mustard-yellow bathrobe, was a small fluffy-headed figure. She was the one I'd locked eyes with earlier.

The one who could quell tornadoes. She leaned heavily on her cane, watching the commotion with narrowed eyes.

"She's the one who called the police," said Pemberton. "If she hadn't spotted your animals and called us, thinking they were strays about to die in the storm, we never would've known where to come. It was your pig who really convinced her though. Apparently he ran right up to her door and pestered her until he saw her pick up the phone."

"He's quite the smart boy," Spencer said, looking at Hamlet fondly. "And we knew as soon as you reported their sighting to the ASPCA that it was them. There was no mistaking their descriptions, and we were fools to think they'd actually stay home."

Pemberton nodded. "It turns out the lady across the street, Eunice Hirsch is her name, had suspected dogfighting in her neighbor's mansion for weeks. She was certainly worried when she saw your animals disappear into this yard. She told the officers who responded to her call they absolutely had to investigate this house and she wouldn't take no for an answer."

"What a hero," said Spencer. "We should go thank her."

"I'm told she doesn't want any thanks," said Pemberton, shrugging. "She's a very private person, and she insisted on staying anonymous. But I thought you should know."

Spencer squinted at the small figure through the rain. Then she glanced at Tahereh, who said, "Maybe we can at least get her address? We could send her a cake or something. She doesn't need to know why. Or maybe we could tell her she won it somehow."

Eddy nodded. "That's a great idea, Tah."

Officer Pemberton nodded. "I'm sure that would be okay."

"So there are two things about all of this I don't understand," said Eddy, stroking Fennec's ear.

"Tell me," said Pemberton.

"Okay, first, how did Chauncey Kane find out Fennec was in Gray Birch, and how long did he know he was there? And second, after Fennec was stolen, how in the world did Bijou, Skunk, and Hamlet know he was here?"

Pemberton shook his head. "I wish I could tell you, but we're still searching for answers. A full investigation has been opened, however. Not only into Fennec's dognapping and the murder of Foggy Lawson, but into this fighting ring. My bet is it expands far beyond just these twenty dogs."

"That's my bet too," said Mariam Short, overhearing us on her march to the ASPCA van where the dogs were being given blankets and water before being loaded. "This may have opened the door for us to save a hundred more lives. It's a long road, but we'll start by tracking these dog's bloodlines back. Most were born into this slavery. If we can find their mothers, fathers, brothers, and sisters, we can bring down fighting rings all over the country."

She pointed at several dogs who were nervously smelling the wet grass and blinking up at the rain. "Some of them have never even been outside. Tonight's been a good night. You all did very well." Her gaze swept meaningfully over Skunk, Hamlet, and me before she walked off.

A loud screech announced the arrival of Agnes into the garden. She was desperately lifting the hem of her dress from the mud and demanding multiple lawyers while Chauncey, who followed her, his wrists in cuffs, told the officers escorting them just *exactly* what his father would do when he found out about this. With a heavy sigh, Pemberton walked over to help herd them toward the squad cars.

Spencer turned to Eddy. "Shall we get these babies to a hotel? The roads are too wet to drive home tonight."

He nodded. "Not to mention we're all exhausted."

Spencer and Tahereh had just scooped up Skunk and I when Blackbeard (i.e., John Smith) was marched past us in cuffs. Immediately Spencer tensed and I unsheathed Dewclaw. But it was Eddy who stepped in front of the man, his face hard as an anvil. "You were in Gray Birch," he said. "I saw you in my bakery the night Foggy Lawson was killed and Fennec was stolen." His gaze slid to the dog head tattoo on Blackbeard's neck. "You committed these crimes."

Blackbeard's lips stretched in a thin, mocking smile. "I quite enjoyed your cupcakes. The brownies, though, were a bit dry."

"Sir, please move aside," the cop holding Blackbeard spoke to Eddy.

But Eddy only stepped closer. "It takes a certain kind of man to murder another man. And you're going to rot in jail for it. But what kind of man brutalizes and kills dogs? What kind of punishment is fitting for such a disgusting crime?"

Sneering beneath his beard, Blackbeard spat at Eddy's feet. "I never murdered any man."

"Oh, please. Don't lie to me. You murdered Foggy Lawson in order to steal Fennec. He wouldn't just hand him over and so you killed him. An innocent old man."

The cop looked between the men nervously. "Sir, *step aside*."

Eddy didn't move and Blackbeard smiled again. This time wide enough to reveal mossy teeth. "You don't know what you're talking about. After I stole the pup, I left that old man still standing and still breathing. All I had to do was show him my gun and he cowered and let us go. I had no reason to kill him."

"No, he was found on that riverpath with his head bashed in," Eddy said.

Blackbeard shrugged. "I'm telling you. It wasn't me."

A Lion Cut

"He's lying," said Eddy on the drive home the next morning. "He killed him."

"I absolutely agree," said Tahereh from the back seat. "Who else would have done such a thing? No one in Gray Birch surely."

"Gray Birch is part of this world, Tahereh," said Spencer, her hands gripping the wheel as she steered the car up a winding mountain pass. "Not separate from it. And it can churn out criminals just the same as anywhere else."

"You don't think he's actually telling the truth though, do you?" said Eddy.

Spencer sighed. "Probably not, no."

Beside me, Tahereh moved her shoulders stiffly, blaming the tension on last night's cheap hotel bed.

I was sore too. But more from yesterday's acrobatics than the hotel bed. Looking out the window at the grove of aspen trees whizzing by, I noticed their leaves had grown overnight, bolstered by the moisture of the storm and now soothed by the sun, which shone brightly. I agreed with Eddy. Blackbeard was lying. Not only had he dognapped Fennec, he'd murdered Foggy, and now he was arrested and that was that.

Prodding Skunk so she'd scooch over on the seat, I settled with my chin on top of Fennec's paw and curled my tail around my nose. I needed Sleep, the great healer.

But moments later, within the delirium of a half sleep, I heard Blackbeard's voice again. *I'm telling you. It wasn't me.*

"The police are going to release Foggy's body," Spencer said, reading the blocky headline on the front page of the *Gray Birch Gazette*. Eddy pulled back the sliver of toast with marmalade he'd been about to feed me, and my jaws snapped jarringly around air.

"So they proved John Smith killed him?"

"Apparently he confessed."

A week had passed since the busting of Chauncey Kane's dogfighting ring, during which poor Fennec had rarely left Skunk's oil cabinet. I'd taken to eating for him as well as for myself, and I eyed the toast with a spot of drool on my chin.

"He probably got a deal with less jail time for confessing." Tossing the toast back onto his plate, Eddy pushed back the bit of dark hair that had fallen over his glasses. "So it's really over then."

"Seems that way. And Chauncey Kane, by the way, got sentenced to three years for his part." Spencer set the newspaper down on the table and folded it.

"Doesn't seem like enough." Eddy was silent for a moment, staring into his coffee. Then he continued, "I thought I would feel differently. More relieved or something."

Spencer reached across the table to squeeze his hand. "Fennec will come around, Eddy. It's going to take time for him to work through everything. But he has us, and Skunk's practically stitched herself to his side since we got home. Leave the marmalade, Bijou!"

But I'd already leapt onto the table, licked the jar, and leapt off again, sprinting for the stairway with sticky lips.

"They convicted Blackbeard," I said, poking my head into the oil cabinet.

"Really?" Hamlet said sleepily from the bed behind me, his light summer sweater rumpled.

"Finally." Skunk waved the flag of justice from inside the cabinet where she cuddled with Fennec. "He's guilty after all *and* I've just realized something. You know how Fennec got so agitated at the grand opening that Eddy sent him to the river to calm down?"

I nodded.

"And you know how we didn't understand what had frightened him so much? Well, I figure he must've seen Blackbeard from the window while we slept. And of course he recognized him from the fighting ring right away. It's no wonder he got terrified. He knew Blackbeard had come for him."

I glanced at the puppy, who was listening to Skunk intently, his brown eyes filled with the truth of her words. "All that and he couldn't tell us."

Hamlet scrambled off the bed and pushed his way into the cabinet, his sweater especially soft as it rubbed against my fur. "But it's all over now, right?"

I kept my gaze on Fennec, wondering if he had more to tell us and couldn't. "I suppose it is. Right, Fenn?"

The little pit bull gave one wag of the tail, but then he turned, his ears limp, and curled up facing the wall.

"Spencer! Wait!"

That afternoon, Spencer and I turned to see Dr. Flora loping up the sidewalk, her normally smooth hair in disarray. Reaching us, she stopped and smiled breathlessly.

"I'm sorry for yelling, but I've been trying to catch you since the stoplight." She pulled a sheet of paper from the stack inside her handbag. "James and I are throwing a funeral for Foggy now that the police have released his body. Well, not *throwing* one. That makes it sound like a party and it's not, though I think Foggy would've wanted it to be. Oh dear, I'm coming off insensitive, aren't I? I don't mean to. This whole affair has me completely out of sorts, and James too. He's been tending his beehives all week in the most horrible mood. And I mean really, *really* horrible." She thrust the paper at Spencer, who took it.

"The funeral is the day after tomorrow?" said Spencer, scanning it. "That's fast."

"We didn't think we should wait. It's already been too long, and a lot of people are helping."

Spencer folded the paper and put it in her pocket. "Of course. What can I do?"

"Well, we figured we'd do the wake at the Drunken Warbler since it's where everyone knew him best. If you could bring a dish, that would be wonderful."

"Absolutely. Is that all?"

"Yes, that will be a big help. Thanks so much." Seeing a few people across the street, Dr. Flora riffled in her handbag for more funeral announcements.

"Are you happier now?" Spencer asked before she could trot off. "With James instead of Foggy?"

Dr. Flora's hands slowed their riffling, and she looked up. "I think so, yes."

"It's adorable, really, that the two of you square-dance."

"Square-dance?"

"Yes, I heard that you and James went to the Do Si Do Barn over in Cherrytown after Witching Flour's grand opening. Lieutenant Tenant told me. Are you interested in competing, or are you just taking lessons for fun?"

Dr. Flora's face paled. "The Do Si So Barn? Oh yes, of course, the place in Cherrytown. We go there just for fun. Only for fun. Now if you'll excuse me, I need to keep passing these around."

Spencer and I watched her hurry across the street with raised brows. Then, with identical shrugs, we continued up the sidewalk for two more blocks before entering the Gray Birch Salon, its door chiming happily.

"Oh, good afternoon, Spencer. Bijou." Bobi Pinn greeted us from where she swept up a pile of salt-and-pepper tresses on the floor. "Take a seat, I'll only be a minute. Just have to finish up with Demelza."

Turning, Spencer and I spotted the freshly cropped woman waiting by reception. "Hello, Demelza."

"Spencer." Demelza nodded.

"How's your nose healing?"

"Well enough. I suppose you heard I'm sending Pim to military school this fall."

Spencer shot me a surprised look. "No, I hadn't heard."

"The boy is turning out too much like his father if you ask me. Killing critters, shirking his responsibilities, and getting into trouble. He'll act out even more now that his father's been denied parole. He needs a firm hand and a nice long separation from his slingshot."

"Well, I hope it works out for both of you, Demelza," said Spencer. "Really, I do."

"Spencer?" said Bobi, putting away her broom. "If you'll just come and sit here, I'll be with you in a twinkling." Bobi gestured to one of the three salon chairs facing a giant mirror. After Spencer sat, I climbed onto her lap and watched in the mirror as Demelza quickly paid in cash, no tip, and left.

"Okay, Spencer," said Bobi, smoothing her apron. "It's been ages since you've been in." She ran her fingers through Spencer's great wave of blond hair. "What are we thinking? Something fresh and exciting? I've just gotten a lovely new purple that would really jazz up your ends. Which, by the way, are quite dry."

"The same purple you've got in your hair now?"

"Oh, yes! I forgot I did that last night. Do you like it?" Bobi patted her purple pixie.

"It looks great," said Spencer. "But I'm just here for my same old boring cut. No purple for me. Also, Bijou needs her summer shave now that it's getting so warm. Maybe the lion cut, same as last year? She really liked that."

I pounded my imaginary shield. Not only had I liked last year's lion cut, I'd *thrived* under it. Never had I looked so fierce and in harmony with my armor.

"Two cuts coming up," said Bobi, reorganizing her shears. "One boring, one lion."

As Spencer rose to follow Bobi to the shampoo station, I strolled along the counter below the giant mirror, enjoying the multitude of obstacles made by Bobi's grooming tools. My agility, I admit, was exceptional. Especially when I bebopped a hair clip perfectly into a hood dryer like a hole in one.

Encouraged by Bobi's subsequent compliment about "cats" and their "knacks," I continued my stroll about the room, and very soon it morphed into a dangerous game of The Floor Is Lava. But then, as I edged past a potted cactus, the evil thing reached out and jabbed my tail. Determined not to touch the floor, I leapt toward the reception desk. Coming up short, I latched onto the top drawer, and it rolled slowly outward while I dangled, my back legs kicking.

"No!" Bobi shrieked, dropping her spray hose into the shampoo bowl and flinging water everywhere. Quickly she lowered her voice. "That drawer is full of my personal things. Spencer, please *do* call your cat away from there."

Frowning, Spencer sat up, suds dripping down her forehead. "Bijou, come away from there. That's not your drawer to go through."

"Yes, it's *private*," said Bobi.

The hairdresser's voice was so guilty I performed a pull-up so I could scour the contents of the drawer.

The first thing I noticed was Demelza's expensive-looking crystal salt shaker. The one I'd seen Bobi pocket from Demelza's kitchen the day Spencer had gone to ask about WC's knife. But that was just one item within a clutter of such. A cache of gold and silver trinkets glittered up at me, dotted with gems of red, blue, and green. In the back, stuffed into a corner, I spotted Spencer's missing necklace. The one gifted to her by her grandmother and lost on grand opening night. But it was something else that attracted, and then held, my gaze. Something that glinted up at me from beneath a set of ornate sugar spoons.

Foggy's ring.

The lucky one that'd been scratched by a cat. The one his grandfather had worn during the Second World War. The one Foggy told me never left the cord around his neck.

I swallowed down a caustic bile, my stomach suddenly feeling chock-full of green persimmons.

Before I could decide on a course of action, I was grabbed by the scruff of the neck and tossed aside. "I *said*, that's private!" Bobi screeched.

"Hey! There's no excuse to be rough with her," Spencer said angrily, rising from the shampoo chair.

I brandished Dewclaw just as the salon door chimed happily and swung open. "Good morning, Bobi," said Dr. Flora. "James and I are throwing Foggy a funeral now that his body has been released and . . ." The sheet of paper in her hand drifted to the floor as she took in the scene, her gaze ultimately falling to the open drawer beneath her nose.

With a cry she grabbed Foggy's ring. "How do you have this, Bobi? It belongs to Foggy, and he never ever took it off. How did you get it? Please answer me!"

But Bobi now stood with her face hidden within her hands, her shoulders sagged and silent.

Dr. Flora stepped forward and shook Bobi's arm. "I don't understand. Bobi, did you hurt Foggy? Did you hurt him and steal this? What did you do to him? *What?*"

Her hair sopping wet, Spencer quickly walked over and pulled Dr. Flora away. But then she rounded on Bobi as well. "Answer her, Bobi. Why do you have Foggy's ring?"

Reaching out and tapping Spencer with a rapid-fire paw, I pointed at the still-open drawer. As expected, Spencer immediately saw her necklace. Untangling it calmly, she clasped it around her neck, her eyes steely blue as she looked back at Bobi. "I think," she said slowly, "that if you don't explain everything right now, I'm calling the police."

"I took the necklace. I took the ring. I take things all the time."

Bobi had slunk into the shampoo chair, her normally arched eyebrows now sunken ships. "One could argue that I have a problem with gambling. That I'm in terrible debt and I've been that way for some time. I take anything that looks valuable. Anything that might pay. I'm not proud of it. But one could argue for self-preservation. I'll be in terrible trouble if I don't pay off my debts."

"Tell us what happened to Foggy," Dr. Flora snapped as I circled Bobi's legs, Dewclaw at the ready.

Bobi shook her head, her purple hair quivering. "I didn't do anything to Foggy. I swear I would never hurt him." Her eyes welled with tears. "I saw Foggy's ring a few months ago at the Drunken Warbler. It was dangling out of his shirt." She pointed at me. "Your cat was with him, and I think he was trying to get her to play."

"That's inaccurate," I told Spencer. "He showed it to me not to play but because I appreciate fine craftsmanship."

"I knew immediately that it was valuable. But I wouldn't dare take it *off* him. No, I found it on the bakery floor the night of the grand opening. It must've slipped from his neck. I swear, I'm guilty only of picking it up."

I shook my head sadly. So Foggy hadn't been wearing his lucky ring when he died. Maybe if he hadn't lost it, things would've turned out differently.

"You're guilty of *stealing* it, Bobi," said Spencer. "Not just picking it up. And the tremor in your voice says there's more to the story. More that you're ashamed of."

Biting her lip, the hairdresser wiped away a spilled tear. "I can't tell you," she whispered. "It's too horrible."

"Spill it, Bobi," snapped Dr. Flora.

"No, I can't—Ow! Your cat clawed me!"

"Good," said Spencer, crossing her arms. "Bijou?"

With a bray, I positioned Dewclaw and struck again.

"Ow! Ow! *Fine,* I'll tell you, but don't hate me when I do." Lifting her feet, Bobi hugged her sword-battered legs to her chest. "It was me. *I* called Chauncey Kane and told him his missing dog was here in Gray Birch."

Spencer's eyes widened. "You did *what?*"

"When you gamble in the places I gamble, you hear about all kinds of wagers, including dirty ones like dogfights. I never attended any fights though, or bet on any dogs. In fact, the whole thing makes me sick. I like dogs. But when I heard about the *reward* Kane was offering for his missing puppy . . . well, I couldn't ignore that. The money was enough to pay off a significant chunk of my debt. I suspected Fennec was the dog almost immediately. He fit the description perfectly. I knew for sure when I glimpsed his tattoo at the river that day you were surfing. So I called. I couldn't believe my luck."

"You called." Spencer's foot tapped angrily against the linoleum. "Tell me, Bobi, did you try to steal him too? Did you break into my inn, my *home*, and try to take him?"

Bobi's head hung limply from her neck. "They offered me an even bigger reward if I retrieved him and they were spared from having to send someone to do it. But I got cold feet, Spencer. Really, I couldn't do it. He was so scared, and when his rope got caught on the barn, I panicked. A light came on in your house then, too, and I thought you'd see me." She reached out for Spencer's hand. "I couldn't do it. I'm really not that horrible."

Spencer pulled her hand away, her voice cold. "You messed with my animals, Bobi. Mine and Eddy's. That *is* horrible."

"And since *you* couldn't steal the puppy," said Dr. Flora, "they sent that henchman to do it for you, and he murdered Foggy in the process. Well done, Bobi. Really, first-rate."

"But that's the thing," Bobi whispered. "That henchman *couldn't* have murdered Foggy. See, I knew who he was and that he'd been sent by Chauncey, so I followed him to the riverpath that night. He didn't know I was there, of course, but we'd both overheard Eddy say he was taking the dog there, and I felt responsible to make sure the retrieval went well. When Foggy showed up with the puppy instead of Eddy there was an argument, but the henchman didn't do anything but give Foggy a shove and wave his gun. After that, Foggy gave up the dog and watched the man walk off with him."

I sat back on my haunches with a *thump* while Spencer and Dr. Flora stared at Bobi in disbelief. Finally Spencer said, "You're saying this man, John Smith, has confessed to, and been convicted of, a murder he didn't commit?"

"I read about his confession in the *Gray Birch Gazette* today, and I'm assuming he confessed in exchange for less prison time. All I can say is I'm glad he did."

"Why?"

Bobi licked dry, papery lips, her gaze flicking to Dr. Flora. "Because *your* man, James Halvah, showed up on the riverpath next, and I figure it's better this John Smith go to jail for murder than him. In this town we protect our own. Especially us Toddy Sisters."

"*James?*" said Spencer, incredulous. "No, that can't be. Tell her, Flora. Tell her about you and James going to the Do Si Do Barn over in Cherrytown."

Dr. Flora's mouth opened and closed like a guppy fish. Her hands gripped each other, her knuckles as white as snow-capped mountains. At last she whispered, "But we didn't. We've only ever talked about square dancing. We've never actually done it. I didn't see James after he left the party. I didn't see him until the next morning."

"My God, Flora," gasped Spencer. "Then why did you lie to everyone, including the police?"

Dr. Flora gave a tiny shrug, her face sallow. "Because James asked me to. He was worried the police would suspect him after his fight with Foggy that night. He said he didn't want there to be any 'messy misunderstandings' or 'cooked-up conclusions.'"

"Uh-huh." Spencer turned to Bobi. "Did you actually *see* James Halvah murder Foggy Lawson?"

Bobi hugged her legs more tightly. "No. But I think I . . . well, I *think* I may have heard it."

Spencer and I exchanged horrified looks. "You heard it."

Her face bloodless and her eyes hooded, Bobi nodded. "The puppy had been retrieved, and I wanted to go home. I'd just turned away and was walking through the forest when I heard it."

"Heard what?"

"That thwack, Spencer. That *awful* thwack."

Wooden Boxes

Spencer's car roared up the dirt road toward the beekeeper's cottage.

The afternoon sun bounced bright and hot off the hood, nearly blinding me where I sat splayed on the dash, my whiskers smooshed against the windshield. In the passenger seat, Eddy flipped his phone back and forth while Dr. Flora and Skunk bounced around in the back seat.

"Eddy, you promised you wouldn't call the police until we'd talked to him," Dr. Flora pleaded, clinging to Skunk for ballast. "He needs a chance to explain. We owe him that."

Eddy didn't reply. But he didn't call either.

My tail floofed, my claws digging into the dash to keep from sliding off, I loosed a war cry as Spencer flew around a corner and hit a llama-sized pothole. My cry only incited speed, and she pressed the gas pedal down even farther.

We pulled up to James Halvah's cottage in a cloud of dust, and I shot from the vehicle as soon as Spencer opened her door. Immediately a throaty hum met my ears, and I saw a small forest of tall wooden boxes dotting the yard. In fact, the hum was so loud it sounded as though a colony of tiny monks occupied each one. Black-and-yellow monks with stingers and sweet and sour attitudes. I kept my shield at the ready.

Halvah, who was dressed in a snow-white suit with a boxy, veiled hat, straightened from where he'd been tending one of the boxes and pushed his veil up in surprise. "Eddy? Spencer?" Dr. Flora exited the back seat. "*Flora*? What are you all doing here?"

Dr. Flora just shook her head, her lips working but dispensing no sound.

My lips had no issue whatsoever dispensing sound, and I sent forth a grand bugle as I charged Halvah's alabaster tibias.

Wide-eyed, Halvah dodged. "What is going on?"

Circling back for another charge, I suddenly found myself swept into the air by Eddy and then stuffed firmly beneath his arm. "Tell me, James. Where did you go the night of Witching Flour's grand opening?" Eddy asked. "After you left the party?"

Clearly rattled from my blitzkrieg, Halvah dry washed his hands. "I already told everyone. The Do Si Do Barn. Why? I saw the paper today. That dogfighting man confessed to everything."

"It seems that perhaps he lied," said Spencer. "He's guilty of just half the crime and falsely confessed to the other half in the name of self-preservation."

"Where did you go?" Eddy asked again, and I could feel his veins throbbing in the arm that held me.

"You've asked and I've answered." Halvah squared his shoulders and marched toward another box, lowering his veil as he approached. "Our business here is over."

"James."

Dr. Flora's voice was so quiet none of us were entirely certain we'd heard it.

"James, just tell me, please. Did you go to the river that night? Did you see Foggy there? They know we didn't go to Cherrytown."

Halvah remained silent, his back stiff.

"I'm not accusing you of anything." Dr. Flora's voice trembled. "But I *need* to know what happened. Bobi Pinn said she saw you there and that Chauncey Kane's henchman stole the puppy but he didn't kill Foggy. She said he left him very much alive. But then you . . . *you* came, James. You came and . . . and I don't know what!" A sniff informed me she'd begun to cry.

Halvah's previously stiff shoulders slumped. A great shudder ripped through him. And then, quietly, he said, "Call the police, Flora. It seems I have no choice now but to confess."

POLICE LIEUTENANT LOU TENNANT: So, Mr. Halvah. You have something to tell me?

HALVAH: Yes. But first let me tell you this. I am utterly broken by Foggy's death. People saw us argue that night, and yes, I was angry, and yes, we didn't always have the best relationship. But I never wanted to hurt him.

POLICE LIEUTENANT LOU TENNANT: Noted. Go on.

HALVAH: Well, I didn't follow him to the river. I had no intention of seeing him again that night. I'd only walked to the riverpath in hopes of clearing my own head and was completely surprised when I ran into him. Instantly my earlier anger bubbled to the surface again. As soon as he saw me, he tried to tell me something. I know now that he'd just been robbed of Eddy's dog, but at the time I was too upset to hear about it. I started an argument. I told him all of the bad things I'd ever felt about him. He tried to calm me. Tried to get away. When he pushed past me, I shoved him. When he fell, Lieutenant, he fell onto a rock. He . . . he hit his head.

POLICE LIEUTENANT LOU TENNANT: Mary have mercy.

HALVAH: I'm so, so sorry, Lieutenant. I'm so, so sorry, and I have to apologize to you because I can't apologize to him. Put me in a cell, Lou. I'm ready to serve my time.

29

A Weighty Burden

Two months later . . .

Exhausted from the unfamiliarity of Crime, summer cloaked Gray Birch in a hot, sleepy haze. August arrived, beautiful and grand, and it found me strolling along Main Street one night, the stars above more brilliant than sapphires. They winked in time with my steps, lighting the pathway home to Fox Burrow.

Spencer was with me, and Skunk, and we each shared in the hefty contentment of an overstuffed bloat. Eddy had just hosted his first dinner party since moving into his apartment above the bakery, and he'd gone all out, inviting not only us but Pete, Harry, and Tahereh too.

Hamlet had worn a gilded mauve sweater for the occasion. I'd proudly sported my new lion cut (done surprisingly well by Tahereh), and Skunk and Delphiki had worn matching pink bows between their ears. Fennec had spent the evening wagging and begging for scraps, which everyone had happily provided.

The little pit bull had grown drastically in the last few weeks. His paws were as big as salad plates, his puppy fuzz morphing into a sleek, sandy coat. His collar was blue now, with a gold tag that said *Fennec the Brave*. For all the changes though, he remained much the same. He still had triangle ears that flopped forward, and he still hadn't uttered a sound or shown signs of hearing anything. But he was more a puppy than I'd ever seen him. At last happy and carefree.

Change, it seemed, was perching again on all of our shoulders, not just Fennec's. Over bruschetta appetizers, Tahereh had asked Spencer if she was going to miss Eddy staying at the inn.

Fingering her grandmother's necklace and lifting a glass of chardonnay to naked lips, Spencer had smiled at Eddy, who was rescuing a lemon sheet cake from the oven. "His stay at Fox Burrow was always temporary, Tah. I need that room for other guests."

"You two are just so perfect together. It's like you're already a clan."

"We *are* a clan." Spencer laughed. "All of us. Just look at Bijou. Look how much she loves Hamlet now."

They'd looked over where I balanced on the piglet's shoulder blades in an attempt to avoid the never-ending ravagings of Skunk and Delphiki.

"She absolutely hated him at first, and now they're two peas in a pod."

More like two warriors in a longship, but sure. In fact, in the final chapter of *Magnum Vikus* we'd learned all about the Viking strategy game King's Board, or Hnefatafl. We'd spent all of last week playing it.

Now, as I trotted up the street, a heady evening breeze

lifted the whiskers from my cheeks, and I inhaled happily. Things had been quiet since James Halvah's arrest. The man was going to prison for some time, much longer than Chauncey Kane and Blackbeard, whose sentences had been reduced. Not that *that* pleased me. According to my moral code, abusing animals was no different than abusing humans.

The truth was out, however, and that was a relief. Even Bobi Pinn seemed relieved when her fellow Toddy Sisters dragged her to a gambling addiction treatment center in Lakewood. From there, she'd written Eddy and Spencer a formal apology letter. Promptly, they'd written one in return, stating their willingness to forgive in exchange for altered behavior.

I myself wasn't so quick to absolve. And even if someday I *did* forgive, I wasn't ever going to forget. Vikings don't often turn their backs on those who've wrongfully pilfered their stores or dognapped a clan member.

With gravel popping and crunching delicately beneath our feet, we turned off Sourdough Drive and onto Fox Burrow's long driveway. Far above, the mountains bared their rocky skulls, all patches of snow finally gone. Closer in, cottonwoods, willows, and aspens swished plump branches, and a soft yellow light glowed from the inn's bay window.

Inside were Widmer, Cork, Miss Tut, Fuzz Aldrin, and several new guests who'd arrived for the end of summer. Feeling extra generous after my magnificent meal at Eddy's, I vowed to perform an extra thorough turndown that night. And if Miss Tut wanted to share her pinot meow or Fuzz, his moscato, that would be fine.

I was in the middle of dominating the porch steps when something black and blocky caught my attention. Falling back, I waited for Spencer and Skunk to enter the house before I turned to investigate. The object in need of investigation sat squat and erudite beneath the porch swing, and I reached out a rapid-fire paw to tap-tap it. It had a familiar texture and scent, like Age itself, and I dialed up my night vision to see more clearly.

"*Magnum Vikus II*." I read the flaking silver scrollwork on the cover aloud, noting the etchings of runes and long-ships that surrounded it. "*A Novice's Guide on How to Be a Viking*."

I sat back. Was Novice a step up from Beginner? Certainly it had to be.

It was then that a cold tingle took hold of my spine, like an icy wind sent down from the mountains. But when I turned, no wind bothered the night. The air was placid and warm, acting every bit the agreeable matron who wanted nothing more than to sit and creepily watch cats sleep.

That's when I knew something else was present besides the wind.

Stepping off the porch, I slid around the apple trees. From there I slithered across the lawn, pulled by a force stronger than myself.

I stopped at the edge of the forest where the trees looked like haughty, rawboned defenders of the gods. I knew they were there before the two blue-gray hairs floated down from the canopy to land between my paws. Breath catching in my throat, I almost didn't look up. *Almost.* But I hadn't earned my now 109 tabby stripes for a lack of bravery.

Cranking my neck upward, I saw four great yellow orbs peering down at me from the treetops. Tails, dappled with starlight, flicked lazily back and forth while paws the size of manhole covers flopped over the branches.

Freyja's great cats had come to see me. Aslog and her brother, Asmund, and both could eat me whole. Truly, they wouldn't even have to chew, just swallow a tiny bit. Licking my lips, I found them desiccated and in need of a Norse balm.

Surely they'd come here to reward me for my recent achievements. Perhaps a nice gold ingot was forthcoming. Or a feather from Freyja's cloak.

But when Aslog spoke she didn't mention ingots, feathers, or rewards of any kind. Her voice, so powerful, so melodious, washed over me like catnip. And when I woke sometime later, Spencer was carrying me back across the lawn to Fox Burrow.

Looking back, I saw that the great cats were gone, but I knew they'd been real. And I knew I had much work to do.

Aslog and Asmund had bestowed upon me my 110th tabby stripe, this one running across my brow like a leather braid. And this stripe, running perpendicular to all of my others, represented not bravery but duty forevermore.

Aslog had spoken of my rescue of Fennec and my acceptance of Hamlet, and she told me I'd found my purpose as a Viking at last. That it had always been there, just waiting for me to see it. And yes, I *did* hold a place in modern society. I held a place as protector and fighter for all of my fellow creatures here on Earth. I was a warrior, and I would never rest so long as they suffered.

I felt weighty with Burden as Spencer placed me gently on the kitchen floor. But it was a satisfying kind of burden. The kind that wasn't really Burden so much as Purpose.

Licking a bit of twig dust from my paw, I watched Skunk creep on a largish crumb squatting smugly beneath the oven. The crumb would win, I presumed, but everyone needed a purpose in life, even Poms.

Turning, I climbed the stairs to attend to my many turndown duties. Along the way I heard Spencer call Eddy and invite him to surf the river tomorrow. All of us would go, the whole clan, and my meep of pleasure echoed down the hall.

Acknowledgments

While writing is mostly solitary, raising a book from a fledgling to an adult with its own place on the shelf takes many people, much smarter than me.

Thank you to my publishers at SparkPress, especially Brooke Warner and Shannon Green. For better or worse, you agreed to introduce Bijou to the world. Julie Metz and Ben Perini, the cover you designed is stunning and makes me smile every time I see it. Crystal Patriarche, Keely Platte, Hanna Lindsley, and everyone at BookSparks, thank you for championing this book and sharing it with unsuspecting civilians. I take all responsibility.

Ty and Virginie, you agreed to beta-read my early drafts and gave me much-needed feedback and support. The next round is on me. Jessica Burkhart, your editorial eye and help in categorizing this book was oh-so-necessary. Thanks for helping me see that, in the end, I actually wrote the story I wanted to write.

Caska, my main girl. My mews. You were my coauthor for this whole book, sitting on my arm, blocking blood flow, and purring. Though you're certainly not a Viking cat, Bijou is inspired entirely by you. Sarge and Novi, I know this book doesn't have horses in it. Please understand I outlined it before you adopted me into your herd. I promise the next one will feature equines prominently.

To all of my family, thank you for your love and support. Most of all, thanks to my best pal and husband, Thomas. You're the first to hear my ideas, read my drafts, and give me endless encouragement. You make me oat milk lattes, straddle horses with me in foreign countries, and are the best fur dad and pawpy west of the Mississippi. All of the animals say so.

About the Author

C odi Schneider was raised in the snowy mountains of Colorado on a steady diet of books. She is a mystery-loving animal enthusiast who, when not writing, can be found traveling the world on horseback. She lives in Denver with her husband, two horses, and a cat who is not a Viking but a lover of REM sleep.

Learn more at www.codischneider.com

Author photo © Thomas Schneider

SELECTED TITLES FROM SPARKPRESS

SparkPress is an independent boutique publisher delivering high-quality, entertaining, and engaging content that enhances readers' lives, with a special focus on female-driven work. www.gosparkpress.com

Indelible: A Sean McPherson Novel, Book 1, Laurie Buchanan, $16.95, 9781684630714. Murder at a writing retreat in the Pacific Northwest, but this one isn't imaginary. Authors only kill with words. Or do they?

Gatekeeper: Book One in the Daemon Collecting Series, Alison Levy, $16.95, 978-1-68463-057-8. Rachel Wilde—sent from another dimension to bring defective daemons in for repair—needs to locate two people: a woman whose ancestors held a destructive daemon at bay and a criminal trying to break dimensional barriers. Helped by a homeless man with unusual powers, she uncovers a rising shadow organization that's changing her world forever.

Firewall: A Novel, Eugenia Lovett West. $16.95, 978-1-68463-010-3. When Emma Streat's rich, socialite godmother is threatened with blackmail, Emma becomes immersed in the dark world of cybercrime—and mounting dangers take her to exclusive places in Europe and contacts with the elite in financial and art collecting circles. Through passion and heartbreak, Emma must fight to save herself and bring a vicious criminal to justice.

Squirrels in the Wall: A Novel, Henry Hitz. $16.95, 978-1-684630-22-6. In *Squirrels in the Wall*, humans and animals share heartbreak and ignorance about the nature of death. Together, they fashion a collage of a human family and its broader habitat, filled with dogs, cats, bees, turtles, squirrels, and mice, illuminating the tragicomic divide between humans and the natural world.

About SparkPress

SparkPress is an independent, hybrid imprint focused on merging the best of the traditional publishing model with new and innovative strategies. We deliver high-quality, entertaining, and engaging content that enhances readers' lives. We are proud to bring to market a list of *New York Times* best-selling, award-winning, and debut authors who represent a wide array of genres, as well as our established, industry-wide reputation for creative, results-driven success in working with authors. SparkPress, a BookSparks imprint, is a division of SparkPoint Studio LLC.

Learn more at GoSparkPress.com